True Beauty

ScanLife

⌈Scan barcode w/mobile device for more information⌉

Other Books by Shelia E. Lipsey

Beautiful Ugly
(Prequel to True Beauty)

My Son's Wife Series
My Son's Next Wife
My Son's Wife
My Son's Ex-Wife: The Aftermath

Sinsatiable

Into Each Life

Always, Now and Forever Love Hurts

Anthologies
Bended Knees – Against the Grain

Non-fiction
A Christian's Perspective – Journey Through Grief

True Beauty

A Shelia E. Lipsey Novel

BONITA & HODGE

ISBN 13: 9780983893509
ISBN 10: 0983893500

First Printing December 2011
Printed in the United States of America
10 9 8 7 6 5 4 3 2 1

Library of Congress Cataloguing Data 2011915920

Bonita and Hodge Publishing Group (USA) Inc.
Attention: Order Processing
P. O. Box 280202
Memphis, TN 38128
Phone: 1-901-654-7388

Cover Designed by Thomas Sign Designs

Dedication

Ebinique Nevels
Charm is deceitful, and beauty is vain, but a woman who fears the Lord is to be praised. Proverbs 31:30 (ESV)

Acknowledgments

Now unto him that is able to keep me from falling, and to present me faultless before the presence of His glory with exceeding joy, to the only wise God my Savior, be glory and majesty, dominion and power, both now and ever. Jude 1:24–25 (KJV)

Father, I thank you for all that you have done, are doing, and will do in and through my life.

—*God's Amazing Girl, Shelia*

What Is True Beauty?

Insight by Evangelist Irma Williams

Since we are living in a world where people are one hundred percent visual when the subject of beauty is spoken of, advertised and marketed, there is no wonder how blurred our vision has become. We ascribe beauty to outward things. Things like what makeup we use and the shoes we choose to go with the outfit we wear. We have gone as far as altering our physical appearance to become more "beautiful."

We are consistently, and methodically, inundated with what everyone else says about how we should look. Countless television commercials, billboard advertisements, magazine ads, and even Internet marketing infiltrate our eyes, and all have stated too vividly, how we ought to look. We have even been forced to accept and believe that sexiness means beautiful. That concept could not be any further from the truth. True beauty has absolutely nothing to do with sex or sexiness.

Our society has determined for us what we should accept as being beautiful, and those who are made to feel less than beautiful have created a myriad of personal issues to accommodate the lack of beauty that society says we do not have. We are more concerned about what the outside of a person looks like than we are with what a person has in her heart. A pair of pretty eyes, or a perfectly shaped nose, voluptuous lips, or even a six-pack and a rugged chin, can never be compared to compassion, love, and caring. These attributes cannot be seen but can only be experienced, but they have more of an impact on making this world we live in more bearable for everyone.

If we had the eyes of the Creator, of all things, we would be able to see beauty everywhere, True Beauty.

Our eyes have limitations. What our eyes see as beautiful is shortsighted, and our vision keeps us from seeing the True Beauty in others as well as ourselves.

1

That which is striking and beautiful is not always good, but that which is good is always beautiful. Ninon de l'Enclos

Layla positioned both hands on her curvy hips, and tilted her body from side to side. She smiled as she stood proudly in front of her floor-to-ceiling mahogany mirror. Her cranberry sheath sweater dress rested just above her knees, and definitely showed off all of her new, shapely curves. She smiled before she leaned slightly forward and puckered her thick lips in front of the mirror. "Lord, have mercy, if I must say so myself," she mouthed, and then swished around and reached for her purse lying on the bed. "Time to play," she said.

"My, my, my, heaven must be missing an angel, girl," the suave-looking Puerto Rican brother said at the same time he got up from Layla's chair. Layla smiled. He walked toward her, reached for her hand, and then sought her lips. Layla, however, reciprocated by presenting him with her dimpled cheek. "So, it's like that, huh, foxy lady?"

"Yeah, it's like that." Layla went to the hall closet and pulled out her military-style hip-length jacket.

Omar was cute and had it going on. He had a decent job, nice ride, a place of his own, and, as far as Layla knew, no steady girl. Not that she worried about whether he had someone or not, because she was still involved with Dennis, close to three years strong, with no intention of getting on a serious tip with any of the men she dated on the side. Meeting men came a dime a dozen now that she had a new body, not only from her massive weight loss but a full-body lift, compliments of the victim's compensation settlement she received after Mike's crazy night of terror.

Sometimes Layla still got goose bumps when she thought about how her ex-boyfriend, Mike, sneaked up on her after she was supposed to be going to church with her parents. The day he appeared at her apartment three years before, she was ready to kick him to the curb—again. She had grown weary of him using her like she was an ATM machine or some cheap hooker on the street. She was a big girl, weighing 300-plus pounds back then. Yes, it took him shooting her before she could come to terms with the fact that he was a vicious user and abuser.

Mike was sentenced to fifteen years in prison for attempted murder. The major surgery she had to undergo because of his assault had been life altering. She almost died, but after the terrible ordeal, she now carried a svelte, healthy one-hundred and twenty pounds on her petite frame.

Now that the past was just that—the past—Layla loved dressing up, spending money on clothes, and going out. She no longer depended on hanging out with her girls, Envy and Kacie; although it was all good, but Layla had a life that was hers, and she was deadset on doing whatever she wanted. Her life was better than it had ever been, and she was going to soak up every moment by living it to the fullest.

"Let me help you with your coat," offered Omar as they prepared to leave for a Grizzlies basketball game at the FedEx Forum.

She reached behind and lifted her thick, neck-length black tresses of twists while Omar helped her ease each arm inside her jacket. "Thank you."

"You ready?" Omar asked.

Yes," she answered.

Omar stepped in front of Layla and opened the door to her apartment.

"Are you sure you want to get out in this weather?" asked Layla. "The sleet is coming down pretty heavy."

Omar waited for her to lock the door before he eased his hands around her waist as if he was trying to shield her from the frigid weather. "I got you, sweetheart. You don't have to worry about a thing when you're with me."

"Who are you supposed to be?" Last time I checked," Layla said, flashing a smile, "God was still in control of the weather."

Omar chuckled and replied, "He still is, but I don't think He'll mind if I offer Him a little assistance." Omar grabbed hold of her gloved hand, popped open his golf umbrella and they walked to his car.

Each step she took toward his matador red sports vehicle was marked with assured boldness and an exuberant confidence. This was definitely not the Layla of yesterday. Her life had changed tremendously. God had certainly taken a bad situation and caused it to work out for her good.

~

Kacie peeped through the double windows in the living room of her new four-bedroom Section 8 home. She witnessed the sleet as it fell from the otherwise dark star-filled sky. She continued to gaze upward, oblivious to the sounds of her kids gathered in the den. They were supposed to be watching one of the assortments of DVDs she had collected over the years. Tonight, the girls had out yelled the boys, which meant for probably the eighth or ninth time they chose to watch *The Princess and the Frog*.

Two-year-old Kyland, three-year-old Keshena, four-and-a-half-year-old Kendra, six-year-old Kali, seven-year-old Keith, and nine-year-old Kassandra were doing God knows what else, in addition to watching the movie, while Kacie tried to escape into a world void of her kids. She didn't hear twelve-year-old Kenny's voice; he was probably in his room on one of the popular Internet social sites.

Kacie's phone rang; it was Envy.

"Hey, girl. What's up? I haven't heard from you in a couple of days," Kacie said as soon as she answered the phone.

"I know, but I've been swamped. It's peak season. You know the New Year ushers in with it a fresh, heavy workload of regulatory projects to tackle. But I'm not complaining; at least I still have a good-paying, steady job."

"You're right, you're blessed."

"Look, when was the last time you talked to that crazy, flipped-out friend of ours? I've been trying to see if she's come down to earth since it's a new year and all."

"Shut up, y'all," Kacie hollered at her children before she responded. "Girl, these kids are about to get on my last nerves. I'm in the living room, trying to get a little peace and quiet, but it seems impossible." Kacie walked with a cerebral-palsied limp and sat down on the oversized sofa. "I talked to Layla earlier. She said she had a date tonight. I don't know if she went or not, since it's starting to sleet."

"You don't have to tell me that it's not with Dennis either," Envy remarked.

"You know it's not."

"I can't believe how she's been carrying on, Kacie. The girl has a good thing with Dennis, and just because she's not a size twenty-six anymore, she acts like one of those uppity superstar divas. I feel so sorry for him. A good man is hard to find."

"Who are you telling? I know that all too well. I mean, it was a tragedy when Mike shot her, but God turned tragedy into triumph, despite the fact that a large portion of her intestine and stomach had to be removed. I hate to put it like this, but girlfriend got a free gastric bypass out of the deal, and on top of that, lost about two hundred pounds. I mean, as if that wasn't enough, she met Dennis. A great, hardworking man who loves the ground she walks on, and what does she do?"

"Step out with every guy that comes her way," finished Envy. "I know one thing, she better watch herself. She doesn't come to church as much as she used to, and she most definitely threw me for a loop when she stopped singing in the choir. She's like one of those girls gone wild."

Kacie twisted on the sofa like she had ants in her pants and switched the cell phone to her other ear. "All we can do is keep trying to talk some sense into her thick, hardheaded skull. I thought my children were hardheaded, but Layla's got them beat by a long shot."

Envy laughed and changed the subject. "How are things going with you?"

"All right. I'm glad we're settled into the house and the holidays are over. My supervisor told me that I might be able to get a few extra hours during the week."

"That'll be great, Kacie. Will it work around your school schedule and child care?"

"Yeah, and since I only have to be at school three days a week, the rest of the days I can work at least until four or five. My child care voucher comes in handy because the kids can stay at after-school care until as late as six o'clock."

"How much longer do you have before you graduate?"

"A little over a year. Remember, I'm only going half-time. And in community college, there are times when a class you need is cancelled if the class minimum isn't reached. That can add up to going there longer than what is supposed to be a two-year program."

"I have all the confidence in the world for you, Kacie. Working, going to Southwest, and raising seven kids cannot be easy. However, think of all the doors that will open when you get your associate of science degree. Plus, Southwest College's courses transfer to most four-year colleges and universities."

"Hold up. Let me finish this round of school first. I can't begin to think of anything but trying to get my Associate's Degree. My mind can't entertain going further than that right now."

"I'm just saying that opportunities await you. You prove that every day. I know it isn't easy with the kids and after finding out that Deacon wasn't Kyland's father, well . . ."

"Don't go there, Envy. That's in the past, and I cannot stand the name of that man. I really thought he was Kyland's daddy. When I stood before that judge, I felt so foolish when he read the results of the paternity test; 'He is not the father.' Girl, I felt like I was on Maury."

"Oh, it wasn't that bad, Kacie. Anyway, we all make mistakes."

"But I just knew that he was the father. Then to make matters worse, his wife sat next to him gloating, which only made the situation that much worse. I tell you, it was one of the worst days of my life."

"Kacie, don't keep beating yourself up over it. Kyland is a beautiful, healthy little boy. That's enough to be thankful about right there."

"But I don't understand. I was so sure."

"Girl, this is me you're talking to. The thing is you wanted it to be Deacon's baby. But deep down inside, you knew that it wasn't."

Kacie paused. The truth could definitely hurt. "Okay, so I had sex with someone else. But usually I can tell when I get pregnant. The two times I was with Reggie from work, he used protection. And neither time did I feel like I had gotten pregnant. Ohh, I'm so glad he doesn't work there anymore."

"Well, what's done is done. At least you get child support from Kenny's daddy. I don't know why you stopped trying to get help from the other daddies. Just like you got a paternity test for Kyland, you need to go to court on the others. Don't let them off the hook."

"I'm tired of fighting their daddies. Anyway, none of them have any more than I do. It'll be a waste of my time."

"Whateva, Kacie. But I'm still saying that every little bit helps."

"Anyway, I thought we were talking about Layla. How did you switch the subject to me?"

"Because I worry about you too."

"I can say the same about you. All the years we've been best friends and you still keep your life on lockdown like a prisoner on death row. At least you know what's going on in mine and Layla's lives. Why don't you start telling me what's going on with you and your admirer, oh-so-smooth-debonair Leonard what's his name?"

"Girl…puhleeze. Oh no, you didn't go there."

"Oh I went there allright." Kacie laughed over the phone. "Stop flogging. The man I saw was a masterpiece. And you won't give the brother the time of day. But you and Layla got some of the same ways."

"Are you on some of that illegal stuff or what? Because Leonard Stein is not my man. He's only a friend and you know it."

"I don't know a thing," replied Kacie. "Hold on a sec. Let me get these kids in check right quick."

"No, no, no, you go on and check on them. I'm not about to get into a conversation with you about Leonard. Anyway, we'll talk this weekend."

"You sure know how to avoid what you want to avoid. I'll let you slide this time, but there's going to come a day when you won't be able to run or hide. I'll holler at you later."

"Bye, girl," said Envy, and they each hung up the phone.

Kacie was right about one thing. Envy, and no one else, could run forever. There was no way around it; whatever's done in the dark always comes to the light, no matter how long it might take for the light switch to be turned on.

2

Beauty? . . . To me it is a word without sense because I do not know where its meaning comes from or where it leads to. — *Pablo Picasso*

Layla unlocked the door to her apartment, after she and Omar agreed to cut their date short and leave the basketball game early. The Grizzlies were ahead by nineteen points, with a minute and a half to the final buzzer, so Layla suggested that the two of them leave and get home out of the worsening weather.

"You sure you don't want me to come in and help warm you up?" Omar suggested.

Layla smiled. "No, I don't think so. Not tonight at least." Her tone seemed to have an edge of hope for Omar.

He didn't put up resistance. "Okay." He leaned in and kissed her lightly on her painted lips. "Goodnight."

"Goodnight, Omar. And thanks for a great evening."

"No problem. I can't wait until we do it again."

"Me too," she replied. He turned and walked away while Layla walked inside her apartment. Immediately she removed her lambskin gloves and coat, and started rubbing her hands together to ward off some of the lingering chill she felt. A burst of warmth filled the room from the automatic central heating unit, like it just read her mind. She soon forgot about the mounting wintry blast of below-freezing temperatures and sleet outside.

Layla first encountered Omar at the upscale hair salon where she rented her booth space; another great move she'd made during the past year. Ever since she was a little girl, she had been fascinated with hair. The first time she enrolled in cosmetology school, she was younger and a little lazy. She would make up one excuse after another and barely went to class, until she dropped out far short from earning the required 1500 workroom floor hours she needed to graduate. Yet, the thought of going back to school, and getting her license, was never far from her thoughts. Sometimes she still found it hard to believe that she'd done it. She was working in a hair salon, with a legitimate license, instead of fixing hair for a few dollars here and there in her apartment. This boosted her wallop of self-confidence.

Omar, a divorced father of two, brought his fourteen-year-old daughter to the salon every Friday afternoon to be pampered like the angel he called her. She would get her natural, thick, brown hair done in a different style each time she came, followed by a manicure and pedicure. From the first time he walked into the salon close to two months ago, Layla could barely take her eyes off him.

When her eyes met Omar's, she smiled with a confidence that the old Layla never possessed. He reciprocated by walking to her station and introducing himself, while his daughter was being serviced by one of the other cosmetologists. Their initial meet and greet was short because Layla had a client, so they didn't waste much time exchanging cell phone numbers.

Omar kept his promise by calling Layla. She was glad the girls in the salon told her that he was divorced because no messing with married men for her. It was weird for Layla because though she often felt guilty about fornicating, she downright feared the wrath of God when it came to anybody who fooled around with a married man. Kacie and Envy didn't realize it, but Layla believed that Kacie's life had taken a beat-down from God when she continued messing around with Deacon after finding out he was married.

That would never be her. She had her faults and shortcomings, but Layla believed she had a few more morals than Kacie, and Envy too for that matter.

The first night Omar called, he kept Layla laughing with stories about his kids. He told her that he was in pharmaceutical sales and had recently relocated from Columbia, South Carolina to Memphis because his ex-wife and children had relocated to the city. He didn't want the distance to affect his children any more than the divorce already had. He and his wife maintained an amicable relationship, he told Layla.

Omar seemed to be a cool person. When she started dating him on a regular basis, she felt like she was betraying Dennis, the man who had stepped in and breathed life into her solemn spirit after Mike's assault.

Dennis may have been the main man in her life, but it did not keep her eyes from wandering. Her mind soon followed. She couldn't help the change. With each extra layer of fat that fell off Layla, there was an extra layer of regret over all that her obesity had caused her to miss in her life. She was thirty-two years old, but she had never had a mutually satisfying relationship with a man, until Dennis came into her life. She had to admit, Dennis was a great person. He loved doing things to make her happy; and he fell for her before she had lost weight. That garnered him an extra special place in Layla's heart.

On the flip side, there was no denying the fact that she had stepped out and started seeing the world with a so-called new pair of eyes, and she no longer wanted to be bound to one man—at least not for now. Dennis would always have a special place in her heart, but no one said he had to have her whole heart.

Layla sat down on the sofa and pulled off her suede boots, just as her cell phone sounded off with Dennis's ringtone. She reached for her purse on the table next to the sofa and pulled out her phone.

"Hi, sweetheart."

"Hi, there," replied Dennis. "How are you? I hope you aren't out in this nasty weather."

"Nope. I was about to turn on the fireplace."

"Want some company?" he asked.

Layla thought for a second or two before she responded. She was by no means a woman who juggled men, at least not in her own eyesight. However, according to her best friends, Kacie and Envy, they begged to differ. They had accused her, on several occasions, of cheating on Dennis. Layla did not see it that way. She was merely catching up for all the times she missed going out on dates, talking on the phone for hours, and having men go "goo-goo ga-ga" over her. She had not gone to bed with any of them, and even when it came to Dennis, she rarely gave in to his sexual advances. She still considered herself a woman with godly morals. She had no problem with men wanting her because of her beauty, because it felt more than good to be desired for a change, but a loose woman she was not.

"Dennis, honey, the weatherman says that it's getting pretty bad, and by midnight it's going to be treacherous. I don't want you slipping and sliding just to come over here for an hour or two." She made sure she added "an hour or two" so he would know that there would be no spending the night—especially not tonight after being out with Omar. It wouldn't seem right.

"You must forget that I'm a postal carrier."

"No, how could I forget? It's how I met you." Layla laughed.

"Well, with that being said, let me remind you of the postal courier's unofficial motto. Neither snow nor rain nor heat nor gloom of night stays these couriers from the swift completion of their appointed rounds."

"Oh, so now I'm one of your appointed rounds." Layla laughed again when she heard Dennis laughing on the other end of the phone.

"Of course, you are, because nothing is going to keep me from the woman I love."

Guilt quietly crept in and Layla felt ashamed, momentarily. "I still don't think it's a good idea," she said in a more serious tone. "I'm turning in early. I have to brave the bad weather tomorrow morning, just like you. I have three hair appointments before noon, so I'm going to lay this body down so I can get up early just in case the weatherman knows what he's talking about. You know I'm still getting used to driving in bad weather."

"I can always drive you to work and pick you up. You know it's no problem."

"Honey, I know, but I didn't go through all the trouble of learning how to drive and buying my first car, just so it can sit in the garage. I love being independent and doing things that I never used to see myself doing."

"And I'm glad for you, but you don't have much experience driving on ice and sleet. The streets can be—"

Layla cut him off. "That's why I need to get out there, so I can get the experience. I promise to drive safely and be on the lookout for those who don't," she said to him in a reassuring tone. "I tell you what . . ."

"What's that?"

"Let's see how things go tomorrow. Maybe we can hook up when I get off work."

Dennis remained quiet.

"Hello, are you there?"

"I'm here. It's just that I haven't seen you for almost a week and a half. I miss you."

"And I miss you too. But remember that absence makes the heart grow fonder," Layla cooed into the phone while she sat down in her favorite chair and propped her legs underneath her bottom.

"I've heard the opposite, that absence makes the heart wander," Dennis responded.

Layla swallowed deeply and cleared her throat. She'd never heard that saying, but it sent another wave of guilt washing over her. "I know how long it's been, Dennis. But now that I'm working and able to drive too, it feels so, so new, like I've been given a chance to do the unthinkable. I'm enjoying my independence for the first time in my adult life. Just think, I don't have to call on you or Envy every time I want to go somewhere or do something. I can drive myself wherever I choose. I no longer have to sit in front of the TV feeling desperate and all alone because I'm too fat to get up and get out, afraid of people laughing and staring at me. So, if you love me like you say you do, try to see things through my eyes, if only for a moment."

"Girl, don't you know how happy I am for you? I know it's only by God's grace that you're even alive, so it's good to see you living your life for once. But I want to be part of your life too. I want to share in some of the things you've always longed to do. Remember when we went to the Desoto County state fair last summer?"

Pleasant memories surfaced in Layla's wandering mind about that day. "Yeah, I remember."

"You said you hadn't been on a ride since you were a little girl. I think we rode just about everything."

"Yeah, we had such a good time. And we're going to make more memories. So please do not make a few nights of not seeing each other into a big deal."

"Look, I guess I am being selfish because I want you all to myself. I know your world has broadened, and like you said, we'll have plenty of time to spend together. And now that I think about it, I'm going to do like you."

"What's that?" Layla asked.

"I'm going to turn in. I have to be up by four, so I need to get some shut-eye myself. But promise me you'll call if it's too bad for you in the morning."

"I promise. Good night, Dennis."

"Good night, sweetheart. I love you."

"Ditto." Layla didn't hesitate. Immediately the tip of her acrylic-layered nail on her index finger hit the red End button on her cell phone. "Ooooo," Layla said, and stretched while she yawned, stood, pulled her dress over her head, and laid it across her right arm. Entering the bedroom, she smiled when she thought about one of Omar's comical stories.

Every day was like a new adventure for Layla. Much good had derived out of a set of horrific circumstances. Along with the massive weight loss, Layla no longer battled dark moments of depression and feelings of low self-esteem. Her quality of life had definitely improved. Instead of being on a road that could lead to an early death and bad health, she gained a new self-awareness of the woman she was becoming. For the first time in her life, she felt beautiful. When she looked in the mirror, she no longer saw the ugly person who used to stare back and make fun of her. There were no more days and nights of eating herself to sleep. God had given her a new life and she made a promise to herself that she was going to soak up every second, of every day, living it.

She treated herself to a soothing, hot bubble bath. Once finished, she stepped out of the claw tub she purchased from a Midtown antique thrift store she frequented. It was love at first sight when she spotted the copper claw tub.

Envy and Kacie were with her the day she discovered it. They told her she had to be missing a few marbles when she indulged herself. Layla could not understand why they had a problem when it came to her buying whatever she wanted; it was her hard-earned money and she was going to do as she pleased. The very same day they called themselves "roasting her" was the day Layla decided she would never allow anyone, not even her two best friends, to stand in the way of something she wanted. Let them and everyone else think what they wanted, because one thing was for sure, and two things were certain, every time Layla lay back in the tub, it reminded her of her self-made promise: "Whatever it takes to do whatever it takes, in order to do me, that's what I'll do."

Prepared to go to bed in less than an hour, she used the precious bit of extra time to go online. Immediately upon walking into her spare-bedroom-flipped-into-office, which was painted brushed lavender and cream cake, Layla tightened the belt on her terry cloth robe and walked to her compact-style workstation. The first thing she did when she sat down in her chair was to log on to her favorite social media site. Like a kid in a candy store, Layla began to interact with her growing number of online friends. Ten minutes of her precious time was spent checking out seventeen new male friend requests.

Her attention quickly shifted to the pop-up box at the bottom right side of her screen. It was Envy. "What is she doing online? She always says she hates social media."

Hey, girl, I was about 2 get worried when I didn't see you online. (LOL)

I don't no why, u're the 1 who is oh so busted. Thought you were a social media hater. Layla typed into the message window.

I am, but I'm bored 2nite. I decided 2 mess around on here 4 a minute or 2. I searched 4 a few old friends from back in the day before me, u, and Kacie became practically inseparable. How was ur date?

Good, but I cut it short cuz of this bad weather. And I have 2 get up at least an hour early because its sposed 2 b pretty slick in the morning.

I think u r about 2 mess up a good thing w/Dennis.

Girl, where did that come from?

U no u've been stepping out on the man, and not just w/ Omar. He's just 1 of many u've dated since u lost all of that weight.

So? I guess u 4get that I lost all this weight after almost being killed. Anyway, I don't feel like going there with u 2nite. Dennis is a big boy. He'll b fine. Until I decide I want a man to put a ring on it, I'm going 2 live my life. (lol)

U r changing like crazy.

What r u talking about?

Don't u get it? It's not just about u dating other guys. What's with all of the suggestive photos u post online?

What can I say, I got it like that. This body will never b hidden again. (lol)

By, silly. U r definitely out of ur mind. U must not no that yur pics can b seen all over the world."

Yeah, I do. That's the best kind of feeling. Men from all over the world have commented on my pics. I get much attention, believe that, and it's all good. I may have even surpassed yur record.

What? I don't sho myself off online.

Oh no, that's right. U just walk around toting yur Bible in 1 hand and yur panties in the other. I'll talk 2 u 2moro. Goin 2 mess around a few more minutes; got some new pics I took last week that I want 2 post b4 I call it a nite.

Whateva, Layla.

Yeah, definitely. I'm out. Talk to u latr Envy/"

Gnite, Layla."

Envy's pop-up box displayed the word "offline." Layla browsed through the photos on the disc she inserted. Staring at each one, some less subtle than others, she got a rush like she'd been given a shot of adrenaline.

Layla Hobbs was new, improved, and ready to live life like she was more than a conqueror—in the "secular world," that is.

3

Secrets are made to be found out with time. —Unknown

Envy shut down her laptop and placed it and its cooling pad on her night table. "Layla, you are playing with fire. Anyone who has the least bit of sense knows that fire burns. Lord, help my friend. She's turning into someone that I don't know," Envy said aloud.

Envy curled up in her bedside chair with her seven-year-old golden Lab, Fischer, lying contently in his doggy bed gnawing away on one of his chew toys.

No matter how hard she tried to concentrate on the drastic change in Layla, her focus shifted to the skeleton stuffed inside her own closet. It was time for her to come to terms with the death of her newborn child; a death that took place over eighteen years ago, one for which she was at total fault. She shook her head like doing so would help erase thoughts about her past.

"No, no, no . . ." She shook her head. "Not tonight. I refuse to go there."

She got up from her chair and went to her bed. She turned off the light, pulled the down quilt up around her neck, and turned over on her left side. Like clockwork, Fischer jumped on the bed, licked her face, and then went and plopped all of his 105 pounds at the foot of the bed.

Covering her nose with her top lip, she said, "Ewe, you are so nasty! How can you lie in my bed and fart? You smell like a bowl of pinto beans gone bad."

Fischer gave her an innocent look before he turned his head from one side to the other, but he never moved from his spot.

Envy pulled the quilt up over her nose, but the sound of the phone ringing forced her to inhale the malodorous odor anyway.

"Hello, what's up, Leonard?"

"How's my favorite girl?"

"Trying to keep from throwing up," she answered. She leaned over and reached for the air freshener when she noticed it on the floor next to her bed.

"Don't tell me. . . Fischer is in his spot at the edge of the bed, sprawled out, and firing off one round after another." Leonard laughed into the phone.

"I don't see what's so funny. Fischer is just like a man. I might as well be married. Every night he gets in the bed, if he isn't snoring, he's farting, or both! I tell you, sometimes I feel like sending him to one of those pet sanctuaries."

Fischer's head popped up and his big black bubbly eyes looked at Envy as if he understood what she had said.

"Lie back down," she told him. "I need you around to remind me why I never want to be married." Fischer obeyed and rested his head between his paws.

"You don't mean that," Leonard said. "I've heard that love makes the world go round."

"You're free to think what you want. But I'm telling you that love is like a rose, beautiful for just a few minutes, but you'll quickly discover that it is full of thorns."

"Envy." Leonard sounded serious.

"What."

"Let me in."

Envy kicked off the cover and bolted upright in the bed, and so did Fischer.

"How many times have I told you not to ever pop up at my house? You don't have it like that," she fussed. "How can you talk about wanting to have a relationship when you're determined to do whatever it is you want to do, when you want to do it?"

"Hold on. For your information, I am at home with my legs propped up on my desk, sipping on a glass of red wine and enjoying the fire I started. So let me hear it."

"Let you hear what?" She snapped.

"An apology for falsely accusing me."

"I don't need to apologize; you're the one that said to let you in."

"Yes, you're right. I did say that."

"Uh, you don't have to tell me that I'm right, Leonard. I'm not sitting here stuck on stupid, you know." She lay back on her pillow and Fischer relaxed again too.

"Of course, you aren't. But what I meant was, let me into your world. I'm crazy about you. I know you go for tough and all, but somewhere inside of that wall of defense you've built, I believe you like me too."

Envy didn't know what to say. She didn't like to be told how she felt, or how she should feel. Leonard was a nice person, and if she thought long and hard, she probably would agree that she could easily fall in love with him. But she kept her heart under stringent protection. Only she had the key to unlock it.

"Look, I've had a long day. It's cold outside and I want to go to sleep. All of your lovey-dovey talk, save it for one of your females who'll fall for it. You should know that I'm not about to go for your empty words. Never have, and never will," she lied to him, and to herself. The strong beat of her heart against her breast betrayed her every single time she talked to Leonard or saw him.

"It's not lovey-dovey talk. It's real talk. I know I'm not exactly perfect." He chuckled. "I may not be one of those churchgoing, Bible-toting men, but I'm still a good man."

Envy's legs flew up underneath the covers. "You are so crazy! This is one time you are definitely telling the truth."

"I love to hear you laugh."

"Uh, mmm," she cleared her throat. "Maybe if you started paying more attention to getting next to God, then you wouldn't spend so much time chasing after something you'll never have. My heart belongs to one man—God. Unlike yours."

"We've known each other for how long, Envy—three years?"

"And?" Envy retorted.

"And you've never bothered to ask me what I believe." Leonard sounded perturbed. "So how can you play the sanctimonious one, like you have the inside track on God? For your information, my mother and father were both evangelists and missionaries. They spent almost every summer of my boyhood going from town to town holding tent revivals and teaching the Word. We even went to Africa to minister once or twice."

If Leonard could see through the phone, he would have seen Envy's hand fly up to her open mouth. *Leonard? A sort of preacher's kid? No way.* "You're definitely a man of many secrets, Mr. Stein. Any more confessions you care to make . . ." She opened her mouth and released a loud yawning sound into the phone, "before I bid you good night?"

"Let me think about that." Leonard paused. Envy waited. "One day you're going to fess up and tell me what I know your heart is already saying—you love me."

"You are so full of yourself. G'night. Be safe out there tomorrow."

"See, I knew you cared."

"I care about all the stray animals out there in the cold too, but it doesn't mean I'm going to bring them home. So until you come up with something better than that tired line, I bid you good night." Envy ended the call without giving him the chance to respond. Easing back underneath the cover, she leaned her head to the side and looked at Fischer for a few moments while he slept.

There would be no sleep for Envy for some time. Her thoughts turned once again to the child she gave birth to in the bathroom stall when she was a teenager. How could she have been so cruel and heartless back then? If only she had told someone, but she didn't. Not even Stanton, the baby's father. It wasn't like he rushed to her rescue, anyway. He was the one who told her he did not want a baby, nor did he want a relationship with her anymore. It was hard to believe that Stanton was one of the kinds of boys she had heard about around school— the ones who ran as quickly as night turns to dawn once they got what they wanted from a girl. She had pegged Stanton as being more mature. Being a college student, and older than she was, how could he have been so uncaring?

Envy shivered at the thought of what she went through back then. How could a mother, no matter how young, or alone, or scared, leave her child to die in a filthy toilet?

Envy tossed and turned. Here she was, a full-grown woman, with a hideous past, who had slept with over eighty men since she lost her virginity to Stanton. How could she be so critical of Layla and Kacie, when what she'd done was despicable and vile. She was worse than the scum of the earth.

Next, Envy's thoughts drifted to the late Mrs. Rawlings; someone she used to consider a nosy, meddling, old neighbor, who turned into a confidante. Mrs. Rawlings was the one person who saw through her. The wise old woman seemed to understand that the life Envy was living was nothing but a cover-up, a façade, for the dastardly decisions made in her past. Envy grew to accept Mrs. Rawlings's uncanny way of involving herself into her life. In the end, their relationship was strengthened; and Envy was grateful that Mrs. Rawlings was genuinely concerned about her.

Ever since Mrs. Rawlings had gone to be with the Lord, there were times Envy sank deep into depression. Her mother was dead; she didn't exactly have the best relationship with her sister, Nikkei, and having a bevy of men at her disposable no longer made her forget about her past.

Several months after Mrs. Rawlings's death, the property owner decided to bail out and sell the duplex property where she lived. It was a great opportunity for Envy when he proposed selling the property to her before offering it up to anyone else. The real estate market had dwindled during the recession, and Envy looked at it as a blessing in disguise.

Not only did she get the first-time homebuyer's credit, but she became a property owner, and within a few weeks of closing on the property, she was able to locate a word-of-mouth tenant who was anxious to rent Mrs. Rawlings's former side. The tenant, a female truck driver in her late forties, was on the road more than she was at home, which suited Envy just fine. She would always love Mrs. Rawlings for looking out for her, but Envy didn't want another neighbor prying into her private life.

Envy smiled and then switched back to wrestling with the decision she'd made recently to turn herself in to the police. The case about her dead baby had never been solved. There was not a day that passed, when Envy wasn't reminded of the life she so crudely turned her back on.

Before she talked to the police or an attorney, Envy had to find a way to tell Kacie and Layla about her past. There was no way she could get around it. If the police happened to lock her up, she would want one of them to bail her out. She had no one else to turn to. What Kacie and Layla would think of her after this—only God knew the answer to that, but she would rather tell them before she told her sister. She was not up to hearing Nikkei's ridicule.

Envy planned to find the courage to tell Kacie and Layla this weekend at their girls' night out, something they did at least once or twice a month when their schedules coincided. This weekend, if the weather permitted, they were going to dine at one of their favorite spots, The Silver Spoon.

Envy's thoughts drifted back to the one and only true person who could help her through the mess she had made of her life. "God," Envy prayed, lifting her head upward, "help me. I don't know what's going to happen to me, but I know one thing, it's time to do the right thing for once in my life."

4

No matter how discouraged we get, God has not asked us to do the impossible. George Grace

Kacie groaned when she heard the shrill sound of the alarm clock. She turned over on her left side and tried her best to reach the table next to her full-size bed to turn it to snooze. It was to no avail, because Kyland lay in the bed next to her and popped up like a jack-in-the-box as soon as the alarm went off.

"Ma-Ma," he said, and immediately climbed up on her side like it was a mini-mountain. "Ma-Ma."

Kacie groaned again and used her right hand to pull Kyland over the side so they were face-to-face. She gave him a kiss on his soft, round, dirt brown cheek. Looking at him, she still could not believe that he was not Deacon's son. He looked so much like him from his fat, juicy cheeks to his thin, curly bush of sandy brown hair.

"Boy, I sure don't need an alarm clock as long as I have you sleeping next to me." She eased herself to an upright position without loosening her grip around his toddler waist. "Go wake up your sisters and brothers," she ordered the two-year-old. After she released her hold, he turned over on his belly, like a big boy, and slid down the side of the bed until his feet touched the carpeted floor; then he ran out of the room.

"Good, maybe now I can catch an extra five minutes of shut-eye." Kacie lay back down on her side, closed her eyes, and drifted into a light sleep.

The ruckus of children pulled her from the dream she was having about a good-looking, sexy man who loved her a hundred times more than Shrek, the ogre, loved Princess Fiona. The mystery man welcomed her and her seven kids into his life. She stood next to him in front of the altar; dressed beautifully in a pure white, one-shoulder, silk-and-chiffon, ankle-length wedding gown. Her hair was coiffed perfectly and a rhinestone and alloy silver tiara rested on top. She and the man in her dream were about to exchange wedding vows when she was awakened by sounds of crying, screaming, and hollering flooding into her bedroom from the hallway.

"What in the world are y'all doing in there?" Kacie rubbed her eyes and sat up in the bed. While she yelled, she placed both feet on the floor, reached hold of the bedpost to steady herself, and then out of the room she went, moving as fast as her deformed legs would carry her.

Kenny yelled at Keshena, who screamed back at him, while Kassandra talked over the other kids, including Kyland, who stood in the midst of the other kids trying to outcry or outyell them all. Kacie couldn't quite decipher the scene unfolding before her at the time. But one thing was certain; they had spoiled one of her best dreams yet.

"Stop it." Kacie pointed her finger. "Stop it right this minute. Have y'all brushed your teeth and washed your faces? Kenny and Kassandra, have y'all started breakfast; and Kali, while you're running your mouth trying to act like somebody's mama, have you even bothered to change Kyland's pamper, and, Keith, you look guilty as−." Before she resorted to using profanity, the way she sometimes did when her children really aggravated her, Kacie gave them a firm warning. "I know one thing, by the time I come back out of my bedroom, dressed and ready to get out of here, y'all best be ready too . . . or else." The kids shot off in all directions like shotgun pellets, including li'l Kyland.

In the short span of time since waking, the full fantasy events in her dream had quickly dissolved, which made her even angrier.

"I'm so glad the holidays are over and y'all are back in school," she told them while she walked away. "Y'all better hurry up and get ready before I come in there and give you all something that's going to give every one of you a reason to holler. You can play me this morning if you want to, but I'm going to show you better than I can tell you."

Kacie went to her walk-in closet and pulled out her red work uniform shirt that she'd washed and ironed the night before. She put on the red top and black trousers. Afterward, she went deeper into her closet until she found her black Reebok tennis shoes. The shoes were one of the few types that relieved the pressure off her ankles because of her bended knees. She could move around better at work and maintain her balance more than she could when she wore shoes with a heel.

"Are y'all getting ready in there?" she hollered at the kids again.

"Yes, ma'am," most of them answered, almost in unison.

She finished getting dressed; and before she left her room to go help the kids finish getting ready, Kacie turned from the closet and walked over to her dresser. She stood in front of the mirror and stared at the reflection. One hand slowly touched her face and rubbed the side of her cheek. In her mind, it was like the mirror had two faces; and Kacie disliked both of them. She looked at the pitiful woman staring back at her. How did you get inside me? Why can't I be beautiful and successful? What do you want from me? What happened to make my life so messed up? God, why did you make me this way? The flurry of questions kept her frozen still, like a block of ice. If only the woman staring back at her would answer. Suddenly, angry at God and the woman in the mirror, she balled up a fist, prepared to hit the mirror, and then suddenly stopped.

Kacie released a long, sullen sigh before she turned her back on the woman in the mirror.

"Y'all better be ready in there," she said again, and left the room to start another day.

5

A woman has got to love a bad man once or twice in her life, to be thankful for a good one. —*M. Rawlings*

Dennis and Steve walked outside after having attended the monthly postal workers' union meeting. Friends since seven years old, and co-workers since eighteen, the ebony and ivory friends hung out as often as time permitted. Their bond of unity was probably as tight as it was because Dennis grew up in a house with seven sisters, and Steve was not just an only child, but the only white boy who lived and grew up in a black neighborhood two houses down from Dennis. Their bond of friendship remained tight, like brothers.

After three months of seriously dating Layla, Dennis formally introduced her to Steve and Steve's wife, Betty Jean. He confided in his best friend that he was in love and wanted to spend the rest of his life with Layla. Dennis often fantasized about living a grander scaled but mirrored life of Steve and Betty Jean. Steve appeared to have a perfect life, surrounded by a woman who always acted as if she adored him.

Dennis never verbally admitted the pinch of jealousy he sensed when he witnessed Steve's children bolting toward their father and repeatedly squealing, "Daddy" when he walked into a room. It was the type of happy, serene life he hoped to one-day share with Layla.

"You going to see Layla tonight, man?" asked Steve as they approached their individual cars parked side by side.

"Naw." Disappointment lodged in the base of his throat. "I don't know, man." Dennis shook his head.

"You don't know what? Trouble in paradise?" asked Steve.

"It's just an unsettling feeling I'm starting to have about me and her."

"Like what, man?" Steve folded his arms like he was trying to fight off the sting of the hawk blowing directly at him.

Dennis apparently noticed. "Man, get in the car. It's brutal out here. I'll talk to you about it later. Anyway, it's probably nothing."

"I disagree. Man, if you sense a change, something different, then it's probably something. I'm not saying anything like her stepping out on you, but females . . . well, all I know is they can be some moody creatures, and that crosses the racial lines. You know Betty Jean and me been together since I was nineteen. Man, I promise you, I've seen so many personalities from that woman until I think I'm loco sometimes." Steve laughed and opened the door to get inside his car.

Dennis barely chuckled. "I'm about to head to the house. See you tomorrow. Peace out." He got inside his Ford Edge. Simultaneously, he closed his door and turned the ignition.

"Yeah, backatcha." Each of them pulled out of the parking lot, almost at the same time.

Dennis pushed the radio button on the steering wheel until he located one of his favorite media playlists. Immediately he started singing along with the song.

Minutes later, while driving away from downtown and toward the I-240 Nashville junction, a call came in.

SYNC identified the caller and paused the music so Dennis could hear and take the call.

"Hi, I thought you would be asleep by now," he said to Layla.

"I was about to close my eyes, but I thought about you, so I called to say good night."

"Umm, awfully nice of you. You know, it's simple things like this that make me love you more each day—that's if it's possible to love you more than I already do."

"Love you too. Are you still at your meeting?"

"Nah, I'm about to get on the interstate. I should be home in about twenty minutes."

"I heard that."

"What? You must want me to come over there?"

Layla sighed, disregarding his question. "Be careful out there. I heard the streets are icing over, and I don't want anything to happen to my most prized blessing."

"Yeah, okay. Look, let me get off this phone so I can concentrate on what's going on out in these streets, and not what I'm missing between your sheets." He repositioned his body as he felt tension and desire warring in his flesh. "I'll talk to you in the morning. Okay?"

"For sure. G'night, babe."

The call ended and the music started up again. *Lord, why does she do me like this? She knows how much I want her. But she's right. I don't want to take the treasure you've given me, and misuse or abuse it. I never want to take her for granted.*

Dennis thought some more about Layla, but this time he wasn't asking God, Why? Instead, his mind drifted to thoughts of making love to her. When it came to that part of their relationship, he and Layla disagreed too. She usually discouraged his sexual advances and innuendos, but there were other times when he managed to win. Afterward, she often acted like she regretted giving in to him by becoming quiet and distant. Her behavior after making love didn't make him feel bad, because he loved her and didn't want anyone but her. So what if she said she was against sex outside of marriage? She wasn't a virgin when he met her, and he wasn't about to start being celibate. If he had his way, he was going to make sure Layla wouldn't have to feel guilty much longer. Her birthday was coming up in a few months, and he planned to ask her to be his wife. Dennis continued his drive home. Everything was going to be all right. It had to be.

Once inside his three-bedroom flat, Dennis removed his burlap overcoat and threw it over the living-room sofa. He sighed as he walked farther into his empty house. It was toasty warm inside. The words of Steve replayed in his mind. The sound of Layla mentally toyed with his body. What if Steve was right? Maybe the change he noticed in Layla really meant something. Was she losing interest in him?

The change had come on subtly over the past few months. She began to make excuses as to why she couldn't see him; whereas she used to want to be around him every day. He used to sleep over at her apartment, or vice versa; but now he was lucky to see her once a week.

There were Sunday mornings that he left his house or Layla's apartment with Layla still in the bed. That was out of character for someone like Layla who used to be at church almost every time the doors opened. How could he have missed the signs?

When she told him one Thursday night, about a month and a half ago, that she resigned from her church choir, Dennis almost choked as he took a deep swallow. She always said that singing was her release. She had a voice that no one could mistake being a gift from God. He loved hearing her melodious voice. Her singing could tame the savage beast, and melt the coldest heart. She used to tell him that she could not see herself doing anything else, because God had made it plain, simple, and clear that she was to use her voice to sing His praises. And she had—that is, until recently.

Dennis processed all of Layla's changes in his mind as he disrobed and stepped inside the shower. It was like putting together the pieces of a puzzle. As he neared the end, the pieces of the puzzle became easier to find. He washed his mocha-colored skin from head to toe while he tried to wrap his mind around what he had not allowed himself to think.

Dennis carried his newly revealed thoughts to the bedroom after he dried off. With his towel wrapped around his midsection, he went to his king-size bed, pulled back the comforter, and sat down. When he spotted his cell phone on top of the cherry wood chest of drawers, he got back up and took two giant steps to retrieve it. The phone and his index finger seemed to have a mind of its own as he pressed the speed-dial button.

Ring, ring. No answer. *Ring, ring.*

"Hi, if you want me to return your call, leave me a message and I promise to get back to you as soon as I become available."

Dennis hit the End button. "She must be asleep already." He went back to his bed. This time he released his towel and climbed underneath the top sheet. With both hands behind his head, he lay on his double pillows. A heavy boulder of pain took the liberty to sit over his heart. He was afraid to say aloud what he already knew on the inside.

Layla is messing around.

6

Beauty and ugliness disappear equally under the wrinkles of age; one is lost in them, the other hidden. —*Unknown*

"I'm so glad we're going out tonight. It's always good to get away from the kids every now and then for some me time."

Envy responded, "Kacie, I don't know how you do it, but I'm proud of you."

"Me too," added Layla. "School, work, motherhood. Ooh wee, you rock, black girl."

"Thanks, y'all. I know my patience with the kids can wear thin sometimes, but it's harder than y'all can imagine. Neither one of you have kids. Here I am with seven."

"Come on, Kacie. Enough already. I'm tired of hearing the same old sob story about you and your seven kids and seven baby daddies. Get over it. Dog!"

Kacie looked at Layla and rolled her eyes.

"Be quiet, Layla You used to have your share of I need to talk moments. I don't care how many times we have to listen to each other's stories and woes, whateva, that's what we're supposed to do if we call ourselves friends."

Layla nodded. "You're right. And I'm sorry, Kacie. Get it off your chest."

"I know you get tired of hearing it, but I can't seem to move forward because I feel ashamed so much of the time. Yeah, I'm in school. So what? Men still think I'm a slut or something when I tell them how many children I have. I can't even find but one, sometimes two, of either of their daddies. That's a shame." Kacie started to sniffle.

Envy leaned forward from the back seat of Layla's car and looked at Kacie. "Kacie, how many times do you have to be reminded that none of us can afford to be seen in anything white." She chuckled.

Layla laughed too, followed by Kacie.

Kacie became serious again. "I keep being used and abused because men think I'm easy. I guess I am. That's the killing part. Then having this disability doesn't help matters either."

"I don't see how having a disability can make a man look at you any differently. Shoots, they're all out for one thing. It doesn't matter how you look, walk, or what size you are. They don't care if you're butt ugly."

"You know, you'll say anything." Layla eyed Envy in the rear view mirror. Stifling a laugh, she turned toward Kacie. A serious expression replaced laughter. "I feel you, Kacie. Disregard the relationship expert," Layla advised.

"If only y'all knew half of what I've gone through with men because of my cerebral palsy, you wouldn't be so quick to speak about what you obviously don't know about, Envy."

"Excuse me. I didn't mean to step on your toes," Envy apologized. Kacie could be sensitive about her disability. Most of the time, she and Layla tried not to talk about it, because just like tonight, Kacie would get upset.

"Forget it," Kacie responded.

As they neared The Silver Spoon, an upscale lounge and restaurant, Envy planned to spill her guts. Hearing Kacie talk about her kids, and her believing that she was the only one who had given birth to a child out of the three of them, had to end, and it had to end tonight.

The ambience of The Silver Spoon was inviting. Low lights, live entertainment, and delectable food made it the perfect place to unwind on a Friday night. Each of them ordered a frozen margarita, different flavors, along with two appetizers they planned to share. The up-tempo music created an atmosphere where the girls could chill and fill each other in on the prior week's events.

"Layla, what have you been up to?" asked Kacie. "I hope you aren't still messing around on Dennis."

"Look, don't start, Kacie. How many times do I need to remind you two," she used two fingers to point at her friends, "that I am just like you? Single. I am not engaged. I am not about to become engaged. I am not married. I am not about to get married. So, do you know what that means?" Layla didn't wait for a response from her wide-eyed friends. "It means that I can do whatever I darn well please, and I can do it with whomever I please."

"Nobody is telling you that you can't, but you shouldn't lead Dennis on either," commented Envy. "You know that man worships the ground you walk on. He loves you for real. I don't want to see him get hurt, the same way I didn't want to see you get hurt by Mike. You, of all people, know how it feels to have your heart broken."

"No, not really, because Mike didn't break my heart. He actually helped build my spirit. Yes, he was a fool, an abuser, and he used me for everything he could. But when I wised up and told that fool that I couldn't take any more of his mess; then he went ballistic. But you know, and I don't know how many more times I'm going to have to say this, but what the devil meant for evil, God meant for my good. Now that's all I have to say about the matter."

"Blah, blah, blah, and blah," said Kacie as she opened and closed her hand to make it appear that her hand was doing all the talking. "I hope and pray that this was your last time saying that. I'm so tired of hearing you talking about God used your situation for good. Okay, I can agree with that, but have you ever stopped, and I mean really stopped to think whether or not God is okay with you flaunting your body, dressing half-naked, flirting, and strutting yourself around like you're His gift to man."

Layla bucked her eyes and leaned back in her chair. "Envy, do you hear this girl? Has she lost her rabid mind or what? Just because I finally have some self-confidence and feel good about myself, she, of all people, wants to call me names? I hope it's not jealousy I'm hearing, Miss Kacie," retorted Layla.

"Jealousy?" Kacie leaned forward like she was about to spring out of her chair, but the server interrupted the heated exchange by bringing their drinks and appetizers.

"Thank you," Envy told the server, they all remained quiet until the server walked off.

"Now, like I was saying, why should I be jealous of you? Just because you lucked out and lost a couple of hundred pounds," Kacie emphasized. "You lost your personality, not to mention your religion, along with it. I don't know why you don't realize that beauty comes in all sizes, not just a size eight. You were beautiful when you were a big girl."

"Don't you talk about me and my beliefs. I don't have to prove to you and anybody else that I'm a child of God."

"Oh, that's funny. When you were fat—and by the way, I mean F-A-T, not P-H-A-T, you acted like you just loved yourself some God," Kacie snapped. "And you do know the difference between the two, so don't get it twisted," mocked Kacie. "Every time we turned around you were up in the church house singing and shouting, getting your praise on as you called it. Now all you sing about are those same old tired love songs, or rump-shaking rap songs. You're a fool and you don't even realize it."

"I bet I'm not a fool with enough children to have her own basketball team. So watch what you say, honey. You talking about you feel bad, shewww, you right to feel bad. Look at yourself. You keep on making the same old mistake over, and over, and over, and over, and over; let me see how many is that? Oh, I need two more. Over and over. Now, take a look at yourself before you try to talk about me."

Kacie's face turned crimson. Fire seemed to blaze in her piercing black eyes.

Envy stopped the heated conversation as they spiraled out of control. "Look, I didn't come out here tonight to listen to the two of you bicker." Envy looked at Layla. "Layla, one thing you're right about, and that is you are a grown woman. You can do as you please." Then she turned to Kacie. "And, Kacie, we need to stay out of her business, unless she asks us to be in her business."

Layla nodded and the frown on her nicely made-up face transformed into a broad smile of satisfaction.

"So you're taking her side?" A deep crease formed on Kacie's forehead as she scowled.

"No, I'm not taking anybody's side. I just don't want to hear this tonight. Let's talk about something pleasant for a change."

Layla jumped right back in the saddle. "Okay, let me tell you about this guy I met online."

"Online? Since when did you start going online to meet men?" This time Envy was the one who appeared stunned. She cocked her head to the side and peered over at Layla sitting next to her.

"I don't go online to meet men. They see my profile and come after me. Anyway, like I was saying," she continued in a mocking type of voice, "his name is Camden, and he is a hottie. He's an electrical engineer, divorced, no children, and he lives in Arlington, Texas."

"Oh, I guess you're going to Texas now, huh." Sarcastic undertones dripped from Envy's lips.

"No, I have more sense than that, unlike some people I know," Layla bit back. "All we do is chat and text. I've talked to him on the phone a few times. He said he might have to come to Memphis this summer for a training seminar. If he does, we'll probably hook up."

"Oh, like that makes it any better," mumbled Kacie.

"You're one to talk. How can the pot call the kettle black? Need I remind you again that you don't have room to talk about anybody? And no use in being jealous of all of this, baby." Layla allowed her hands to highlight her body.

"Stop it!" Envy slammed the flat of her hand down on the table so hard that their margarita glasses started to shake. "Stop all the fighting. Dang. Y'all getting on my nerves with all this."

"Envy, there's no use in getting upset. The truth hurts some people. I can't help that I look good now. I can't help it that men are waiting in line to meet me. Matter of fact, I met one literally in line at Whole Foods the other day. His name, let me see . . ." Layla twisted her mouth, placed her thumb and index finger on her lips, and exhaled. "Oh yeah, Landon. Now, talking about one fine brother. Y'all know that song that came out a while back by Usher called 'OMG.' Well, this brother gotta a body like pow, pow, pow," she sang to the tune of the song. "Oh, and before I forget, he and a couple of his friends might come through here tonight." She smiled a devilish smile.

"Oh no you didn't invite him here," Kacie bit on her bottom lip, and inhaled. "This is supposed to be girls' night out. No guys are included, and you know that. I'm worried about you for real." Kacie pushed back from the table and stood up. "I'm going to the bathroom. Suddenly I feel like I need to…to sit on the toilet."

"Last time I looked around, this was a public establishment. I don't need your permission to tell a friend about this place. And, as long as you meet the legal age limit and pay your money to get in, then there's nothing you can do about it." Layla jerked her head from side to side.

This time Envy couldn't stifle her need to laugh. "I don't know what I'm going to do with the two of you. Y'all kill me."

Kacie stormed off. "Humph," she said as she walked away.

"Now you know you were wrong for that," said Envy.

"Wrong for what? Kacie gets on my nerves. Trying to act like she's so perfect. You and I both know all you have to do is look at her and all the baby daddies she has. Plus, when she tried to pin Kyland on that man from church. Now that's what you call dead wrong."

"That was three years ago, Layla. Plus, none of us should be judging each other. Kacie is just looking out for you. She means well and you know it. So go easy on her. And another thing."

What?"

"She's right about Girls' Night Out. It *is* supposed to be for us. No men."

"Yeah, that was only because we didn't have any men to include. You won't give that Leonard dude or any other man the time of day. And Kacie, well, she only keeps a man long enough to get knocked up. She needs to go on strike." Layla leaned her head back and laughter spewed forth.

"See, that's what I mean. I agree with Kacie. You're so condemning—like you haven't ever made mistakes."

"The truth is the truth. Call it what you want."

Kacie returned to the table. "Whatever y'all were saying, please don't stop on my account."

"Don't worry. I won't," replied Layla. "Oh, my gosh." Layla's hand flew up to her mouth, and she quickly bowed her head.

"What is it?" asked Envy. Kacie looked surprised as well.

"It's—it's the guy I told y'all about. Landon."

"Why are you ducking and dodging? You just said he was coming with two of his—"

"Friends," Kacie quickly added. "Is that Dennis standing next to him?"

Envy looked toward the entrance of the lounge. Sure enough, Dennis and two other gentlemen were entering. One of them peered around like he was searching for someone.

Kacie's surprise was accompanied by laughter. "You're caught if one of them is Landon with Dennis, and you're still caught if Landon is coming and Dennis is here already."

"Shut up. Are they looking over here?" she asked, her head still bowed like she was picking up something from off the floor.

"Affirmative, and they're coming this way," said Envy." I think Dennis just spotted me and Kacie."

"What do I do?" Layla sounded frantic.

"Handle your business like a grown woman," Kacie remarked harshly. "Hi, Dennis," Kacie said as soon as he and the two men approached the table.

Layla looked up. "Hi. What are you doing here?"

"Hi, Dennis and friends," added Envy.

"Hi, Envy. Baby, I didn't know y'all were coming here tonight," remarked Dennis. "Me and Steve told our co-worker here, Landon," Dennis patted Landon on the back, "that we'd meet him here. He's hooking up with this female, and just in case it doesn't go too well, me and Steve were going to be his way out.

"You know Layla?" Landon frowned and looked at Layla and then Dennis. Steve stood back, quiet, with his arms folded.

"Do I know Layla?" Dennis pointed at himself. Without any warning, his expression changed. "Man, what kind of question is that? This is my lady. I need to be asking, how you know her?" His mind seemed to go into overdrive as he looked to his side at Landon, then slowly they reverted to Layla. "Man, don't tell me she's the female."

Landon threw both hands up in the air in a state of surrender. Envy, Kacie, and Steve watched. Thick intensity filled the space.

"Hey, man, I had no idea." He pointed at a pale-faced, speechless Layla. "Girl didn't mention she had a man. I told y'all I met a chick a couple of days ago, man. Y'all already know what's up. Hey, man, I'm sorry." Landon extended his hand toward Dennis.

"Man, it's not your fault." But he still shook Landon's outstretched hand. 'She's the one who needs to do some explaining." Still standing, Dennis bit his bottom lip and shook his head in disgust. "Why you play me like this?"

Layla rolled her eyes up in her head. "Don't try to make this my fault. If you weren't interested in meeting some other female, why did you agree to come along with him?" she asked. "And, Steve, last time I checked, you had a wife and kids, so seems to me like I'm not the one in the wrong here. All I did was have an innocent conversation with Landon. Told him about The Silver Spoon." She eyed Landon with raised eyebrows and a distorted face. "Don't play," she said to Landon and cocked her head to the side. "And," focusing her attention on Dennis now, "It's not like I owe you an explanation when I haven't done anything in the first place."

Envy's mouth slightly hung open, but no words formed. Kacie looked away and started picking on her sweater.

"She's right, man," Landon said. "I'm the one who misunderstood."

Dennis looked over at Landon. "I'm no fool, man, so don't try to cover for her." He switched his focus back on Layla. "Even Kacie and Envy can't vouch for you. You're busted. For the past couple of months, I knew there was something that wasn't right, but I couldn't quite put my finger on it." Dennis looked over his shoulder at Steve. "Man, you tried to tell me, but I wouldn't listen."

Steve placed his hand on Dennis's shoulder. "Look, man, let's just get out of here before things get out of hand," recommended Steve. "You're upset right now and this is awkward for everybody. You and Layla need to talk about this in private."

Dennis jerked away from Steve. "You're right. Let me get out of here." Dennis turned around and walked out of the lounge.

Landon looked at Layla like he was unsure of what to do.

"I'm out too, man," said Steve. "I'll holler later."

Landon was the last man standing.

"Come on, Kacie. Let's move closer to the band. Let the two of them talk."

Kacie nodded but didn't say a word. She got up and followed Envy.

"What's up with you, lady?" asked Landon and sat down. "So you messing around with my co-worker?"

Layla looked embarrassed, but she quickly tried to change embarrassment to a look of self-assuredness.

"Not that it's any of your business, but yeah, Dennis and I are friends. I also told you that I wasn't married. I care a lot about Dennis. I wouldn't ever want to intentionally hurt him."

"But that's the thing. Hurt was written all over my man's face. He's good people." Landon used both hands to cover his face for a second. "Ugh, this is messed up. I haven't known Steve or Dennis for that long. I just started working the same shift with them a few weeks ago. This was our first time hanging out."

Landon shook his head. "Man, why didn't you just say you had a man and leave it at that. I don't want to be part of no mess."

"Aren't they waiting on you outside?"

"We drove our own cars, because like I said, I told them I was meeting you. Steve was just getting out for the enjoyment. Nothing was on his mind about cheating on his wife. The same with Dennis. He told me he had a beautiful woman, and she was crazy about him. I can't lie. You're gorgeous. Tell me, why you gave me your number?"

"I'm not going to sit here all night, Landon, and try to explain things to you. I did not intend to form a forever-after relationship with you. As for Dennis, if he loves me so much, then he should have put a ring on it, not that I would accept it, because I'm happy. I've held back on living life for far too long, and I'm not going to take it for granted ever again. If that means that someone gets hurt in the process, oh well, sorry. But I've got to do me now."

The look on his face was difficult to read. "Look, you're one sexy, fine, and confident woman. I have to admit that you turn me on. I would have loved to get to know you better, a whole lot better," he said, and laid his hand on top of hers.

"Landon, there are enough worries for today to waste time worrying about what might have been. It was nice meeting you." Layla turned away from him. Landon walked off. *Another one bites the dust. If only Dennis hadn't shown up.*

Kacie and Layla returned to the table after Landon departed.

"What happened?" they both asked, almost at the same time.

"Nothing really. I just told him that he was never meant to be a forever-after relationship."

"What about Dennis? What are you going to do about him?" asked Kacie.

"The man looked crushed," said Envy. "I felt terrible when he realized Landon was here to meet you. Girl, could things have been any worse?"

"Yeah, I could still be a big, fat, ugly woman sitting on the couch in front of the TV, munching on Church's fried chicken. Oh, there are many things that could be worse, and have been worse, besides wondering how I'm going to get things back right with Dennis. If anything, he had better realize the jewel he has in me. 'Cause I'm telling y'all something that men like Landon realize every day—I'm priceless."

Kacie gave Layla a crazy look and rolled her eyes up in her head. "Come on, y'all. I'm ready to go. My sixteen-year-old babysitter is probably pulling her hair out right about now," said Kacie.

"What's the rush? Isn't Kenny helping her with the kids?" asked Layla. "It's still early and it's not like we have to get up early in the morning. We can have another margarita and finish our girls' night out. We sure won't have a lack of things to talk about, not after all the drama tonight." She smiled while Kayla and Envy looked at each other and then at Layla with faces that looked like they had been etched in stone.

"Kacie's right," remarked Envy. "Let's go. Kacie wants to see about her kids, and I don't want to start thinking about how you can sit here and act like everything is all good when you probably just blew off the best relationship you've had in your life."

Layla shooed them off with a wave of the hand. She took another sip of the last few drops of her margarita before she proceeded to stand. "Y'all are some real party poopers. If I'm not sitting here pulling my hair out, then I sure don't see why the two of you are making a mountain out of a molehill. But that's fine. Let's get out of here. I have plenty of numbers I can dial if I really want some company, and that includes Dennis and Landon. I don't know what it's going to take for y'all to see that I'm not the old Layla Hobbs; this time I'm the shot caller." Layla pointed at herself, reached across the chair, picked up her coat, and proceeding putting it on.

Kacie and Envy remained silent while they put their coats and gloves on too. The three of them walked outside and were welcomed by the cold.

The ride home was full of continuous banter by mostly Layla. "Watch this," she said as she turned on Ridgeway in the direction of the interstate. She turned off her Bluetooth, and put her phone on speaker.

"Fool, what are you doing?" asked Envy.

"Yeah, you do not need to be talking on the phone and driving. Shoot, it's not like you have that much driving experience. And haven't you heard of the Oprah Winfrey No Phone Zone pledge about not talking or texting while driving?" Kacie shot Layla an irritated look.

"No, I never was an Oprah fan, and you know it. There's nothing someone like her, with billions of dollars, can tell me. She has a chauffeur driving her around so she can talk whenever she pleases. Forget Oprah, and shut up and listen."

"Hello," Dennis said; he was on speaker for all of them to hear.

"Dennis, I'm sorry about tonight. I can explain everything, if you'll give me a chance." She looked over at Envy and eyed Kacie who was in the backseat as she sped along the interstate.

"Look, I don't want to hear your excuses. I know what was going on, so don't try to play me. I'm not going for it." Hurt more than anger resonated in his voice.

"Dennis, please. I know you love me, so don't play games. Let me stop by. I need to talk to you for real."

Silence filled the air. Envy and Kacie appeared glued to the conversation between Dennis and Layla.

Envy peered over her shoulder at Kacie and shook her head.

"I'll give you fifteen minutes. That's it." He sighed into the phone.

"That's all I need. I should be there in about thirty, no later than forty minutes."

"Remember, you still have only fifteen minutes of my time when you get here."

"I'll see you in a little bit. Bye, sweetheart." She hit the End icon on her phone. "Didn't I tell you that I have that man in the palm of my hands," she said, and gestured with one hand off the steering wheel.

"Girl, slow down. It's probably still some ice out here from the other night. While you're trying to prove to us that you're some . . . well, I don't know what you're trying to prove," chided Kacie, "but right now, all I need you to prove is that you can get me home safely."

Envy and Layla laughed and the three of them engaged in conversation about everyday happenings they'd heard about around the city.

"Kacie, what's up for you when you get home?" asked Layla.

"I don't know. I don't have a man in my life. Girl, my little red book got so much dust on it, it's beginning to take on the form of a mountain." Kacie laughed.

"I'll have to see what I can do to help you out. You need to do something fun, and go somewhere daring, where the fine men hang out."

Envy spoke up. "Do not listen to this wild child, Kacie." The three of them laughed while Layla drove toward the intersection.

"Come on, let's make the best of this ride home."
Layla turned the radio to classic soul and Jennifer
Hudson was singing. "You hear that, y'all? She said she's
invisible for the last time. Sing that song, girl."

Kacie started laughing. "Will you watch where
you're going! You've only been driving for a minute, you
know."

"Don't try to talk about my driving. I'm getting
better every day. Stop trying to avoid the song. You
hear that?" Layla asked, and then started singing, "'And
now I'm gonna live my life for me.' You better wake up,
girlfriend."

"If you ain't crazy, I'll pay somebody my paycheck,"
Envy said, cracking up while banging her back against
the seat cushion.

"All I know is that the last thing I need is a man.
You used to say that all you had to do was look at food
and get fat; well, all I have to do is look at a man and I
get pregnant," said Kacie.

The three friends spent the ride home singing,
talking, and laughing. None of them knew or cared what
tomorrow might bring. There were plenty of worries to
last them through the night, without the fresh worries
they were sure to face on tomorrow.

7

By trying, we can easily endure adversity. Another man's, I mean. Mark Twain

Kacie unlocked the door to her house. Before she could make a complete step inside, a stream of light guided her along the cherry wood floor and toward the den. One of Kenny's favorite rappers serenaded her from what she recognized as his most prized possession, an IPOD his daddy had given him. "Everybody must be sleep," she whispered for no apparent reason.

She removed her coat and hung it, along with her faux Coach bag, on the coatrack inside the foyer. In a butler's dozen of steps, she was in the den. The first stop was Kenny's IPOD dock. She reached down on the table to switch off the dock, and almost stumbled and fell when she saw two figures lying on the floor.

Her hands covered her open mouth. "Oh, my God, what is this?" Her voice seemed to startle the couple lying on the floor. Twelve-year-old Kenny was in his boxer shorts and the sixteen-year-old babysitter was butt naked. She hurriedly pulled the quilt up to shield her body.

"What in the . . ." A list of expletives poured from Kacie's mouth. She had been scared out of her mind, thinking that something tragic had happened. Something had—the babysitter had molested her son. "Get up. Get up right now!" she screamed. "How dare you come into my home and rape my child. I'm calling the police right now." Kacie felt each pant pocket for her cell phone, but quickly recalled it was inside her purse.

The frantic looking babysitter jumped up, holding on to the quilt while she searched around the parameter of the room for her clothes.

Kenny was up just as quick. "Mom, stop tripping, will you? Jackie did not rape me. So don't be calling the police. We weren't doing anything, man. Anyway, I'm going to be thirteen in a few," he said.

The cracks in his voice rendered Kacie speechless for a few seconds as she thought about her oldest boy being right at the door of puberty. She shook her head. "I don't care how old you are. You can be a hundred and thirteen, but know this," Her voice rose in anger. I'll whoop your behind then too. Kacie walked up on him and pointed her finger so close to his face that she could have scratched his eyes out if she chose. "Boy, you don't know anything. You still have milk on your breath. This fast-tail girl took advantage of you, and she's going to pay." Kacie pointed at a terrified-looking Jackie.

"Ms. Mayweather, please don't call the police," Jackie pleaded. "I didn't do anything. I promise I didn't. Nothing happened. Please, Ms. Mayweather." The girl cried uncontrollably.

Kacie turned abruptly. She saw two of her older children, who must have heard her screaming, watching from around the corner. Their eyes were huge as hokie marbles. "What are y'all doing? Y'all got somebody in here too?"

With looks of terror, they shook their heads and said, "No, ma'am."

"Then get your butts back in your rooms," she yelled at Keith and Kassandra, "and I mean right now." The kids disappeared within seconds.

Jackie managed to gather her clothes. And within moments, the girl was fully dressed, while Kenny remained half-naked in front of his mother. For the first time, Kacie looked with different eyes at her oldest child. She studied his almost-six-foot frame, which he'd taken after his father. She looked at his forming abs and muscular shoulders. She even noticed stubbles of hair on his chin. When did all of this happen? How had it happened without her noticing? The sound of his voice telling his mother that she was wrong brought her back to a state of reality.

"You are in serious trouble, young man, if you are having sex in my house," she continued to yell. "And you, Miss Hot Tail, I'm calling your parents right now. They think you're over here babysitting, and you're, well, you're nothing but a slut and a pervert. Messing around with a child. What kind of neighbors are y'all?"

Tears continued to pour from the girl's eyes.

"Too late for tears now. Sit your behind down on that sofa until I get your parents on the phone. Then I'll decide about whether or not to call the police on you."

"Momma, stop it, will you? Don't you see you're scaring her?"

"Boy, if you don't shut up talking to me and get some clothes on your behind." Kacie's face was scarlet. She formed two fists like she was getting ready to fight. "And remember, the taller they are, the harder they fall. I might be shorter than you, but I will still knock your butt out. I will not have you disrespecting me in my own house. I don't care if you're twelve or forty. Do you understand me, son?" She didn't flinch for a second. She stood at his chest, mere inches from him. Her face had a snarl on it that could probably curl the devil's toes. She was just that mad.

Kenny obeyed his mother. He hurriedly found his pants and T-shirt and put them on just as quickly as Jackie had put on her clothes.

"Now sit down. Over there." She pointed toward the recliner. Kacie left the room and went to retrieve her cell phone. She called Jackie's house and began telling whoever answered the phone what she had walked in on when she arrived home. "Y'all need to come over right now, because I am about to call the police on your daughter."

Kacie threw her cell phone on the couch and returned her focus to Kenny and Jackie. "See, if I had walked in here, and you, Miss Thang, were a boy, and Kenny was a girl, well, there would be a murder committed up in here because I would have done everything to take you out of this world . . . and I still feel like it. But you think since he's my son and you're a girl that you can just do what you want to him and not suffer any consequences? Well, honey, you've met the wrong mama now."

"Ma, please. Stop it. It isn't my first time being with a girl. I know what I'm doing. Anyway, I made the move on Jackie, not the other way around." Kenny bit on his bottom lip and paused like he was deciding whether to keep talking or be quiet. Kacie's temper could get out of hand at times, and this was definitely one of those times. He timidly spoke again while Jackie sat on the couch and rubbed her hands together. "And we weren't having real sex, anyway, Ma."

"What do you mean you weren't having real sex? I didn't know there was such a thing as not having real sex," she said in an angry voice. "Why don't you enlighten me by telling me the kind of not-real sex you were having? Tell me that!" she yelled.

"Just oral sex. It was nothing."

"What did you just say? Boy, are you on drugs? I know you didn't say that you've been having oral sex? Where? Up in my house? Don't you know what God teaches about fornication, sex outside of marriage?"

"Ma, I don't mean no disrespect, but look around our house. You have seven of us and we all have different daddies. I know how to use protection if I was going all the way. Anyway, a lot of kids do it. It's no big deal."

Kacie hauled off and slapped Kenny so hard that his face turned sideways and her handprint formed before he could turn back to face her. She hit him repeatedly. "Please, please, Ms. Mayweather. Don't hit him anymore," Jackie cried and pleaded.

The doorbell rang and saved Kenny from another blow against his face and head. His eyes were watery, but no tears fell. Jackie, however, was almost hysterical. When she heard the voice of her father coming inside, she jumped up from the couch and ran into his arms. Her slender frame and long legs made her look like a wobbly giraffe.

"Yeah, run to your daddy, but your daddy can't help you up in here."

Jackie's mother wasn't with him. Kacie surmised that she must be at home with Jackie's younger sister and brother.

"Calm down, honey," he told his daughter while he surveyed the scene in front of him. "Ms. Mayweather, can we sit down and talk about what you said happened here?" he asked in an almost raised tone.

"We sure can. Have a seat," she instructed more than offered. The man held on to Jackie's hand and led her to the sofa.

Kacie remained standing. "It's simple, Mr. Cheney. Like always, I called your daughter to babysit my kids while I went out with my friends for some me time. I've been gone about two hours, only to return home to find my house dark with music playing right here in my den. I almost fell down when I stumbled over your daughter and my son underneath the cover you see over there." Kacie turned her head in the direction of the cover and used a finger to point as well.

"I know you probably don't want to hear this, but your daughter was butt naked, laying all up against my twelve-year old child. She's sixteen years old. She should know better. She molested my son. She gave him oral sex. How disgusting is that?"

"Hold on, Ms. Mayweather," the man said, and put his hand up like he was stopping traffic. "I don't think my daughter molested your son. Look at him." Mr. Cheney focused his attention on the young man sitting in the chair. His face was still beet red with handprints that looked like they had been professionally engraved on each side of his cheeks. "I don't know if you've noticed, and I'm certainly not trying to take any blame from my daughter's alleged actions, but Kenny does not look anywhere near like the average twelve-year old. The boy is almost as tall and as big as I am. And to be honest, he doesn't need a babysitter."

"What does that have to do with anything? And for your information, if you felt like my children didn't need a babysitter, why did you let Jackie come? You never had a problem with it before."

Mr. Cheney sucked in his breath until he looked like he was about to burst. "I let her come because you were paying her, and because I believed she would be safe. Apparently, I was wrong."

"Look, I have six other children and I'm not about to leave them for my son to watch by himself. And it's my business, not yours, whether I choose to have a babysitter or not. And apparently," Kacie emphasized, "I was the one wrong for believing Jackie was a respectable, trustworthy young lady. She obviously had other things on her mind, none that included looking after my children. No telling how long this has been going on," Kacie retorted with a show of force like she was backed by a full troop of soldiers.

Mr. Cheney rebutted angrily, "Well, if Kenny didn't want anything to happen between my daughter and him, he was certainly able to stop it." Mr. Cheney turned toward his daughter. "Jackie, did you and Kenny have sex? You can tell me the truth, honey. And if he made you do anything you didn't want to do, you can tell me that too. I'm here to protect you."

Jackie put her head in her hands and cried.

"I didn't make her do anything!" Kenny yelled.

"Shut up!" Mr. Cheney suddenly bounced up from the sofa. "You shut up right now. If you did anything to hurt my daughter, I swear—"

"Look here, don't you even try to turn this thing around and blame my son for what that little tramp did."

"I don't see how you can stand in front of me and call my daughter a tramp. Take a look at yourself in the mirror," he said with force behind every word. "That's why I hate that you people on Section 8 can move in our decent neighborhoods and then mess it up with kids like your hoodlum son, and you, Miss Mayweather," he said in a sarcastic drawl, "need to watch who you're calling a tramp."

"Daddy," Jackie hollered. "Please stop it."

Kenny sprung up. "Don't you call my mother a tramp," he yelled at Mr. Cheney. "Me and Jackie are friends; friends with benefits," confessed Kenny. "We've been having oral sex practically since we moved over here. I like her, she likes me, and age doesn't matter. A lot of teenagers are doing it; and she can't get pregnant 'cause we're not going all the way. Just because I'm twelve, y'all act like I don't know anything. But you got me messed up. Tell 'em, Jackie. Tell 'em that we care about each other." Jackie nodded but looked embarrassed.

Kacie reared her head back and started laughing. "You see, that right there shows just how stupid and immature you are, boy. This girl"—she pointed mockingly at Jackie—"could care less about you. No telling how many boys she's been doing that to."

"My daughter has been raised in a Christian home. That's one of the things I made clear to you when she was referred to you by one of our church members. Nothing like this has ever happened, until now. One thing your son said that makes sense is that age doesn't matter, especially when he's the size of a full-grown man. So don't start pointing accusatory fingers at my child. You're talking about calling the police, go right ahead. I bet you'll see that it's my daughter who's been violated, that is if anything happened." He looked over at Kenny with bloodshot eyes. His daughter remained silent.

"That's a hoot. Everything you're saying is a bunch of bull. You really want people to believe you're Christian folks? What kind of Christian allows their daughter to run around having sex with underage boys? What kind of Christian allows their daughter to act like she's so innocent and pure when she's no more than—than—than. . ." Kacie was at a loss for words.

"We don't have to justify our faith or beliefs to you. It's you who needs to take a look at your life and all these stray children you have."

"You don't know a thing about me or my children," yelled Kacie, "but the police are going to know all about your child." Kacie dialed 911 while Kenny yelled for her to stop, and Jackie sobbed into her daddy's chest. "Yes, I need the police right away. My son has been sexually assaulted."

~

Envy took Fischer for his walk before she settled in for the night. It was clear, quiet, and the stars shone bright. Her mind reflected once more on the death of her child. Her plan to talk to Kacie and Layla tonight had been foiled.

"Maybe it was for the best. Sometimes God has to intervene in situations in life before we make even more mistakes. Maybe God didn't want me to tell them tonight. Maybe I need to talk to a lawyer, Fischer, before I do anything else. That's exactly what I need to do." She spoke aloud to the dog like he understood everything she was saying.

One thing was for sure, if there was any chance of moving forward in her life, she had to go back and clean out the damage of her past. What the decision to talk to a lawyer would lead to, Envy had no idea, but she arrived at the conclusion that now was the time. Not another day, month, or year could go by without her confessing her crime. Throughout the years, she often prayed and asked God to forgive her, but it was never enough for Envy. She believed her full healing and forgiveness would come once she paid for what she'd done. It was the only way she could forgive herself.

"Come on, Fischer. You've finished doing your business. Let's get out of this cold. Tomorrow is going to be a better day. Just wait and see."

~

Layla tapped on Dennis's door. She pinched her cheeks until they turned red and forced tears to pour from her eyes, just as soon as he answered the door. Without waiting on an invitation, Layla walked inside Dennis's house like a sad puppy dog. She walked over to a nearby chair and placed her oversized bag on it. Immediately she fell into his arms.

She loved the power she wielded over Dennis. She made sure she kept him on his toes; she didn't want him to think she would be at his disposal 24/7. In this way, she could love him from a distance while she played around just enough to catch up on all she had been missing in her life before possessing a figure that most women would die for, and men drooled over.

"Dennis, please listen to me. I'm sorry. I know you think I was up to no good, but really it wasn't what it looked like."

Dennis, with a sickening look on his thick, mustached face, and light beard, pushed her away and walked into the open-floor-plan house. He stopped at the family room and took a seat, quickly placing his head in his hands. "Why? Just tell me why, Layla?"

"Come on now, Dennis; there is absolutely nothing to tell. It was all completely innocent. I love you." Layla slowly sat down next to him. Her body leaned against his, sensually, she spoke into his ear. "How could you ever think I would consider cheating on you?" Layla tenderly removed one hand and then the other from his face. She cupped his chin and tilted his head so they were eye to eye. "I'm no fool and neither are you. If I wanted to mess around with, Landon, why would I tell him that I was going to be at a lounge with two of my friends? Think, Dennis. That doesn't make sense. And he was lying because he never told me that he was coming to The Silver Spoon. We spent some time talking, and the subject about some of the cool places in Memphis. I thought about hooking him up with Envy or Kacie, nothing written in stone. It was just a thought." She fell into his arms, looked up at him, and flashed her captivating smile.

Dennis couldn't suppress his feelings any longer. Layla was enticing. The enticing smell of her perfume, the soft look in her hazel brown eyes, and the sincerity that dripped from her lips like honey appeared to have him spellbound. He leaned in and kissed her with passion, and she allowed him to do whatever he pleased with his hands. Tonight was the night to remind him, at all costs, what he would miss if he ever thought about putting her out of his life. She was not going to let a man win ever again. She would be the one to say when things were over. No matter what she had to do, she planned to prove to him that if he ever walked out of her life, he would be the loser, not her—never her again.

8

*Whenever you're in conflict with someone, there is one factor that can make the difference between damaging your relationship and deepening it. That factor is attitude. —
William James*

Kacie despised every minute she had to sit and look at Jackie and her father. Clinching her teeth, she was furious. Kenny was still sitting over in the chair, brooding like the young boy he was.

The police arrived full of questions. They barely gave Kacie a chance to talk. All the commotion must have awakened all the kids because they stood outside the entrance of the den whispering.

Her voice bellowed. "Get out of that hallway and get back to your rooms."

They scurried out of Kacie's sight but remained in the hallway within earshot.

Kacie was fire hot with anger after Kenny had the audacity to support Jackie's version of what happened. No this boy didn't just go against me? She closed her eyes, clinched her fist, and inhaled deeply. What planet did he think he was from? Mars or something? She was about to bust him in his head but up stepped Cheney like he was so holier than thou.

"Officers, I am just as upset, if not more so, as Miss...uh Miss Mayweather here. But I believe these kids, especially my daughter," he said while glancing at her. "As you heard, both of them stated that nothing happened."

Kacie couldn't hold back one minute longer. Like an oral version of Old Faithful, she blasted out long, unintelligible swears, and spewed out vicious, verbal assaults at Cheney.

"Look, ma'am, you better shut up before we give you a special ride downtown," one of the officers said. Sounding like a master sergeant, he barked, "It's over. We'll fill out a report, and if anything changes, you can come down to the station and report it."

The second police officer spoke up; his stare directed toward Jackie and her daddy. "You two, you're free to go."

"You mean you're not taking her to juvenile detention? You're just going to let her walk out of here like—"

The officer pointed one lone finger a smidgeon away from Kacie's nose. "I don't want to hear another word from you. Now, goodnight."

Kacie tried her best to slam the security door as hard as she could when they walked out of her house. Like a whirlwind, she whipped around and met seven pairs of eyes glued to her every move. "You know what?" she said and moved closer to the children who seemed paralyzed in their spots, because they sure didn't attempt to move. "Y'all better get out of my sight before I do something bad, real bad, to you.

As if pricked with a pin, they suddenly jerked and scurried away like squirrels.

~

The following morning, Kacie made it a priority to call Envy and tell her what had happened. By the time she finished telling the story, she'd made herself even angrier.

"Girl, I'm so doggone mad I can really, really hurt somebody right about now."

"Don't say stuff like that. If the wrong somebody hears you talking like that, you could find yourself locked up. They could say you threatened them. And as for Kenny, he's growing up, Kacie. He needs some male guidance. And as tall and big as he is, I don't think he needs a babysitter. I mean, he used to take care of all of the kids when he was younger anyway, and he still does when you can't find someone to babysit. He'll be a teenager in a week, so why do you need to pay a babysitter? You could pay him the money you pay a babysitter. That way he could have a little pocket change to do some of the things he wants to do."

Kacie exploded over the phone. "Do you realize how foolish you sound, Envy? I see why you don't have children. Why in the world, after finding my son and the babysitter naked on the floor of my living room, would I consider trusting him to keep his sisters and brothers? You sound like booboo the fool."

"Look, don't take your frustration out on me," Envy snapped back. "I will not hold this phone and listen to you insult me. I'm only trying to give you a way out of this mess. You see the police aren't going to help. Why don't you consider signing him up at the YMCA. There's plenty going on there for him to do."

"Look, I'm not going to the "Y" every day or every other day, so that's out of the question."

"Why don't you let him participate in the weekly youth groups at church then? It will be good for him. They have activities for the boys. I heard that they teach them things young men their age should know, all within in a Godly environment. If you aren't careful, this is only the beginning of a situation that can easily get out of hand. Kenny is at the age where he's beginning to what the old folks call 'smell himself'. If you aren't going to allow his father to spend more time with him, and if you don't get a hold on him now, or get a mentor or someone in the church to help him, you're going to have your hands full. And he's the first one. You have six other ones that are going to follow in his footsteps, so you better get on it sooner rather than later."

"Oh, don't you worry. After the police left, I took my leather strap and beat his naked behind. Then I took his cell phone from him and removed the computer monitor out of his room. He won't be calling or chatting with no fast-tail girls for a while. Believe that," Kacie said like she'd won the battle.

"I still say that when we go to church tomorrow, you should sign him up for one of the youth groups. Plus, it would be a good idea to start the other ones, who are old enough, in age-appropriate Bible classes too. It might even help you out, because you can get some studying done while they're at church."

Kacie remained quiet for a moment or two. "You know what, that might not be such a bad idea. I'll think about it. But I still want something done about that babysitter and her self-righteous, lying daddy. They need to pay, and I'm going to find some way to make sure they do. I guarantee that."

"'Vengeance is mine,' says the Lord,'" Envy told Kacie.

"Yes, I know that. But this time He's going to get a little help from His friend - me."

"Whateva. Whenever you get like this, there's no talking any sense into your head, so I'm going to change the subject. Have you heard from Layla?"

"Nope. You know Saturday is usually her busiest day at the salon, plus she gets her hair and nails done too, so it's likely that I won't talk to her until sometime this evening."

"But she still usually answers her cell phone."

"She might have her hands in a jar full of perm. What's up?"

"Shoot, I want to know if she patched things over with Dennis."

"Who can tell with her. You already know that girl is sitting on s-t-o-o-p-i-d. She's stuck on herself, and frankly, I hate to say this, but she's not fun to hang around with anymore. She's changed way too much for me. Got the nerve to try to act like we're beneath her. Then on top of everything that went down last night, she expected us to lie for her? Not me, girl," Kacie stressed over the phone. "God just can't bless some folk because they don't know what to do when He does."

"Kacie, you are going to have me rolling this morning. You are so funny, but you're telling the truth at the same time. You know good and well that Layla has been our friend for far too long to cut her off. Think about it, suppose you were in her shoes. Suppose one day you woke up and God had healed you of your cerebral palsy. Suppose you no longer walked like you do? There's no telling what you would be out there doing!" Envy laughed again.

Kacie laughed too. "Ooh wee, I don't want to think about it. If I had some sexy legs and walked without this limp, and my legs were suddenly straight, I don't know what I would do with myself. I mean, first, this sister would not have seven kids. I would give Layla a run for her money because, I don't care what nobody says, I know I look better than she does on my worst day. People always talking about beauty is only skin deep, but that's a lie. Beauty is to be seen; it's expressed on the outside. And when it comes to us women, we definitely have to have it going on for a man to even step to us."

"See, that's what I'm talking about. You sound just like Layla. You have no confidence or self-worth about yourself. Imagine how she feels now that she's thin. It's like going from a negative one-fifty in your bank account to waking up and finding you purchased the winning Powerball ticket worth millions of dollars."

"Powerball? You gamble?" inquired Kacie.

"Is that all you heard out of everything I said?" asked Envy.

"No, but I still want to know if you play the Powerball."

"All I can say is you can't win if you don't play. Now I have to go. I'm going to do some shopping now that the ice and snow has melted, and the temperature is climbing."

"Knock yourself out. I have some homework to finish, and I promised the kids I'd take them to Wal-Mart and buy them a few movies later on. I'm going to make Kenny sit in the car while me and the other kids take our time shopping."

"Now, that's mean. It's going to be cold in the car."

"He better think about the warm body he was laying next to last night like he was grown."

"You're too crazy for me. Let me let you go. I'll try to call Layla a little later on. If I don't talk back to you, I'll see you at church tomorrow."

"Okay."

"Oh, and think about what I said about Kenny."

"Yeh, um, hum, bye, Envy."

"Bye, girl."

Layla stood in front of Dennis's steamy bathroom mirror. She used a hand towel to wipe away the steam so she could finish getting dressed. She and Dennis had fun making up, although afterward she hated herself for using her body to please him. No matter what she did now, she couldn't push away the lessons she'd been taught ever since she was a girl in church. Her parents took her and her siblings to church, Sunday School, and midweek service every week. If the word "church" was in it, the Hobbs family was sure to be there.

Layla understood that the Bible taught that fornication and adultery were a sin. She understood that a long time ago, but it was the only thing she had to offer to men when she was fat and ugly. Now instead of being used by men, she made it her mission to be the one to call the shots. Dennis wasn't meant to be included, but the fact that he was a man could not be overlooked. Whenever she engaged in sex with Dennis, it was because she chose to do so. She never felt pressured by him, even before she lost all of the weight. She had to admit that he was a good, kind, decent Christian man. But she was also ready to tell him to step, if he ever tried to control her. Last night she had almost let him go, but she decided that it was worth giving him one more chance. Plus, it felt good being in a position of power. She felt like Delilah. Like Delilah, she used her seductive words and captivating body to make him do as she pleased. It was fun. It felt good finally to have the tables turned.

"Layla," Dennis called out, and interrupted her beauty regimen.

"Yes, sweetheart," Layla answered.

"Do you want some breakfast before you leave for the salon?"

"Sure, that would be nice," she answered.

The extra set of scrub uniforms she kept in her car came in handy. She finished dressing and breathed in the aroma of freshly brewed coffee as she neared the kitchen.

"Ah, it smells good in here," she complimented him. He walked toward Layla and kissed her. "I made you an egg whites scrambler, with turkey crumbles, diced tomatoes, a slice of pepper jack cheese, and red peppers."

"Yes, just the way I like it." This time she kissed him. When she felt that he was getting heated, she eased away from him and walked toward the dining-room table. She loved teasing him.

Dennis had the food arranged beautifully on the table like they were in a five-star restaurant.

When he took his seat next to Layla, he reached for her hand, which she placed inside his. He said aloud, "Father, thank you for this day. Thank you for bringing Layla into my life. . . ." He prayed for family, friends, and the food they were about to receive, while Layla prayed secretly for a carefree life, without having to keep safeguarding her relationship with Dennis.

9

Whatever God's dream about man may be, it seems certain it cannot come true unless man cooperates.—Stella Mann

Kacie, Layla, and Envy arrived at church within minutes of each other. Kacie headed toward the nursery and children's church to sign in the younger kids, while Kenny went on his own to youth church.

Layla and Envy had saved a space for Kacie on the purple fabric-covered pews. The praise and worship team started to sing, and people all over the church joined in. Layla's voice sprouted forth as if it had a mind of its own. Kacie and Envy looked at each other.

Kacie leaned over and whispered into Envy's ear, "She needs to be back up there."

Envy nodded.

After praise and worship, Minister Washington extended an invitation to the congregation to come to the altar for prayer. Envy was the only one out of the three of them to walk toward the front of the church, along with a large group of other churchgoers. When he started praying, Envy started pleading to herself for God's guidance. She was not going to let anything or anyone keep her from going to talk to an attorney about her situation. Whatever she had to face to get rid of the guilt and to remove the self-condemnation out of her life, she was willing to do. She also prayed for strength to reestablish some type of civil relationship with her sister, Nikkei. She missed her nephew and niece, and she missed Nikkei. Since their mother's death almost three years ago, Nikkei had little to do with Envy. At first, it suited Envy just fine. They always butted heads when they were growing up, and it had carried over into their adult lives.

Nikkei had a great marriage with ideal children. She lived in a nice home inside a gated community. Envy looked at her as a trophy wife because she only worked when she got bored. Other than that, Nikkei spent her days transporting her children to school, after-school activities, and church.

Envy returned to her seat with her eyes filled with glistening tears. Neither Kacie nor Layla said a word.

Pastor Betts walked up to the pulpit. "I feel good this morning. I feel the presence of the Lord in this place. I don't know how y'all can sit still. His eyes appeared to roam the sanctuary. "If you're here this morning, that ought to be enough to make you stand on your feet and give God some praise," he bellowed. "I know the choir is about to show out, but before they come, I see someone that you and I know can pull the blessings on down."

Envy watched as Pastor Betts' eyes shifted in the area where they were seated.

"Sister Layla, come on up here."

Layla gasped, One hand flew up to her neck. It was evident that she was stunned. She looked around like perhaps another Layla was being called.

The sound of thunderous clapping began. Envy and Kacie joined in the clapping too. They took a step back so Layla could pass by them.

Layla stood frozen.

"Come on here, Sister Layla. God didn't give you that voice for you to keep quiet." He focused on Layla until she slowly crept up to the podium like a frightened kitten.

"You know what I want to hear," he told her. The musicians began to play the tune of the song, in Layla's key. She swallowed, looked at Pastor Betts as he went to sit on the bench, and suddenly the words of the song poured from her mouth.

"Amazing . . . grace," she sang. It was like having the old Layla back again. Her body was indeed different, but her voice was stronger than ever.

By the end of the song, the congregation was in an uproar. People were shouting and praising God all over the sanctuary.

"Layla, girl, you sang that song," Kacie told her when she returned to her seat. "You tore it up, girl."

"Thanks," she responded, "but I wish Pastor Betts hadn't put me on the spot like that."

Pastor Betts stepped back to the pulpit. "Thank you, Sister Layla. Did y'all hear what I heard? She said—just in case you were thinking about what you were doing last night, or rather this morning before you got to church—she said God's grace is amazing. That's enough right there to make you want to get up and shout."

The congregation roared and clapped; the percussionist and guitar players went wild on their instruments. The pianist followed suit and then the choir stood and began to sing the song, again.

"All right, all right," Pastor Betts said. "That's enough. Y'all keep on like this and we won't ever get out of here." He chuckled as he picked up his Bible from the podium. "I want you to turn to Acts, chapter thirteen. I'm going to read one verse from the New International Version. Verse thirty-eight says, 'Therefore, my friends, I want you to know that through Jesus the forgiveness of sins is proclaimed to you.'"

Envy looked at the passage of scripture in her Bible and thought about her life. *Forgiveness? But I don't know if you can ever forgive me, God. I've slept with so many men that I've lost count. Lord, I left my own child to die. Surely, you cannot forgive me. I'm ugly, so ugly, maybe no one can tell from the outside, but I know, and you know, that I'm ugly all on the inside.*

Pastor Betts spoke with firmness and assurance. "Let me say that again. I want you to know that through Jesus the forgiveness of sins is proclaimed to you." He pointed toward the congregation. "Allow me to tell you what the Britannica Dictionary says about the meaning of proclaim. It means 'to cry out'; 'to declare publicly,' and then it says 'to praise or glorify openly or publicly extol.' Forgiveness is not something that God doesn't want you to know about. He publicly, proudly, with a show of praise and glory, forgives you."

Pastor Betts stood on his toes, which meant he was really getting into his message. "God is a forgiving God. He proclaims that you are forgiven. There is nothing that you can do, say, or become that God will not forgive. He says that He is faithful and just to forgive you of your sins—not some sins, but all of your sins. All-inclusive. Jesus is the perfect sacrifice so that you and I"—he pointed to himself—"can be forgiven. The question remains, are you going to forgive yourself? When are you going to let go of the past mistakes you've made? When are you going to look in the mirror and see yourself the way God sees you?"

Envy couldn't take it anymore. It couldn't be possible. She'd done too much wrong; she'd made too many mistakes. Without forewarning, she stood up, eased across Kacie's legs, and hurried toward the exit of the sanctuary. Just as she made it to the door leading into the vestibule, her eyes met up with Leonard's. Next to him sat an attractive woman. Her fingers were intertwined with his. Envy dashed out the door and raced into the nearest women's bathroom. Tears gushed from her eyes. She didn't understand why she was crying. Was it because of what Pastor Betts said, or was it because she saw Leonard with another woman, and of all places, Cummings Street, when he knew this was her church. As long as she'd known Leonard, she rarely heard him acknowledge church. If he thought his selfish act would make her jealous, he was dead wrong. It only solidified the belief that men were no good and were out to use a woman for whatever they could. Whatever the reason for her tears, it all added up to a sense of shame and self-disgust.

"That low down dog, how could he?" she said aloud, not caring if there was anyone else in the bathroom besides her. Envy sat on the toilet inside one of the stalls and pulled out her mirrored compact. She regarded her red eyes and tear-streaked face. Suddenly she could see clearly. It had taken her eighteen years to see what a terrible and ugly person she was. The mirror didn't lie; it couldn't lie. She felt such shame until she became physically sick to her stomach. She jumped up off the toilet, lifted the lid, and vomited until all she saw was a black tarlike substance in the toilet.

The door to the bathroom opened. "Envy? Envy, are you in here?" Envy hurried and quietly let the toilet seat down and sat on top of it with her legs propped up.

"She's not in here," she heard Kacie say.

"Well, where did she go?" she heard Layla ask Kacie. Envy remained still and quiet as a church mouse, until she heard their footsteps retreat, and the door close behind them. For several minutes, she remained in the stall until she was sure they were gone.

As fast as her trembling legs could carry her, Envy ran out of the church and across the street to her parked car. Once she was safe inside, she released a new wave of tears. Turning the ignition on, she put the car in gear and, luckily, sped off without hitting a car parked close to her.

For the remainder of the afternoon and on into the night, Envy refused to answer her phone. After she received so many calls and text messages from Kacie, Layla, and Leonard, she turned off the phone and curled up in her bed in a fetal position. She cried until she cried herself to sleep.

An incessant knocking noise jarred her from her turbulent sleep. She stumbled out of the bed. The over-sized digital clock in her living room said 7:30. For a moment, Envy was confused. Was it seven-thirty a.m. or p.m.? The constant knocking irritated her even more. "Who is it?" she yelled.

"Leonard."

"Get away from my door," Envy yelled. "I have nothing to say to you."

"Please, Envy. Open the door. I want to explain."

"You have nothing to explain to me, Leonard, because you don't mean a thing to me," she yelled even louder. "Now get away from my door before I call the cops!"

Silence came. The kind of silence that made her feel like something had been ripped from her heart.

Certain that Leonard had left, she peeped outside the picture window and saw that it was dark. Her mind began to come back into focus about the day's events. She returned to her bedroom and turned on her cell phone. Message tones began to flood her phone one after another. The calls were all from Kacie, Layla, and

Leonard. She thought of whom she could call that would give her the least grief. All she wanted to do was let Kacie and Layla know that she was all right.

She decided to call Layla, who was far less dramatic than Kacie.

"Girl, why did you leave out of church like that? We've been worried sick about you. Where have you been, and why did you turn your phone off?" Concern filled Layla's voice.

"I . . . I got sick. I'm sorry. I had to leave out of church before I threw up all over you, Kacie, and everybody. I made it to the ladies' room just in time," she continued to lie. "I thought I would feel better if I splashed some cold water on my face, but I only started to feel worse, so I left and came home. I must be coming down with the flu."

"You still didn't have to turn off your phone like that. You could have just picked it up and told us what was wrong."

"Look, I'm sorry, okay? I don't feel like being put through the third degree. I told you what happened, and you're right, I shouldn't have turned my phone off, but the constant ringing was making me feel even worse, if that makes any sense," Envy replied, trying to sound a little less edgy.

"I'm sorry. I didn't mean to badger you. I know how bad the flu can make you feel, and it comes on you so quickly. Is there anything you need me to bring you? Soup, crackers, aspirin, anything?"

"No, I keep chicken noodle soup in the pantry and I have some crackers too. Just do me a favor?"

"Sure. What?"

"Call Kacie and tell her what happened. I still don't feel up to talking to anyone. And you and I both know how dramafied Kacie can get. I can't take it tonight. All I want to do is crawl back under the covers and go back to sleep."

"Okay, but please keep your phone on, even if you have to put it on vibrate. Call or text me if you need anything."

"Thanks, Layla, I will."

Envy laid her cell phone beside her on the bed. She cried some more. She was hurting over everything that she'd done wrong in her life, and it was time to do something about it.

Fischer sat at the side of her bed and looked at her with his large brown eyes. "Come on, Fischer. At least you love me, no matter what I've done." Fischer jumped on the bed and plopped himself next to her with his chin resting on her chest.

"Fischer, tomorrow is the day that I'm going to start clearing up the mess I've made of my life. But for now, all I want to do is sleep." Envy got up, went into the den, and looked inside her minibar full of mostly red and white wines. She chose a bottle of Moscato. On the way back to her bedroom, she stopped by the kitchen to get a wineglass. Fischer trailed behind her. She sat on the side of the bed and drank several glasses of wine until some of the pain subsided and she fell back to sleep—but not for long. The wine mixed with the contents of an empty stomach made her sick again, and she woke up and rushed to the bathroom.

When she returned and got ready to lie back down, the phone vibrated and moved around on the nightstand. She picked it up and saw a familiar name—Tyreek. Her first inclination was to ignore the call, but like she always did when she was depressed and feeling guilty, her quick fix was to let her physical body take control.

At least for a time, she could hide her problems with a man beside her.

"What time can you be here?" she asked Tyreek without giving him a chance to speak.

"Give me forty-five minutes."

"I'll give you twenty-five," she said, and ended the call. She got up, took a hot bubble bath, and prepared to spend the night letting Tyreek take her to another place in time, one that wouldn't include the trappings of her sordid life.

She met Tyreek a few years back at one of her secret getaway spots, Precious Cargo. Neither Layla or Kacie knew that she spent quite a bit of time at the downtown restaurant and bar. She would have a few drinks after work, get her buzz on, and then meet up with the bartender afterward, who was none other than Tyreek. He was just her type: handsome, suave, single, and with a physique like a soap opera hunk. He was always impeccably groomed and his conversation was smooth as butter. Yeah, he definitely had it going on, and Envy set out to add him to her stable of available "mind relaxers," as she'd come to call the men she used. This part of her life, she kept on the down low.

There was no way she would ever confide in Kacie or Layla about her secret sex life. And they would call her "crazy" or "psycho" if she told them she had an alter ego who visited her every time she stood in front of the mirror. Her alter ego was powerful, almost more powerful than Envy. She reminded Envy that though she may have been beautiful on the outside, she was filthy and wretched on the inside. The face in the mirror looked beyond her outer beauty and saw her true ugliness. Envy despised the face in the mirror, because it revealed a part of her that she wanted to escape, if only for a little while.

Tyreek had come to understand Envy. He really liked her when he first met her, but time had shown him that he would never be more than a quick lay for her. He was someone who could satisfy her sexually—tell her all the words she longed to hear—only for her to almost push him out of her bed until the next time she called. He used to want more and expect more from her, like possibly building a relationship, but Envy reminded him through her words and actions that her heart was not up for grabs.

Tyreek soon became content being Envy's nightcap, her mind relaxer, her boy toy, like many other men who'd come and gone in Envy's life, always with no strings attached until she pulled them.

Leonard Stein was a different story. He was the only man out of all the men she had bedded over the years to capture a portion of her heart. But after seeing him with another female today, she threw him in the same pile of mess that she placed all of the others. He was only good for one thing, and now she wasn't so sure she'd use him for that anymore either. He pretended that he wanted to be with her, and that he loved her, but his actions today showed an entirely different story. He was someone she used, like she did Tyreek, Cedric, Chris, Ronnie, Tyrone, Pete, and an endless list of other men, some of whom she'd forgotten their names. None of them meant anything to her but a good or halfway de-cent time in bed for as long as she wanted. After the sex ended, she wanted them to leave. She made sure never to allow any man she slept with to think that it could be more to it than what it was: sex. Some—like Leonard, Tyreek, and Cedric—always came back for more; while others were merely a one-night stand that she initiated. It was her game, and the game was played according to her rules, until it came to Leonard.

Envy couldn't quite grasp what it was about Leonard that was different. He was really no different from any of the others in the beginning. She didn't like that he always seemed to want more from her than she was willing to give. She had managed to get Tyreek to understand what she wanted, and things were fine between them, but Leonard was a horse of a different color. He was special in his own way.

Leonard was the one who stood by her when her mother and her neighbor, Mrs. Rawlings, died. Leonard was the one whose kisses were full of passion and true desire. Sure, he understood, or said he understood, that she wanted nothing serious with him, but somehow Leonard was able to step beyond her hardcore exterior and walk away with a tiny fraction of her heart. He had a way about himself that made her believe she could trust him. So there were times she talked on the phone to Leonard or visited him at his home, something that was definitely off limits with the other men that had come and gone in her life.

Today was a tough one, even for a woman like Envy who had the backbone to stand up against anyone and almost anything. Today opened her eyes and revealed her true weakness. Stanton had walked away from her when she got pregnant as a teen, and not since then had she given a man the opportunity to crush her heart. She was not about to start now. What she saw at church today was for her own good. She needed a wake-up call; she needed to be reminded that she was slipping, and that was not part of Envy Wilson's persona.

The doorbell took her from her thoughts. Fischer barked and Envy walked to the front door to let Tyreek in. She had prepared for his intimate visit by putting on a thigh-length grape satin kimono wrap and a splash of her favorite fragrance.

She opened the door, and ordered Fischer to sit and invited Tyreek to come in.

"Girl, you look—"

Envy hushed him with a kiss, which almost cut off his breath. She rarely kissed him. It was something Envy just didn't do. Kissing meant there was a deeper connection. It took the mission she was on out of perspective—the mission to satisfy her sexual desire and escape from her present battle with herself. But if she chose to change the rules from time to time, so be it. It was all on her terms and in her own way. Tyreek slammed the front door closed with one hand and returned her hot passion with that of his own. He kissed her face, her neck, and moved to her shoulders. Without breaking away from her, he pushed her toward the bedroom.

Tyreek remained in Envy's bed most of the night, satisfying her urge, and bringing her to the fever pitch she loved to reach. When she was spent, he lay back next to her on the bed without touching her.

Envy proceeded with her normal routine. She lay in the bed for approximately ten minutes in total silence, except for the slight inhaling and exhaling sound she made. Afterward she got up, went to the bathroom, and closed the door behind her. She turned on the shower, but before she got in, she said her signature line: "Remember to lock the door when you leave."

10

You can clutch the past so tightly to your chest that it leaves your arms too full to embrace the present.—Jan Glidewell

Two weeks after Kacie walked in on Kenny and as Kacie called her, "Little hot in the pants, Jackie, she went to Juvenile Court and insisted her complaint go before a judge. Whether she bullied herself into a court date, or the counselor couldn't take anymore of Kacie's loud, boisterous mouth, she left with a piece of paper and a court date.

Layla had things pretty much back on track with Dennis. She had become a cleaner version of Envy. She didn't sleep with the men she met, but she sure had a fun time making them think she was going to give it up.

Envy had returned to doing things the way that had worked for her in the past. It wasn't difficult to have the stable of men in her life come calling again. She also made contact with a prominent criminal defense attorney, whom she planned to see later on today.

The three friends planned to get together for a late lunch at a nearby restaurant. It was midweek, the temperature hovered around sixty degrees, the sun was shining, and it was a great day for them to get together, since not having seen each other since the past Sunday.

Kacie arrived first because her job was the closest to the restaurant. She asked the host to seat her and ordered a glass of strawberry lemonade while she waited on Envy and Layla to arrive, which wasn't more than ten minutes. Exchanging chatter, the women paused to check out the menu and place their lunch orders.

"Kacie, what did the prosecutor say about the case against the babysitter?" asked Envy while she took bites from her burger and onion straws.

"He told me that it depends on what Kenny says. If Kenny continues to lie about them not having sex— well, oral sex, which he keeps telling me is not sex at all—and me finding them being naked, then I'm definitely going to look like a fool."

Layla spoke up. "Girl, you already know that he's not going to admit anything. So why are you going through with this?"

"Because it's the principle of the thing. I want to send a message to that girl's arrogant, cocky father and to her, that nobody can come up in my house and mess with my children. Kenny is a minor and she is too, according to the state law, but I don't care. She should have sex with somebody her own age, and I don't care what kind of sex they call it. It's all the same in my book."

Envy's hand flew up to her chest. Layla immediately stopped the forkful of food that she was about to put in her mouth.

"Do you think he meant to say oral sex?" Envy asked like she was hoping that she didn't hear what she heard. "I cannot believe he's engaging in any kind of sex, but especially oral sex. And at his age?"

"He said she's giving him oral sex, but he didn't do it to her. That boy told me that it's not the first time a girl has done it to him. Y'all, I don't know what to do. This is so far out of my league."

Envy entered the conversation again. "Kids these days are scandalous. Some of them start having sex as early as ten and eleven years old; and I'm talking about boys and girls. Did you sign him up for the youth group, like I suggested? The boy needs some mentoring from a man. It's a shame that his father hasn't stepped up to the plate."

"Girl, when I called and told his daddy about it, he had the nerve to say, 'That's my boy.' Like it was something to be proud of. He told me that boys will be boys, and that Kenny is at the age that he's going to try things. Said I ought to be glad that he isn't gay. I hung up in that fool's face. He can make me so mad with his ignorant self." Kacie took a bite of her chicken strip.

"And if they did have sex, I wonder if they used protection?" asked Layla. "Now, that would be something if that girl comes up pregnant and it's Kenny's baby. He'll be a father at thirteen." Layla shivered. "Ewe, I can't imagine that. He's still a baby himself."

"Don't speak that kind of negativity over my son, Layla. It's something I refuse to let happen. I've talked to him about sex, like I should have done a long time ago. But he had the nerve to tell me that he already knew about sex, and furthermore his mannish butt told me he knows about using protection. Then he went so far as to tell me that he can't get a girl pregnant if she's giving him oral sex."

Envy pushed her designer eyeglasses up on her nose. She started analyzing the situation by going into her story about what she'd read or seen. One of the things she loved to do was read. She read anything put before her. Envy also spent any television time watching health documentaries, Discovery Health, History Channel, Nancy Grace's program, and Current TV. Anything that had to do with anything—if it was a documentary, she was sure to watch it or TiVo it.

"Well, just because a girl can't get pregnant by performing oral sex, it still doesn't keep either party from contracting an STD," Envy informed. "I know most studies say that you're less likely to contract HIV from oral sex, but bad oral hygiene, like bleeding gums, cold sores—and I won't go into everything else that some people do when it comes to oral sex—but I know from reading surveys and studies that oral sex can turn into high-risk behavior. I bet most of these kids don't realize that you can still be infected with gonorrhea, yeast infections, and several other STDs."

Layla said in a self-righteous tone, "The Word of God makes its plain that it is wrong to engage in premarital sex, and I believe that includes oral sex too. I say if you're not married, and if it doesn't lead to procreation, then it's fornication and adultery, and it's wrong in God's eyes. And before you give me the evil eye, I know I've had sex outside of marriage, but I've asked God to forgive me, and I know He has." She didn't mention that she'd just asked forgiveness for sleeping with Dennis—again. "And I sure wouldn't think of doing something as nasty and disgusting as oral sex. Yuck, these children are gone mad," she said, a frown noticeably filling her face.

All three of them were still sexually active; yet they were on one accord when it came to protecting young kids like Kenny from the perils of engaging in sex outside of marriage and taking it so casually.

Envy spoke up after swallowing some of her food. "I hate to see kids making the same mistakes as us. It's the main reason I want kids like Kenny to understand the ramifications of having sex—not only from a biblical standpoint, but from a physical and emotional aspect too.

It's wrong; and it can lead to so many other things other than pregnancy."

"Yeah, but who are we to talk, when we're doing the same thing?" Layla actually looked frightened.

"You're right. But that's what I'm saying; we've got to do more to educate our young people. Depending on teachers in the school and their peers to teach them is not enough. I admit that I have not been a good example for my kids; and with Kenny being the oldest, he probably looks at me and gets the idea that sex is okay. And why wouldn't he, when he has six brothers and sisters, so how much can I tell him?" Kacie looked confused and tormented at the same time. She pushed her plate away. "I can't eat anything else. I just lost my appetite thinking about how I've messed up my life and possibly the future of my kids."

Layla reached over and placed her arm around Kacie's shoulders. "Look, don't let the devil make you feel guilty. Try to remember what Pastor Betts said at church when he talked about forgiveness. He said that your past is forgiven. Remember that?"

Kacie nodded and tears fell from her eyes and onto the table. "My past may be forgiven, but that doesn't stop me from feeling guilty about my children's futures. And it doesn't stop me from having to suffer the consequences of my sinful actions. Kenny will be thirteen tomorrow, and he's already sexually active. Who's to say that I won't be a grandmother before I turn thirty-four or thirty-five years old? Who's to say that he won't turn out like me, or his father, for that matter, running around thinking he's a pimp because he can get any girl he wants? He has his father's good looks, he's charming, and he's really a nice kid. He can probably talk a girl into giving it up in no time. And let's be real, y'all; I don't even know what to teach him or how to teach him about oral sex. This is so messed up. Who would have thought I would be talking to my thirteen-year-old son about something so, so delicate?"

Kacie continued to cry as Layla and Envy tried to console her.

"Look, we're going to pray about this, and I mean it, y'all," said Envy. "Beginning today, we are going to start interceding on behalf of not just Kenny but all of your kids. Agreed?" She looked at Kacie, who nodded, and then Layla, who nodded too. "Now, let's talk about something else."

Kacie wiped her eyes before the tears that had formed escaped. "Yeah," she said, grinning. "Envy, what's the latest on you and Leonard? You still aren't talking to the man or what?"

"Girl, puhleeze. There's no way I'm going to let him get into my personal space again."

"I don't know why," said Layla with much attitude. "You said he didn't mean anything to you, anyway, so I don't understand the attitude when you saw him with another woman."

"It's not that I got mad about seeing him with someone else. It's the fact that he was at our church! I will not tolerate any man disrespecting me like that. He could have gone to any church in the city of Memphis, but he bought his behind to ours. No, that's totally unacceptable."

Kacie and Layla laughed so loud that a few heads turned toward their table. "You are a mess with yourself," said Kacie. "You can't tell that man what church to go to. Anyway, she must go to our church, since they were there together. The church is growing so fast that it's impossible to know who's a member. And even if they were just visiting, that's their business. You don't have any claims on him, remember."

"Kacie," Envy said with a raised eyebrow. "Don't play. When you were messing around with Deacon, would you tolerate him bringing his wife to the church?"

Kacie's face turned red. "I didn't know Deacon was married when we first started messing around; and just to remind you, Deacon and I were a couple, unlike you and Leonard. And, on top of that, Deacon's wife was not a member of our church. She was still attending her home church."

"You have to admit, she has a point," said Layla. "I mean, Leonard has been after you for—what—two, almost three years? You know the man has some deep feelings for you. He wants a relationship with you, but he's probably getting tired of being turned away. And you know that if he thought he was going to run into you at church, that he wouldn't have come. Come on, now. Give the brother a break. I don't understand why you try to be so tough all the time. It'll do you good to give your heart to someone instead of sleeping with this man and that man, thinking that nobody knows about it. And you sit up here talking about saving kids like Kenny."

"I do not sleep around." Envy denied, and rolled her eyes. "It's a new year and I've changed my ways. I've got to get my relationship with God where it needs to be, and if that's ever going to happen, I have some other things in my life that I have to change too. I'm tired of yo-yoing with my life, and straddling the fence when it comes to my relationship with God."

Kacie nodded her head in agreement. "You're right. I feel the same way about my life. I'm worried about my kids; I'm worried about the decisions I've made; I'm worried about the way I say I trust God one minute, and then the next minute, I'm sitting up in church lusting over some good-looking brother in the next pew. I hate the fact that I'm handicapped. I hate this limp I have, and I hate the stares people give me. I feel like a freak, but then I keep hearing in my head that I am fearfully and wonderfully made. But when I look at myself in the mirror, I don't see this wonderful, unique person that God formed. And, anyway, why did He let me be born with cerebral palsy? Why couldn't it have been Nikkei? So I feel what you're saying, Envy. I really, really do. But you'd be fine with your life if you only knew what I go through every day."

Layla looked back and forth from Kacie to Envy like a foreigner sojourning in a strange land. "I can tell both of you that I know the feeling too. I mean, there was a time when I looked in the mirror and saw how terribly unattractive and ugly I was. I know I still have some issues; and I sure know that I've taken a step back when it comes to my relationship with God. But I feel like He should understand. After all, I've lived most of my life being made fun of because I was fat, but I never stopped singing for God. I never stopped going to church. It was the only place I felt partially accepted. But now that I'm no longer a whale, I want to enjoy life on the beach. And I believe that God should understand that."

Layla took a swallow of her strawberry lemonade and stirred her fork around in her salad plate. "I mean, all the years I've given to Him, can't He at least allow me to have some time doing what I want to do for a change? So what if I like to flirt? So what if men finally look at me and want to get to know me instead of making crude jokes about my weight? It feels good to be beautiful. And I'm going to take a break from being all holier than thou. I'll come back to God full-time after

I've experienced life from a different perspective." Layla changed her focus to Envy. "And, Miss Envy, why are you looking at me like I'm the chief sinner or something?"

"I'm not. That's you being paranoid. It's your choice what you do about your relationship with God. I have to get me right," Envy said, and pointed at herself. "I'm the last one who should judge you or anyone else. But if you're wondering why I was staring at you like that, it's because I respect you for at least telling us what you feel." Envy looked over at Kacie. "And you too, Kacie. Since y'all have spilled your guts, I might as well share my deepest fears with you. I've been meaning to do it for some time now, but it just seemed like every time I made up my mind to talk to y'all, something stopped me. What I'm about to tell you is a terrible part of my past. You two are my best friends, and I need you to promise that you won't turn away from me. I need your support more than ever, if I'm going to go through with my plan."

"Whatever you have to tell us is going to stay among us. I don't think any one of us can judge the other. We all have our secrets and misunderstood idiosyncrasies." Layla reached across the table and placed her hand on top of Envy's.

"She's right, you know," said Kacie, and she placed her hand on top of Layla's. "Now, tell us what's going on."

Kacie and Layla sat in total silence.

"What is it?" Layla asked. Her voice appeared etched with concern and worry.

Envy took a sip of her beverage. Her eyes shifted away from Layla and Kacie. She sucked in a deep breath and then slowly released it. "Eighteen years ago, I fell in love with this guy named Stanton, he was a college student. I just knew we were going to spend the rest of our lives together. Long story short, I ended up getting pregnant. When I told him, he blew up; said he wouldn't let anything interfere with his college studies, especially a baby. I'd never seen him act the way he did. He cursed at me and accused me of trying to trap him. But it wasn't true. I was barely fifteen years old, for God's sake, and in love with him. I would never do anything to hurt him. But my words were ignored because Stanton told me he wanted nothing else to do with me. He told me to have an abortion, but I refused. He warned me not to tell anyone that I was carrying his baby. And I didn't. I hid it from everyone. Thank God, I didn't gain much weight at all, and my stomach was round but small, so I didn't have a problem hiding the fact that I was pregnant."

Kacie's mouth hung open, and she removed her hand from the top of Layla's, while Layla's hand remained firmly planted on top of Envy's. It was apparent by their gazes that they were all ears.

Envy continued to tell them the story of her past. "Week after week, I hoped and prayed that Stanton would change his mind, and admit that he loved me and wanted to spend the rest of his life with me and our child, but it wasn't the case. I couldn't stop thinking about his reaction to the child we'd made. How could such a smart, intelligent, kindhearted man—a person who loved dogs and cats and Xbox, who smiled at little babies whenever he saw them on the street, who was obsessed by his major in nuclear physics, who confessed his undying love for me—end up being someone I never really knew at all?"

"It happens like that sometimes. Did you ever go to see a doctor?" asked Layla.

"No. I was too afraid. I told you, I didn't want my mother or anyone to know. The way things turned out, I didn't have to worry about anybody finding out."

"Why?" asked Kacie. "What happened to your baby? How did you keep it hidden?"

"I started to grasp that there was no way I was going to be able to keep hiding my pregnancy from my mother, so I planned on telling her. I was also going to tell her that I was going to give the baby up for adoption, so he or she would grow up in a family where it would be loved, and given the kind of home that I never had."

"So you're saying you have a child out there somewhere? Envy, with today's technology, don't you know that you have a good chance of finding your child?" Kacie advised.

"No, you don't understand. I never got the chance to tell anyone. The horrible fact is that I will never see my child. I'll never know how my baby looked, if it had features like me or Stanton."

Kacie stopped Envy again. "Yes, you can. We'll help you find your child. Won't we, Layla?"

Still shocked, Layla could barely answer. "Of…of course."

"You can't help me because my baby is dead. And it's all my fault."

Layla snatched back her hand from lying on top of Envy's. Kacie leaned back against the back of the booth. "What are you talking about?" asked Layla.

"A lot of it is still a blur, but I remember it was on a Friday afternoon, at the end of sixth period. I got this urge to use the bathroom really, really bad, so I asked my teacher for a hall pass. She told me I could dismissed since it was only minutes before class ended, so I hurried off to the bathroom." Envy spoke with her head down. "From the time I went to the bathroom, all I can really remember is seeing blood-soaked hands against my face. I was terrified and my stomach was cramping so bad. Thank God no one came in the bathroom. I eased up from the toilet, and that's when I saw—"

"What did you see?" Kacie asked. Her voice horror-pitched.

"I saw," she answered, then paused. "I saw something, something that looked like a rope with a doll attached to it. It looked so strange in the toilet. It was bloody and its skin reminded me of a dark gray sky. You know how it gets dark before a storm? It was that kind of gray. I said to myself that this couldn't have come out of me. This couldn't be my baby. But it was. I became so terrified. I couldn't think clearly. I just remember saying, 'No, God. Not here, not now.'" Envy started crying, and so did Layla and Kacie.

"I knew I had to get the rope out of me. I searched in my purse and found some nail clippers, and I . . . I cut the rope. I think I had to tear it too. I don't know. There was so much blood. The next thing I recall is looking at the ceramic walls of the stall, a sense of claustrophobia came over me, and fear like I've never felt before consumed me."

"Did you get help?" asked Kacie.

"I tried with all of my might to gather my senses, but I couldn't. I listened to see if there was any one else in the bathroom, but there wasn't, so I hurried out of the stall, leaving my baby in the toilet. I rushed and locked the bathroom door and ran to the sink to clean up the stall and wash as much blood as I could off my hands and uniform. I got so sick that I threw up in the sink. I kept cleaning and scrubbing with paper towels until I got up all traces of the blood. I couldn't look at the thing in the toilet: I didn't believe it was a baby. I don't know what I was thinking at the time. I rushed out of the bathroom and took the side stairs, where I was sure no one would see me."

"What happened after that? Did you go to the hospital? Didn't you call the ambulance to go get your baby?" asked Layla.

"Don't you understand? I think my baby was dead. I never heard it cry or make a sound. I couldn't tell anyone. I was too scared, so I left it there, in the bathroom, skipped seventh period. I walked home so no one could see the blood stains on my clothes. I didn't call Stanton; I didn't call anyone. I hid in my bedroom the whole weekend. I still cramped and passed a huge lump of blood later that night that looked almost like another baby. Later I learned that it was probably the placenta. I've never been through anything so terrifying. I thought I was going to die. I cried all night. I couldn't sleep. I can't tell you why I left my own child. I've asked myself that question every single day since then."

"What happened after that?" asked Kacie.

"The next day, there was this article in the Memphis Commercial Appeal, and it was on all of the local news stations. The newspaper said something like a newborn was found dead in a bathroom toilet at Germanside High School. The next week, everybody was talking about it all over the school. Seemed like everyone, including me, was trying to figure who the girl could be and why she would abandon her baby in the bathroom. There were theories about who the girl was, but no one thought of it being me. I was too uppity and far too pretty to be involved in something that was so tragic, or so people thought. My mother asked me if I had any idea who the girl could be. Of course, I told her that I didn't know anything about it."

"Then what happened? Didn't your mother ask why you were stuck in your room all weekend?" questioned Layla.

"No, I told her I had a school project. I avoided her as much as possible. Don't you understand? I was a child myself. I lay across my bed frightened that at any minute the police would come storming inside my room, lead me out in handcuffs and my face would be plastered on every TV screen across America. Everyone would know what a terrible person I was to leave my newborn child alone, in a school toilet, to die. God would never forgive me. No one ever would. To this day, I still can't forgive myself. I was a mean, wicked, wicked girl, who's now a mean, wicked woman."

Layla's eyes bulged and her hands slid across the smooth surface of the table. "This is too much to take in right now. I need some time to think."

"Think about what?" asked Kacie. "There's nothing to be done. It's over with. It happened eighteen years ago. You were fifteen years old, for Christ's sake. No one ever suspected you, right?" Kacie looked at Envy as if she was desperate for an answer.

"No. No one ever came; no one ever questioned me. Nothing. I began to feel better physically a few days after the birth; and the bleeding stopped. I called Stanton up one day, and it just so happened that he decided to answer my call. I told him that I lost the baby; he never questioned me about the details and I have not seen or heard from him again. Before I realized it, not only had the school year passed, but it's like I looked in the mirror one day, and I was a grown woman. Because of what I did, I know it's the reason I will never be able to have children."

"What makes you say that?" asked Kacie.

"Because back when I was in my twenties, I started having extremely painful periods, so I went to an OB-GYN and asked for a complete workup. The doctor ran a battery of tests. She said I had fibroid tumors. I haven't been on any contraceptives. I know it; I'm barren."

"A lot of women have fibroid tumors, Envy. It doesn't mean they can't have children," said Layla.

"She's right, Envy. The doctor should have told you the same thing. Girl, you are not barren." Kacie waved her hand and shook her head.

"Whateva, that's not the issue here anyway. The thing is I've relived that day every day for the past eighteen years. I can't do it anymore. I have to take responsibility for what I did, or should I say, didn't do."

"What do you mean?" asked Kacie. "What are you going to do?"

Envy looked at her cell phone. "I'm meeting with a lawyer downtown today at two o'clock."

"A lawyer, for what?" Kacie further inquired.

"I'm going to tell him what I did. I'm ready to face the consequences, whatever they may be."

"You're turning yourself in?" Layla spoke up. "Why? You said no one ever found out who the girl was. Why would you drudge up something from your past? We're talking about eighteen years ago, Envy. That case is long closed. And if you haven't asked God to forgive you, now is the time. You know He will. But I don't see any reason for you to go to a lawyer and confess a cr . . . something that happened when you were a child."

"I agree with Layla," responded Kacie.

"You were just about to say crime, weren't you, Layla?" remarked Envy.

"It . . . It wasn't intentional, and I didn't mean it like that."

"But that's just it; you're right. It was a crime, and if it was a crime back then, it's still a crime today. I'm not going to be able to forgive myself until I own up to what I did." Envy opened her purse, pulled out her wallet, and laid enough money on the table to cover the check for the three of them. "I'll call y'all and let you know what he said, but right now, I need to go. I don't want to be late." Envy eased from the booth, stood, and used her hands to press the skirt of her two-piece gray business suit. She swallowed and then exhaled. "Say a prayer for me," she said, and then she turned around and walked toward the exit.

11

Worry, worry, worry, worry. Worry just will not seem to leave my mind alone. —*Ray LaMontagne*

Attorney Casper Stephens was often described by his colleagues and clients as a brilliant strategist, bold and sometimes controversial, who had a winning record of cases. He listened intently to the fashionably dressed, vividly attractive woman sitting across from him in his luxurious office that commanded a spectacular view of the Mississippi River.

Envy's demeanor was reserved, close to being aloof, but Casper found himself drawn to the woman. As he listened to her story, he became even more fascinated with her. Much like he did with all of his clients, Casper tried to insert himself into the set of circumstances that brought her in to see him. This time it was immensely difficult. He did not quite understand why. But the need to visualize her as a fifteen-year-old girl from eighteen years ago, in comparison to the beautiful trappings of the woman she was now, had to be done, if he was going to be able to help her.

"Now that you've heard my story, what do you think?" asked Envy.

Casper clasped his hands together and rested his elbows on his cherry wood desk. He was not one to rush. Plus, he dared not admit that he was pulled to her like a moth to a flame. He never allowed himself to become entangled with his clients—well, except for one time, and that was ten years ago, when he had just entered into his law profession. The client had been a victim of brutal domestic violence, and he was a young prosecuting attorney. The relationship was doomed to fail from the beginning. Her Asian culture and beliefs that women were often looked upon by Asian men as lower members, and the fact that she had been so poorly mistreated by her ex-husband, did not leave room for her to trust another man. Initially she clung to him like paper to glue, and it was her need to want him around constantly that drew them apart after a short six-month stint.

"Attorney Stephens—"

"Yes?"

"Did you hear anything I said?"

"Of course. You'll find that I'm one who, should I say, savors what I've heard before I answer. Your story fascinates me. And, please do not misconstrue what I mean."

"Can't promise anything," was Envy's response.

"I simply believe it is a case that I would be interested in accepting."

"Thank you." Envy released a long sigh and nodded.

"But I would like to ask you something?"

"Ask away," she replied.

"What made you want to rehash the past? I mean, honestly, this is definitely a cold case, filed between a slot in the Cold Case Archives. Next, even if someone came along and decided to reopen it, the statute of limitations is up, unless it was murder, which from what you've told me is unlikely. Second, you probably wouldn't be charged with a crime because of the lack of evidence."

Envy twisted her hands together in a nervous fashion and inhaled before she spoke. "That all sounds good, you know, about the statute of limitations and lack of evidence, but I'm not trying to find a way to get away with what I did. There's no statute of limitations for me. This is something I know deep in my spirit that I have to do. I believe God is pushing me to do it so I can move forward into the rest of my future. I can't live my best life now if I have the trappings of my past clinging to me," Envy explained.

Her sincerity enamored him that much more. At that moment, he knew that he would do everything in his professional power to help her. He used to be a praying man and a criminal defense lawyer. Now Casper Stephens was a criminal defense lawyer only; his prayer life all but gone. He was noted as one of the best attorneys in the Mid-South, but earning his reputation didn't exactly come by way of him toting a Bible and wearing a cross around his neck. He had to be hard. There were times, on more than one occasion when he knew a client was guilty, but Casper gave his all to assure the client got a fair trial, and the best sentencing or plea deal.

Envy Wilson was different. He could sense it. Whoever was involved in a relationship with her was definitely a lucky man.

"I tell you what, "Miss Wilson, give me some time to research your case. No telling how much or how little there is in the Cold Case files on this one.

"Please." She paused. "You can call me Envy."

"Okay, Envy, I'll be able to tell you more about the direction we'll take once I review all the files and evidence."

Envy stood up and extended her hand out to Casper. Casper scooted back from his desk and walked around to where Envy stood. He accepted her hand into his and shook it. Her hand felt like mink. He told himself to remain focused on being professional. He definitely did not want to scare her off before he had the opportunity to do everything to set her free.

"I'll be waiting for your call," she told him as he released her hand. Envy turned around and walked to the door. She paused with one hand on the door handle as if she was about to say something.

Casper had made it by her side and his hand gently rubbed against hers as he opened the door. He was like that toward any woman. His grandmother had raised him. There were two main things she taught him; no drilled into him: to revere God, and always, always treat a woman with the utmost respect.

Envy's eyes met his. "Thank you, thank you so much, Mr. Stephens. I have a good feeling about this. I think I'll be able to have a good night's sleep for a change, knowing that I've taken the step toward making things right in my life."

Casper cleared his throat. "Don't thank me yet. Let's see what I find first." He smiled and then stepped aside so she could leave. "Have a good afternoon, Envy."

Envy returned his smile and walked away.

Casper lingered at the door until she disappeared. Once she was out of his sight, he informed his administrative assistant to hold his calls and returned to his office behind closed doors. The story she'd told him was so magnetic that he began to work on it immediately. He had to find out exactly what had happened all those years ago. He contacted the Cold Case Investigations Unit and began his search to either prove if the alluring Envy Wilson was guilty of murdering her baby or just a young, naïve, frightened girl who panicked at the site of the formed human being in the toilet.

Envy got inside her car and said a prayer. "Father, thank you for giving me the courage to take the first step toward my redemption for the sin I committed against my child and against you. Thank you for Attorney Stephens having an open mind and for him not passing judgment on me. Let your will be done."

She remained sitting in her car, in thought. Today felt like a heavy burden was lifted. Now she would have to face the demons of her past, and it terrified her. Leonard's assigned ringtone intercepted. Initially she started to push Ignore, but instead she instinctively answered.

"Why are you calling me?" she replied in a low voice.

"Envy, please do not hang up on me. I know you're still upset."

"No, actually I'm not. After I thought about us, I came to the realization there is no us. You were a friend with benefits. That's it. So don't get it twisted. You have every right to be with who you want to be with, and take her where you want to take her. It just took me off guard to see you at church, that's all. But that did not give you the right to pop up over my house. Maybe you were concerned about me when you saw me rush out of the sanctuary. I'll give you that much credit, but I had some other things on my mind, which had nothing to do with you. Believe me, Leonard, you give yourself to much credit."

"I'm going to ask you again, Envy. When are you going to let me in?"

"Look, Leonard, I am not going to keep doing the same old thing I did last year, and the year before, and the year before that one, if you get my drift. It's time for some changes to be made in my life. All of this laying up with you whenever I feel like it; well, it's not going to happen anymore. Not because of you and some woman, but I've got to get things right with God so I can get things right with me." It was good that Leonard wasn't sitting across a table from her, because he would be able to see the tears that trickled down her face, and she didn't want that.

"See, that's what I'm talking about. You think it's all about coming to your place and laying up, but it's not. I want you to let me into your heart. Give me a chance to love you. I'm almost at the end of my rope here. I believe there can be something special between you and me. Really, if you think about it, there already is. You've been involved in my life for over three years. If it was about laying up with you, I could get anyone to do that. But it's not about that."

"I won't allow you or anyone else in my life, my heart, nowhere in my space, especially at this point in my life. Can't you see that I'm a wreck, Leonard," she tearfully admitted.

"Why don't you come to see me? So we can talk face-to-face. I can't close the chapter on us with a snap of my finger. I want to see you one more time. No funny stuff. No trying to get you in bed. None of that."

She was filled with a haze of feelings and desires. "Okay, I'll come. What about six o'clock?"

"Six is good. I'm finishing up at the office. I will be at home by the time you get there."

"Sure, okay."

"Envy?"

"What else is it?" She tried to discipline her voice to maintain complete control.

"Thanks."

Envy listened to the silence infiltrate the phone call. Leonard had hung up. She put the key in the ignition, turned on the car, and then drove off. There was something else she had to do to get things moving forward in her life, and that was to talk to Nikkei.

She left downtown and drove in the direction of her sister's house. At first, she was going to call and let Nikkei know that she was going to stop by, but she decided against it. Knowing herself, and knowing Nikkei too, they would probably end up arguing on the phone, and the chance to really sit down and air some things out would be lost. The death of their mother had widened rather than closed the gap that existed between her and Nikkei. There was no need to pretend that they had mad love for one another.

Envy believed Nikkei had always been jealous of her good looks. Their mother often told Envy, "When you walk among women, don't forget your whip. Girls are going to always be jealous of you, Envy, because you've been blessed with an aura of untouchable glory and sensuous beauty." She would pull Envy in front of the mirror and tell her to look at the strikingly beautiful girl who stood before her. It used to make Envy feel weird, but as she grew older, she began to embrace her beauty to the point where both her mother and sister began to act jealous.

When they were younger, people in their neighborhood used to tell Envy how pretty she was and say nothing about Nikkei. But through Envy's eyes, Nikkei was an extension of her. They bore many of the same features. Nikkei had a rich, fawnlike beauty. She wasn't into wearing makeup other than just enough lipstick to show that her mouth was perfect.

Nikkei may not have seen things the way Envy did. Envy had a jealous streak. She was always trying to live up to other people's expectations of her, while Nikkei was content in being who she was. She did her own thing regardless of what people thought. But when it came to being constantly compared to her older sister, Nikkei seemed to develop a bitter ache in her heart for Envy.

It was now time for the sisters to let go of the bad blood and allow new, fresh blood, which should be shared by a family, to pour into their hearts and minds. The only way to do that was for Envy to act like the older sister she was and try to make amends by talking to Nikkei.

Envy pulled into the driveway of Nikkei's five-bedroom, ranch-style brick house. The doors to the three-car garage were closed, so Envy couldn't tell if Nikkei was at home or not, but she didn't regret her decision to drop in on her.

She pushed her glasses up on the bridge of her nose before she opened the door and extended her flawless Tina Turner like legs out of the car. Like a bad habit, she used her hands to straighten any sign of wrinkles from her skirt. She buttoned her overcoat before she walked along the concrete pathway that led to Nikkei's front door.

She pressed her always perfectly manicured nail to the doorbell and lightly pushed it. She waited for a few seconds, but no one came to the door. Envy pressed it for the second time. Again, there was no answer.

"We will talk," said Envy. "Real soon." She turned around, strode boldly to her car, got in, revved her motor, and drove home so she could get ready to go and meet Leonard.

12

It is amazing how complete is the delusion that beauty is goodness. —Leo Tolstoy

Layla sat at her computer after spending a long day at the salon. She had taken another group of photos and was getting ready to upload them. Each pose revealed a certain self-assuredness and was meant to show off every curve of her body. She smiled as she thought about how good she looked. These particular photos were taken when she went with a group of cosmetologists to a hair show in Nashville. She hadn't bothered to show them to Kacie or Envy. She would hear about it soon enough when they saw them on her social media site. For Layla, it was apparent her friends couldn't accept the fact that she was far more gorgeous than either of them.

It only took about ten minutes for her to get all of the pictures uploaded. After she completed that satisfying task, she ran some bath water and planned to light some scented candles around her claw tub, put on her facial scrub and eye mask, and just relax in the tub until the water turned cool.

Before she could take a step into her bath, Dennis called. Layla pinched her lip with her lower teeth, sighed, and answered the phone.

"Hi," she said.

"Hey, there."

"Hey."

"How was your day?"

"Good, but long. I was about to get in the bathtub and soak. Whuzzup?"

"What's on your agenda after that?"

"I'm going to chill; rest my mind and body. I have more early appointments tomorrow. You know how some of my clients like to get their hair done before they go to work."

"I sure want to see you tonight. Mind if I come over and rock you to sleep?" he asked, and then laughed lightly into the phone.

No, no, and no. "Can I get a rain check?...Dennis. Dennis, are you still there?"

"Yea, I hear ya."

"Let's get together this weekend. We can go see that new movie, and since this weather is turning more spring like, we can ride downtown and walk along the river. That would be nice, don't you think?"

"Yeah, it sounds nice. I just miss you, Layla. We haven't spent time together in weeks. You're always so busy."

"What do you mean by that? I have a lot of things on my plate now, Dennis, other than food."

"Look, I didn't call to argue. I can't help it if I miss you, so I thought I'd call and come over. No pressure to make love to you, or anything like that. Just to hold you, maybe spoon a little. That's it. We can sleep in each other's arms, and I could wake up early in the morning and fix you a nice, healthy breakfast."

Layla listened; he was a good man, but she was getting oh so burned out on him. There was so much adventure to experience, so many things she wanted to do, places she wanted to go and see. The crazy thing was she didn't want to do them with Dennis. He was becoming more like a kid who wanted to cling to his mama's skirt tail. She, in turn, was a wild, lively, spur-of-the-moment woman. The more she thought about it, the less she wanted to be tied down to one man. As long as she was tagged as Dennis's lady, she would run the risk of him thinking she was cheating on him every time she didn't call him for a few days, or didn't want to see him. Too bad that things had gotten to this point, but it was time he faced the music.

"Dennis, look. What does it take for you to get the message?" She didn't mean to come off harsh, but she was sick of sugarcoating everything when it came to the two of them.

"What message is it that you're sending, because I guess I'm totally missing it? Since when is it a crime for a man to want to see his lady?" Agitation was present in his voice.

"That's just it. The fact that you're my man and I'm your woman. It just doesn't feel right anymore, Dennis. You're settled in your ways. You're used to going to work every day, coming home to watch whatever it is you TiVo'd for the day, calling me, and hopefully coming over here to watch some more TV. On Sunday, you go to your church and I go to mine. We may meet up afterward, have lunch, and the routine starts all over again."

"And what's wrong with that? You used to love spending time with me. What's changed?"

"Put it this way; I just returned from a wonderful weekend in Nashville. The hair show I went to was spectacular. I got a chance to meet other people from all over the Southeast. I had fun. I laughed. I went to the club. I danced. I had a ball. I love that, Dennis. Your idea of a vacation is coming back late from lunch," she said with sarcasm.

"So what are you really saying, Layla? That I'm no longer good enough for you?" His tone escalated. She could tell that she'd pushed his button one time too many. "What, you're Miss Thang now, with a new attitude to go along with your new body? Is that what this is about?"

"How dare you talk to me like that, Dennis Parker." She tried to discipline her voice, to maintain control, but it didn't come across that way. "I guess now that I'm not the fat girl anymore, and other men find me attractive, you want to keep me locked away. Well, that was the old Layla," she raved, blithely ignoring the silence on the other end of the phone. "You are so typical. As long as you thought I was full of low self-esteem and walked around like some sorrowful, needy victim, you were fine because I depended on you. So I guess you want me to be forever grateful. Okay, I'll give you your props. Thank you for being there for me. But I will not be made to feel like I'm wrong for wanting to experience everything that life has to offer."

"You know what? I am so sick of hearing you use the poor, fat girl scenario to justify your actions. It may have taken me a while, but I think I finally get the picture." His voice cracked and trailed away. "You are one piece of work. And here I thought you were genuine when you're really counterfeit."

"Excuse you?" It wasn't a question; it was an inquiry.

"Oh, let me finish, sweetheart." His voice had bite. "When I first saw you, do you think I looked at you and said, 'Hey, there's an overweight sister; let me take advantage of her'? Is that all you thought of me? I loved you for the person you were. I loved your smile. I loved your voice. I loved your full hips and your breasts. I loved holding you and kissing you, all of you. What I'm saying is that I loved you for you, not because you were a certain size.

I've dated lots of women. All sizes, all colors, with different personalities and attitudes. Some were drop-dead gorgeous, with the worst attitude known to man, and others were awright-looking, but their personalities, their spirits, made them beautiful. I'm sorry to say that you sound like the ones in the first category." His voice brimmed with distaste. "If being thin is what you believe makes you beautiful, then I'm about to burst that bubble, because that woman is gone. And all that's left behind is an ugly stain. Like I said, I get the message. You go on and have a good life. You don't have to worry about me being the one you say tried to stop you from doing you. And one more thing I want to say: beauty may get the attention, but it's personality that gets the heart."

Layla heard Dennis's phone click off; she set the phone on the bed before she slowly retreated to the bathroom. She touched the water with the tip of her pedicured foot. It was still nice and warm—just right. She placed one foot inside the round tub and then the next. As she lay back against the tub with her head resting against the bath pillow, she pulled the eye mask over her eyes and refused to allow the words that Dennis had spoken invade her mind and spirit. It was Dennis who had the problem dealing with her because of the strong, independent woman she'd become. It was his loss, and frankly, she was glad that things had ended. Now no one could stop her. Not Kacie, not Envy, not Dennis—no one at all. Layla Hobbs had it going on. Better Dennis's heart be broken, or any man's heart, than hers. Anyway, if she wanted him back, she could get him back—no problem.

Layla remained in the bathtub until the water started to cool. She removed her eye mask, stepped out of the bathtub, grabbed her robe hanging on the robe rack nearby, and put it on. After she rinsed the facial scrub from her face, she placed some natural moisturizer on it. She dried off her legs, one by one, then stepped into her slippers and went into her bedroom. For a few minutes, she had to admit that she thought about Dennis's stinging words, but she was not a whiner anymore. She would shed no tears. Instead, she picked up the phone and called her mother. It had been a few days since she talked to her. Her schedule was so full that she didn't have the time to call her every day, like she used to do.

It was almost eight o'clock. Her mother and father were probably already asleep.

"Hello," her mother said in a drowsy-sounding voice. "Momma, I'm sorry to call so late."

"Honey, is everything all right with ya?" her mother asked.

"Yes, ma'am. Everything is fine. I just wanted to check on you and Poppa since I haven't talked to you in a few days."

"I know, honey, and that's all right. Poppa is already sleeping. He was saying just the other day that our baby is so busy now. You have so much going on in your life. Told me that I shouldn't be sitting up worried about you because the Lord has you in His hands."

"Poppa's right, Momma. I'm fine. I'm going to try to get over there one day this week to see y'all. Okay?"

"Oh, honey, that would be so good. We miss you, baby," her mother said.

"I miss you and Poppa too, Momma, and I love you."

"We love you too, Layla."

"Now go on back to sleep. I'm about to turn in myself. 'Night, Momma." Layla blew a kiss in the phone.

Her mother laughed. "Good night, sweet angel."

Layla changed from her robe to her pink silk boxer pajama set. She knelt down beside her bed and began to make her prayer requests known to God. Her main prayer was for her to stop allowing those who were envious and jealous of her to rattle her and make her upset.

She finished her prayers, climbed into bed and propped up her pillows against the headboard. Her left hand grabbed the remote and simultaneously pushed the POWER button. Flipping from channel to channel, she stopped on SoapNet. With. her legs underneath the cover, she started watching her favorite soap opera, *The Young and the Restless.*

13

Abstinence is approved of God. —Geoffrey Chaucer

Kacie and Kenny entered Division I of Juvenile Court, along with the mediator. Layla and Envy pooled their money together and bought Kenny a classy looking, two-button, chocolate brown pinstripe suit, with a crisp button-down white shirt and a matching necktie. Kacie told his father he needed a pair of new dress shoes, and Thomas, much like always, provided what his son needed.

Kacie didn't know if the judge would look at Kenny and see him as a sixteen-or seventeen-year-old instead of the thirteen-year-old that he actually was. The lawyer had suggested she make sure he was neatly dressed, but he hadn't specified whether that meant a shirt and slacks or the suit that he wore. She prayed that all would turn out fine.

Envy and Layla accompanied them to court, but they were not allowed to come into the courtroom until the bailiff gave them permission. Kacie walked in and saw Jackie accompanied by both of her parents.

Jackie was dressed the opposite of Kenny. In contrast to Kenny, she looked like a twelve or thirteen-year-old. Her hair was pulled back in a ponytail, and the dress she wore was simple and cute. She had on no makeup or jewelry. It was hard for Kacie to look at her like she was sixteen; so how would the judge weigh in on the case? Kacie could only pray for a fair outcome.

Kacie exhaled when she saw Envy and Layla enter the scant courtroom. Several other people came in along with them, but they sat behind the girl's family. Why hadn't she thought of asking people from church to come out in support of Kenny? She believed if she had asked youth minister, Cecil Brunson, he would have come. He had taken a liking to Kenny ever since Kacie, following Envy's advice, enrolled Kenny in the church's youth group; she already saw a change in him. He was livelier, talkative, and enjoyed going to Super Wednesday, an excellent program designed around youths aged twelve to seventeen.

Kacie had a strong desire to start doing better when it came to her kids. She no longer left them at home alone the way she used to do. Nor did she hire teenagers to watch her kids when she wanted to have girls' night out or occasionally work extra hours. She called on their fathers more often, something she had refused to do, even though most of their daddies were willing to keep their kids. They may not all have paid child support, but it was still a relief when she gave in and allowed her kids to get to know their fathers' sides of the family. Plus, Kacie felt her kids were safer in the hands of their fathers.

Kenny's father, Thomas, walked into the courtroom, accompanied by his wife of one year. Kacie didn't trip about it. She had no interest whatsoever in Thomas anymore. He had his evil ways, but he could be cool when it came to his son. He paid his child support on time every month, and except for taking what Kenny did as just being a boy, Thomas was a good father, but their relationship had been volatile at times because of Thomas's short temper. Kacie was glad when their relationship ended shortly after Kenny was two years old.

Kenny enjoyed visiting his father, but Kacie usually had some excuse as to why he couldn't. Part of her was frightened, thinking that Thomas might get upset with Kenny for some reason or other and explode on him, just like he'd done many times before toward her.

Now that Kenny was growing up and looking like he was already grown, Kacie had started to understand that he needed not only the direction and guidance he got from the youth group, but Kenny needed his father in his life too. Soon after the incident with Jackie, Kacie relented and told Thomas that he could spend more time with his son.

Thomas's attitude toward Kacie seemed to soften ever since she told him that. He used to avoid talking to her when he called her house. He would never come to Kacie's house to pick up Kenny. He always insisted that Kacie drop him off at his mother's house. Now, in the weeks since the incident, Thomas called Kenny almost every day.

Thomas, his wife, and Kenny sat in front of Layla, Envy, and Kacie. Kenny was busy talking to his daddy.

"I'm glad to see Thomas here," Layla whispered to Kacie. "I felt if you would give the man a chance, he would step up to the plate and be the father Kenny needs."

"Okay, so you told me so. I accept that."

"What are y'all talking about?" Envy leaned over to get in on the conversation.

"About Thomas being here," Layla told her. "Is that his wife with him?" Layla asked Kacie.

"Yeah, that's Shania."

"How is she?" asked Envy.

"She seems pretty nice. I don't interact with her much, but Kenny seems to like her."

Envy patted Kacie on her shoulder. "Everything is going to be okay. I don't think you have to worry about Kenny. He's going to be just fine."

"I hope you're right. I just hope this judge isn't biased against my son, that's all. You know how some of them can be when it comes to young black men, and it's even worse when they find out they come from poor families."

"Don't even think like that," Layla told her. "The judge still has to listen to this hearing fairly, and everything will work out. And please don't let me hear you identify you or your children as being poor."

"Well, we live below poverty guidelines. What's the difference?"

"Stop talking nonsense. It is not going to help one way or another. We've already prayed about this, and God has everything under control. You talk like this is a murder trial or something, when it isn't a trial at all," snapped Envy.

"I know it's not a trial," Kacie snapped back. "But this hearing will determine if the case can be settled today, or if it needs to be set up to go to court and possibly before a jury."

"It doesn't matter," Envy told her. "Watch how God works things out. I believe everything will be settled today. Kenny, and you too for that matter, will be vindicated. Just watch."

The bailiff ordered everyone in the courtroom to stand for the entrance of the judge, and the hearing began.

The judge listened as both sides presented their versions of what had taken place five weeks prior. Kacie was pleased with the manner in which the mediator presented her side of the case, but she cringed when she heard Jackie Cheney's attorney. He made the whole incident sound like it was a figment of Kacie's imagination.

Kacie was soon called to stand before the judge.

The mediator addressed her. "Miss Mayweather, please tell the court what you witnessed the night of the alleged incident."

Kacie retold the story just as she had numerous times already to the mediator, Child Protective Services, the police, Rape Crisis, not to mention Envy, Layla, and Thomas.

Jackie Cheney's attorney asked the judge permission to question Kacie.

"Miss Mayweather, when you walked into your den, it was dark. Am I right?"

"Yes, and?"

He had his hands clasped together in front of him. His white face, black tailored suit, and black striped tie, with a white shirt, somehow gave Kacie a feeling of powerlessness.

"Did you see my client engaging in a sexual act with your son, or did you assume there had been a sexual encounter?"

"I didn't have to see her doing anything. Her being naked—"

He cut her off. "So did you or did you not see them engaging in sex? Yes or no?"

"No," Kacie answered, and shifted her weight from her right side to her left.

"Has your son admitted to having engaged in sexual intercourse or any sexual act before this alleged incident, Miss Mayweather?"

"My son is the one who was violated."

"Just answer the question, please." The lawyer sounded irritated.

"I don't know why you're asking questions about my son, when you should be talking to your client. She's the one who's a sex-crazed maniac."

"There will be no name-calling in my court, Miss Mayweather," the judge told her in a stern voice. "She's the child molester." Kacie looked over at Jackie and pointed a finger at the girl. "And you want to stand there and act like my son is at fault."

"I said, settle down or I'll dismiss this hearing right now," the judge warned, and hit his gavel.

The mediator stepped closer to Kacie and whispered something in her ear. She nodded.

"So, Miss Mayweather, will you answer the question?"

Kacie looked down. She felt defeated. No one had to tell her that this was not going to turn out as she'd hoped.

"Yes, but it's not like you think—"

"Thank you, Miss Mayweather. That's all the questions I have."

"You may have a seat, Miss Mayweather," the bailiff told her.

Jackie Cheney was called next. When Jackie stood before the judge, she denied that any wrongdoing had occurred on her part or Kenny's. Her testimony was that the two of them had been listening to music and they both fell asleep.

"Your Honor," the babysitter said, speaking in a mild-mannered tone, "What Miss Mayweather said, simply isn't true."

Kacie wanted to jump up and choke the girl until she turned two shades darker than her high-yellow skin. She was just about to do it too, if it had not been for the fact that she was sandwiched in between Layla and Envy. Both had a tight hold on each one of her arms, like they knew what was on her mind.

Listening to lies being told about the incident caused Kacie's head to start pounding. Kenny had moved from sitting next to his father and was now sitting next to Kacie. She dug her knuckle into his back where no one could see. "You better get up there and tell the truth," she warned him.

The mediator peered over his shoulder. "Please, Miss Mayweather, you have to be quiet," he whispered.

Kacie groaned and leaned back against the hard wooden seat. Envy patted Kacie's hand in a comforting manner.

"Kenny Mayweather, please come forward," the bailiff ordered.

For the first time since the incident, Kacie looked at Kenny and saw a frightened boy. She watched as he stood in front of the judge and promised to tell the truth, the whole truth, and nothing but the truth.

Prosecutor Otis Morgan asked Kenny questions about his version of what had happened.

"Nothing happened."

"Why do you think your mother would say that Ms. Cheney was naked and you had on your underpants?"

"Because it was dark in the room." Kenny fidgeted as he stood before the table and in front of the judge. The look on his face revealed his embarrassment of being put in a situation where people could possibly judge his manhood. His mother would be furious, of that he was certain, but he couldn't allow himself to be put on display like he was one of his little brothers or sisters.

Much to Kacie's surprise and dismay, Kenny answered his questions almost identical to that of Jackie

Cheney. The mediator sucked in his breath, bit his bottom lip, and listened to Kenny tell about what had occurred that night. He had briefed Kenny more than once about his testimony, and still the boy stood before the judge with a very different version of what they had talked about in his office.

The mediator stopped Kenny from relaying any more damaging testimony. "That's all of the questions I have."

Jackie's attorney, Lawrence Denton, quickly walked forward. "Why was it dark, Kenny? Did you want my client to engage in sexual acts with you?"

The prosecutor jumped up. "I object. My client is thirteen years old. He cannot make a decision to engage in sex."

"Sustained."

"We were listening to music that I had downloaded from off the Internet," Kenny said.

"I see. Tell me, Kenny, were you lying on the floor with a quilt covering your body?"

Kenny stuttered and paused. "Yes, b-because it was more fun that way . . . and the house was a little cold. My mom always tells me not to touch the thermostat." Kenny did not look at all in the direction of his mother.

Kacie sat back and her eyes looked cutting. Her face was so red it looked the color of a fresh ripe tomato. Her legs trembled and she shook her head from side to side. Layla squeezed her hand.

"So you're standing here this morning, Mr. Mayweather, stating that Miss Cheney and you did not engage in any sexual contact whatsoever, including oral sex?"

"Yes, no. I mean, no, sir. Nothing happened—"

"Prosecutor Morgan," the judge interrupted. "Why would you bring this case to court? There is no evidence

of inappropriate sexual conduct on the part of Miss
Cheney. I've looked through these files and the only
witness is Miss Mayweather. I do not plan on wasting
the remainder of my morning listening to this
nonsense."

"But, Judge . . ."

"Judge Johnson, may I say something?" asked
Attorney Denton.

"Yes, you may," the judge replied.

"I ask that the allegations against my client be
dropped, and as of today this matter be considered
closed. Mr. Mayweather has been questioned openly, as
well as by a child advocacy counselor, and he continues
to say that nothing occurred between him and my client.
What we have, Your Honor, is a case of a mother who
left not one, but all seven of her children at home with a
young, inexperienced babysitter so she could go out and
party."

Kacie jumped up on her shaking legs. "How dare
you!" she yelled. "You don't know anything about me.
My son was molested, assaulted, and maybe even raped
by that—that hussy." Kacie pointed at a scared-looking
Jackie Cheney, and her father looked like he wanted to
get up and knock Kacie to the ground.

"Order in the court," the judge yelled. "Sit down
now, Miss Mayweather, or you will be found in
contempt of court and escorted out of the courtroom to
jail."

Kacie reluctantly obeyed.

The judge hesitated before continuing. "After
hearing the plaintiff and the defendant, along with the
witnesses; after reading the reports from Child
Protective Services, the Rape Crisis Division, and the
police report, there is not enough evidence to support

the allegations of sexual misconduct on the part of Miss Jackie Cheney."

"What?" Kacie bounced up again.

"This case is dismissed." He hit his gavel on the judge's bench. "Get this woman out of my courtroom."

The group stood and filed out. Kenny's father walked along with his son, talking to him.

"The next case is. . . ," the bailiff stated as they departed.

Once they were outside in the heavily overcrowded foyer, Kacie let loose. She blasted the mediator and she totally went off on Kenny for what she called blatantly lying and making her look like a total idiot.

"Hold up, Kacie," Thomas said as he stepped between her and Kenny. "Settle down. It's over with. Let it go. I told you in the first place that you were taking this too far. Let the boy move on from this. He's already embarrassed enough."

"He's embarrassed? Oh no, you did not just go there. He should be getting his butt kicked for making a fool out of me in there," she screamed, and pointed back toward the courtroom.

"Calm down, Kacie," Envy encouraged her, and rubbed her shoulders.

"Yeah, she's right, Kacie. You're not making things better. The judge has ruled, and it's over with," Layla said.

"Let me take Kenny with me. I'll bring him home later this evening. It'll give both of you some time to settle down," Thomas suggested.

"Oh, it'll be a while before I settle down after what he just pulled. You're right, you better take him with you because the way that I feel, I won't be responsible for what I might do to him if he comes home with me."

Kenny cowered next to his father. The facial expression on his face showed a real fear of what his mother would do. Kacie was definitely hot-tempered, and it was nothing for her to punch or slap her kids when they got on her nerves or did something that made her angry.

"Good decision," said Layla. "Let's get out of here. I've never seen so many men, women, and children gathered in one small place like this."

"Kenny, are you all right?" Envy asked before he walked away with his father.

"Yes, ma'am," he said barely above a faint whisper, and then looked off.

Jackie, her father, and her arrogant, highfalutin attorney passed by Kacie and her friends. They glanced in Kacie's direction as they walked toward the exit.

Kacie gave Jackie, Mr. Cheney, and Lawrence Denton the evil eye. Thank God, looks couldn't kill.

The three women proceeded to walk out of the building behind Cheney and his entourage.

"Where are you two headed?" asked Kacie.

"I'm going back to the office," said Envy. "I have some projects that need my attention, but I had to come to support Kenny, and you, of course."

"I'm going to visit my parents before I go to the salon. I have five clients. I want to finish them at least by six, no later than seven. I have a date tonight, so I don't plan on being at the salon all night."

"With Dennis?" Envy asked in a hesitant voice. She arched her eyebrows as she waited on Layla's response.

Kacie waited in silence too.

Layla played them off with the wave of her hand. "No. Gosh, how many times do I have to tell y'all that Dennis is not the only man on the face of the earth? Y'all act like I'm supposed to be so gung ho over him," she said, talking nonstop with her hands gliding through the air. "I had to let Dennis know that I'm no longer interested in saving all my love for him, as Whitney used to sing."

"What are you saying? You broke up with him?" asked Kacie, an astonished look on her face.

Envy's mouth hung open. "What did you do?"

"I didn't do anything but let him know that enough is enough."

"Wow," said Kacie. "Poor Dennis."

"I can't believe you two." Layla brushed them off with a throw of her hand. "Whateva."

"Excuse us, then," said Envy. "We didn't mean to get your panties in a wad."

"I know that's right," Kacie agreed. "But, tell us."

"Tell y'all what?"

"About who you're meeting," said Envy. "Is it Omar again?"

"Since y'all insist on being all up in my business, no it is not Omar. I met this guy at Precious Cargo a few nights ago. I went with some of the girls from the salon."

Envy's eyes widened. "You didn't tell us." She turned and looked at Kacie. "Unless she told you about it," said Envy with curiosity dripping from her surprised lips.

"Nope. This is the first I've heard about it."

"Dang, I didn't know I had to tell y'all every move I make. A few of us went after work to get a bite to eat and listen to some spoken word. I heard about Precious Cargo, but never bothered to go to the Pinch District. But I'm glad I did, because there was this cutie behind the bar, with eyes the color of midnight and a smile that could knock a girl off her feet. Whew," Layla said, and feigned like she was about to pass out. "I went to the bar, and he offered me my drink of choice on the house. I asked for a ginger ale on the rocks. I think it was the best ginger ale I've ever tasted."

Envy stumbled. A stunned look crossed her face, but she remained silent.

"Be careful, girl," Kacie told her when she saw Envy trip and almost fall.

"Thanks," replied Envy. "My heel got caught in between one of the cracks on the concrete." She took a deep swallow before she continued to speak. She addressed Layla. "I had no idea you hung out at Precious Cargo."

"I don't. It was my first time going. It was a spur-of-the-moment thing. But I will tell you this, it may have been my first time, but believe me, it surely won't be my last. Anyway, I'm meeting him tonight after he gets off work. We're going to hang out."

"What's his name?" Envy asked. Her eyes narrowed suspiciously. Maybe it was the part-time bartender, Spencer, but she doubted it. He wouldn't be Layla's type—too hefty, for one thing, and not so easy on the eyes.

"Tyreek. Isn't that an appealing name?"

"What can you and this Tyreek fellow possibly have to do late at night, Layla? Girl, you better be careful. Sounds like you're about to be somebody's booty call." Envy faked a smile.

"What is your problem?" Layla asked Envy. "Don't even go there with me. Kacie, you better tell your girl about herself, because she is not one to talk about anything I do, with anybody."

"Both of y'all need to stop tripping. If I didn't know for myself that you all are best friends, I'd think the way y'all getting all heated up about nothing, y'all are arch enemies. Layla, listen. I think Envy is just concerned about you, that's all. Frankly, I am too. We're not used to this new you. Every time we look around, girl, you calling out some other man's name that you've met. Dennis is getting pushed farther and farther on the back burner."

"Tell you what—y'all start the violin music for Dennis while I say this one more time, because you two just don't get it for some reason. Okay, Dennis was there to pick up the pieces after Mike. I'll always be grateful to him. But I do not owe him the rest of my life, duh." She continued to speak as they arrived near their parked cars. "Y'all have heard of the cliché, I'm sure, 'People come into your life for a reason, a season, or a lifetime.' I'm afraid that Dennis's season has come to an end."

The three of them stood next to Layla's car.

Kacie's voice was controlled, almost tight. "So which part applies to this guy, Tyreek, and what about O . . . Omario?"

"Girl, his name is Omar, not Omario!" Layla laughed. "Like Martin Luther King said, 'Longevity has its place.' And Omar's place has ended," she laughed again. "Let me get out of here. I'll talk to y'all later."

Layla got in her car, and Kacie and Envy walked to their cars, parked several spaces apart in the private parking lot.

"I don't know what to say about her. She's gone bananas," Envy told Kacie.

"Oh, she's just having fun. Trying to enjoy her new life, and I don't blame her too much. You only live once, and for the past thirty-two years, she was on life support. Now she's fully resuscitated; and she has her whole life before her. She'll be all right. She just needs to be careful out there, and knowing Layla like we do, she's not going to take any mess off anyone. I have to say that I'm glad for her."

"Humph, well, you can think what you want, but I think she's treading on dangerous ground. But it's her life, like you said. I'll talk to you later," Envy told Kacie when they arrived at Kacie's car.

"Thanks for coming to support me and Kenny. I'm praying that he'll get himself together before he goes too far with some girl out there and ends up with a baby."

"Kacie, Kenny will be fine. You'll see." Envy pecked her on the cheek and squeezed her hand. "If you're going to worry, don't pray; and if you're going to pray, don't worry. Remember Pastor Betts preaching about that one Sunday?"

"Yeah, I do, and you're right. I'm just scared. I don't want him to turn out like me."

"Look, don't do start badgering yourself. You're a great person." Envy's cell phone rang. "Look, I gotta go. We'll talk," she said, and walked away while she pushed the green button on her phone. "Hello."

"Hello, Miss Wilson?"

"Yes, this is Miss Wilson."

"Casper Stephens. I was wondering if you could meet me sometime today."

Envy stepped up the pace until she reached her car. She clicked the remote to open the door and climbed inside quickly.

"What is it? Can't you tell me on the phone?" she asked.

"No, I prefer to talk to you in person. Do you have any time today?"

"Well, I'm on the way to my office. I had an outside appointment this morning. I have some projects that really need my attention. They should take a few hours to complete. I can meet you after work, say around five-thirty?"

"Five-thirty sounds fine. We can meet at my office, or if you'd like, I'd be glad to do a dinner meeting." He took a chance and laid it on the table. He wanted to see more of her outside of his office. A dinner meeting would be the chance he hoped would open the door for him to get a little closer to the mysterious Envy Wilson. After learning about her past, and seeing the woman she was today, he couldn't help but be intrigued by her. It took a woman of courage and great strength to open a cold case where she was the missing link to solving it. For that, he admired her. She was ready to face whatever the outcome would be. She was special in his book.

"Dinner? Umm, well, that'll be fine. Any particular place you have in mind."

Since you live in Midtown and I work downtown, I think it'll be easier on the both of us if we met somewhere in between. There are several fine eating establishments. There's Soul Catfish Café on Cooper; Huey's and Boscos both on Madison; Sekisui, on Belvedere; the Cupboard on Union . . . ."

"What about Sekisui? I haven't had their famous sushi rolls in a while."

With a certain alarming thrill, Casper Stephens said, "Sekisui, it is then. I'll see you at five-thirty."

"I look forward to it," responded Envy.

Envy drove back to the office with a mixture of emotions. What if Casper had terrible news? What if he was going to tell her that she had to turn herself in to law enforcement, and be locked behind bars in a cell for the rest of her life? Casper sounded hopeful, but maybe she had read him wrong. It was hard to tell what a person was thinking while talking on the phone. She felt dismayed at the prospect of everyone finding out how wretched she was—that she was a child murderer.

14

Guilt: the gift that keeps on giving. —*Erma Bombeck*

Envy spent the afternoon at the office working like a lunatic. When her assistant, Bobbie, asked questions about some of the projects they were working on together, Envy's words were spiced with irritation. She wanted to get everything done, so she could get out of there. Her face tightened and she felt like she was in the middle of the nightmare she always feared would come true.

A flurry of second thoughts saturated her already cluttered mind. She never felt loved by her mother. Her father had deserted her. The only love she felt was love at a distance, never giving in to it, or allowing it to approach her. But sleeping with man after man was something she was able to control. She was the one who kept herself from being hurt. But the trauma she had experienced all those years ago never left her. She never smoked before, but now she thought if she had a cigarette, it would help calm her down.

"Miss Wilson?" Her assistant's voice invaded her thoughts.

"What is it, Bobbie?" Her tension level rose a few points.

"I need your signature on these reports." She passed three coiled booklets to her. "Once you sign them, I can finish the rest of the projects and enter them into the database." She seemed to sense that something was not quite right with her boss.

"Give them here," Envy said in a bitter tone. "All I want to do is get this stuff done so I can get out of here. I have somewhere else to be that's far more important than being stuck here in this office."

"Yes, ma'am."

Envy signed the reports and immediately gathered her coat, purse, phone, and keys.

"Send all of my calls to my voice mail, unless it's something you can handle. If anyone asks where I am, tell them I had an emergency." Envy pulled open the door to her office. "Shut down my computer before you leave this afternoon, and do not," she emphasized, "do not call me. Whatever it is can wait until tomorrow."

"Yes, Miss Wilson."

Envy, highly frustrated and worried, stormed out of the office, down the hallway, and to the elevator. She pushed the button repeatedly, until she became frustrated when it didn't come quickly enough, so she ran down the flights of stairs leading from the eighth floor to the garage.

She looked at her watch. It was four-fifteen, still too early to meet with Casper Stephens. What could she do? She drove aimlessly around downtown until she suddenly spotted the massive Catholic Church, built with Victorian-era elegance, and pulled up in front of it. Their doors remained unlocked for prayer. She remotely locked her car and hurried inside. Once inside, the setting sun's light sprawled over the ceilings. She felt dwarfed by the opulent, plaster-relief ceilings.

Envy continued to take careful, quiet steps farther into the overwhelming sanctuary so as not to disturb others she saw kneeling at the altar or sitting on various pews in meditation. She took a seat midway the cathedral and loosened her taupe-and-ivory coat, revealing her sooty gray pantsuit jacket and the warm onyx-colored pullover she wore underneath. She leaned forward and rested both hands in praying style on the pew in front of her and made her petitions known before God.

Whatever she was about to hear from Casper Stephens would determine where the rest of her life was headed. Her heart began to beat profoundly. *Lord, I'm terrified. I need your help. Give me strength to endure whatever it is I'm about to face.* Envy remained in the church praying and thinking about what Casper had to discuss. It was after five when she looked at the time on her cell phone. Now she had to hurry to get to Sekisui on time.

~

While he sat at Sekisui and waited on Envy, Casper Stephens studied the thin folder of scant information he'd recovered from the Cold Case Investigations Unit Evidence Room. It was five-forty. She told him she had some things to finish up at work, so he blamed her tardiness on that. He nursed a glass of water with lemon as he waited for her arrival. He looked at the timepiece on his left wrist, and before his eyes could deflect toward the door, the sound of her voice gave him cause to look up. He cleared his throat, stood up, and greeted her.

"Hello, Envy," he said, and extended his hand in the direction of the empty seat across from him.

"Hello, Attorney Stephens. I'm sorry that I'm running late. I left work in plenty of time," she said as he pulled out the seat for her, "but I made a stop and then ended up getting caught in five o'clock traffic."

"No problem. You're my last appointment. And while I was waiting, I had a chance to go over your file some more."

Envy looked flushed. "I don't know what to say behind that. Should I be glad or sad?" she inquired.

"Before we discuss anything further, why don't you look at the menu and let me know what you would like to eat."

"I'm not really hungry. All I want is something to drink. They have great sweet tea here. That'll be all for me."

"But I thought you wanted to dine on their famous sushi rolls?" His eyebrows raised in an inquisitive manner; then he smiled.

"I did, but I'm afraid I'm so nervous that I've lost my appetite."

"I hope it's not on account of me."

The server appeared before she could respond. "Hello, my name is Jason. I'll be your server this evening. May I interest you in our two-for-one house hot sake and an appetizer?"

Casper looked at Envy. She shook her head.

"No, thank you. But the lady will have a glass of sweet tea with lemon."

"And for you, sir?"

"I'd like a small bottle of hot sake and, um, the nigiri sushi," Casper said, and closed the menu. "Are you sure you don't want an appetizer or a salad, or something?" he asked Envy.

"No. Really, I'm fine. Thank you."

"That will be all," Casper told the server.

"Thank you, sir. I will be back shortly with your order, sir, and your tea, ma'am."

Casper nodded. After the server left, he opened the file folder. "Did you say something?"

She shook her head. "No."

"Well, let's get to your case. I did quite a bit of research through the Cold Case files for information involving your child."

"And?" She looked at him with raised eyebrows.

"And," he replied. "I located the file."

The server returned promptly with a glass of tea, with a slice of lemon wedged around the glass, along with the bottle of hot sake.

"Thank you," Envy and Casper said.

"I guess I should be glad, but I can't say how I feel." Envy looked at him. Her face was almost crimson. She removed her eyeglasses and fidgeted with them.

"That's understandable. It's been eighteen years since the unthinkable happened. You were a teenager. I can't imagine the torment you went through back then." Casper took a swallow of his sake. "I keep thinking about the courage it took for you to rehash such a painful part of your past." He looked at her with empathy. If he had been in a different place in his life, he would have tried to holler at her, perhaps make something happen between the two of them. But his life was too full of his own personal problems, not to mention a thriving, but draining, law practice.

"Like I told you, there was no way I could expect my life to get better until I closed the door to my past. But before I can close it, I have to open it."

"I understand where you're coming from."

"Good, I'm glad you don't look down on me."

Casper studied her. She appeared rigid and troubled. He did not want to keep her in suspense any longer.

For the second time, the server approached the table before Casper could respond. "Your order, sir." The server set the plate of food in front of Casper, and then reached for a pitcher of tea and refilled Envy's nearly empty glass.

"Thank you," Casper said, and the server retreated. Casper patted the folder resting next to his plate of food. He blessed his food quickly, took a bite, and paused long enough to chew and swallow it. "Um, this is good. Are you sure you don't want anything?"

"Yes, I'm sure. I just want to know how long I'm going to be in jail."

Casper picked up a napkin and wiped his mouth. "I think it's highly unlikely that you'll be going to jail. Let me show you what I found."

Casper pushed his plate of food to the side and placed the folder in front of him. He removed the old newspaper clipping from the file and placed it in front of Envy. Instantly, he saw tears form in her brown eyes. His heart turned even softer for the beautiful woman sitting before him.

"Please understand, I get no pleasure in showing you this. I'm sure it brings up terrible memories for you. But I need to show you everything that is in the file."

Envy nodded. "I understand."

Search Continues For Mother of Newborn Left in School Lavatory
Memphis, TN (Memphis Commercial Appeal). The body of an infant, said to have been only hours old, has been found under shocking circumstances. The baby's lifeless body was discovered in the toilet by one of the janitorial staff at Germanside High School. Police state the body appears to have been in the second-floor bathroom toilet for as long as five hours. Homicide detective Monica Bell said the newborn girl was well developed and was more than likely full-term. A postmortem examination of the newborn will be done to determine the cause of death. "One of the major concerns now is to locate the mother of the infant," states Bell. "We are concerned about her health physically and psychologically." Detective Bell further states, "Everything is being done to locate the mother. We urge anyone who has information that will lead us to the mother to contact 555-TIPS. We are also pleading with the mother to contact police right away."

"You're right. It is hard to read." Envy breathed an exasperated sigh. "Though I've read it over and over in my mind for all these years, it's still nothing like seeing it in print again." She appeared to quiver while she read the newspaper clipping.

"Are you cold?" he asked. His tone pensive.

"No, no, I'm fine. Just nervous, on edge about all of this."

"I understand."

Envy pushed the clipping back to Casper and took a swallow of tea. "What else is there?"

"The police report, which I will go over with you. I think it will help you to relax a bit."

"What does it say?"

"Even though the case was initially being investigated as a homicide, detectives stated they were looking into the possibility that the baby's death could have been an accident."

"Are you saying that I may not have killed my baby?"

"Yep, that's exactly what I'm saying." Casper scratched his forehead and left it with the makings of a frown. "But there's something that puzzles me." Casper showed Envy another newspaper clipping. It was a small one, probably hardly noticed by readers back then. "In their search for clues, police were looking for evidence of a homicide and the instrument used to cut the baby's umbilical cord. I'm curious; what exactly did you use?"

"At first, I didn't know what to do. I was too shocked.

I couldn't believe that I had given birth. Then I tried to think, and I remember seeing something on television that showed a father cutting his newborn son's umbilical cord. Back then I didn't know that's what the cord was called. It looked like a rope to me. I remember searching through my purse to find something I could use to do like the man. I found a pair of nail clippers. I used them to—"

Casper showed the palm of his hand. "Stop. No need to go any further. I get the picture. There's something else."

"What else?" The familiar look of terror Casper had come to recognize covered Envy's face.

"Autopsy results." For a third time, he presented Envy with more information from her past. "An autopsy was done on your baby. It was determined by the medical examiner that the baby was stillborn, which means that you are not a murderer, Miss Wilson. What you did was wrong. I'm not denying that, but you were young, foolish, and pregnant. You were scared and you didn't know which way to turn. Gosh," he said, and leaned against his chair, "I'm sure when you went to the bathroom that day you had no idea you were about to give birth. Even after having given birth, at your age, you probably weren't aware that a stillbirth is supposed to be reported."

"No, I had no idea what I was supposed to do. I guess I hoped it would all go away. That I would wake up and find that I'd been in a nightmare for the past nine months."

"I'm sure it was a nightmare, only one that you actually lived through."

Envy glanced at Casper. Maybe he really did understand what she went through back then. She couldn't hold back her tears. She cried quietly with her head in her hands.

Casper passed her a napkin from off the table. At that moment, he felt an odd sense of closeness to her.

"Everything is going to work out." He tried reassuring her.

While she continued to cry, he sat quietly and gave her some time to digest what he had shared. As he sat in silence, thoughts about his own past flooded his bank of memories. The way things looked, Envy would have a chance of being set free from the guilt she'd carried around all of these years, but he didn't know if it would be that easy for him.

He could relate somewhat with how she felt. He'd done quite a few things when he was young that he truly regretted. He often played in his mind a tune by one of the old-timers, Tyrone Davis: "If I Could Turn Back the Hands of Time." The key word was "if." If only he had asked Lillie, his one true love, to marry him; then he wouldn't be an over the top workaholic, a man whose entire life was structured around his profession. But he was far too busy back then trying to do well in law school, so he could one day have the means to marry her and take care of her in the manner in which she deserved. But Lillie didn't want to wait. She accused Casper of making excuses. He never had time to see her. He was always too busy studying. When he wasn't studying, he was working a part-time job to help cover some of his tuition. But she wanted more. She wanted to be by his side, to become his bride. She pleaded with him, told him she would work while he finished law school, but he wasn't having it. His father would never approve of a woman working to send a man to school. "A real man makes his own way. A real man provides for his family," his father used to tell him, repeatedly.

Time spent between him and Lillie lessened more and more. The day she told him that she had met someone else, and was moving on with her life, the news almost struck him down like a bolt of lightning. He was in too deep with his studies, commitments made to his parents, and obligations to complete what he had always wanted—a law degree.

Casper had played tough; he had gambled on Lillie's love to be there for him always, and he had lost it all. But there was a flip side to Casper's personality that was only evident in his work. He was a hardheaded idealist who believed good things came to those who waited. Envy Wilson had been waiting for eighteen years. Unlike him, there was still a chance for her to come out a winner.

He reminisced about the day he located the autopsy report on Envy's baby. He was about to call it a day when he ran across autopsy results, stuck like glue on the back of a police report inside the folder. "Bingo," he had said aloud when he read, '...determined the fetus was stillborn.' "Yes!" Casper looked up at the ceiling. "Thank you for being my friend in high places."

Envy finally stopped shedding tears. She looked at Casper with reddened eyes and a smile that forced him to smile back.

Her voice sounded quiet, almost tranquil to Casper. "I don't know what to say. I don't know whether to be happy or hurt. Should I be smiling, or am I supposed to keep on weeping because I lost my baby? I have so many conflicting emotions running through me right now. I don't know what to do."

Casper reached his long arm across the table and patted her on the shoulder. "I can't tell you how to feel. That's something you have to deal with, but what I can tell you is that we still have some work to do."

He could feel her body stiffen just as he removed his hand. "You're talking about turning myself in?"

"Not literally turn yourself in like going to jail. But if you really want to ride this out all the way, we have some things we still need to do. I don't see the district attorney prosecuting this case. For one, it was a stillbirth which means that it would not have been viable outside of the womb; and number two, you were a minor back then, so different rules, laws, and regulations will apply. If there is a charge, it might be for desecration of a corpse, but it's unlikely that charge won't stick because of the statute of limitations. However, it's going to be your confession that will solve this case. There was no DNA taken from the baby; at least there is no evidence I could find that shows they took DNA. What is important for you right now is the medical examiner's ruling, the statute of limitations, and the case would likely have been a misdemeanor, anyway."

"A misdemeanor? Really?"

"Yes. You see in the state of Tennessee, both misdemeanors and felony cases must prove that you, the suspect in this instance, committed an unlawful act with criminal intent. You did neither."

Envy's hands trembled as she put her eyeglasses back on. "Oh, my gosh. Thank you, Lord." She cleared her throat. "So, uh, what's the next step?"

"I have a criminal case I'm trying that starts tomorrow, so don't be alarmed if you don't hear from me during the day. I'm going to contact the district attorney's office after I leave court. I might have to call you after hours, if that's all right."

"Yes, whatever time you call is fine. Now that I know I didn't murder my baby," Envy paused. "It's . . . well, it's unexplainable what's going through my mind right now. But yes"—she threw up both hands—"call me, whenever."

"Good. As soon as I go over everything with the DA, I can let you know what to expect after that. But I don't want you to do any unnecessary worrying."

"What can I do? How can I thank you, Mr. Stephens?"

"I'll get all the thanks I need when I see this case settled once and for all, and you can be at peace. But until then, you can do me one favor." He smiled and so did Envy. "Please call me Casper."

Envy chuckled lightly this time. "I hope you don't mind," she said. "But I think I'd like to eat some of those sushi rolls, after all . . . Casper."

Casper laughed. "Great."

After her dinner meeting with Casper, Envy felt as if a heavy burden had been removed from her shoulders— a burden that she had carried unnecessarily for all of these years. She got in her car. Before she left the parking lot, she tried to call Layla, but her phone went directly to voice mail. Next, she called Kacie.

Kacie answered. "I can't talk right now, Envy. Kyland just cut his foot on a piece of glass. I'm headed to the emergency room."

Envy heard Kyland screaming in the background. "Is he okay? Is it bad?"

"I think it's going to require at least a couple of stitches. But I need to make sure there's no glass in his foot. Look, I gotta go." Kacie ended the call.

Envy then decided to do what she attempted to do a couple of weeks ago, and that was talk to Nikkei. No matter how distant their relationship, the truth about her past needed to be told. She dialed Nikkei's number. Surprisingly, she answered the phone.

"Hello, Envy," she said, having apparently looked at her caller ID.

"Hi, Nikkei. How are you, the kids, and my brother-in-law?"

"Everyone is fine. What's going on with you?"

They both sounded dry over the phone. It always seemed like they had to force a conversation with each other.

"I was thinking about coming over there. I stopped by a couple of Sundays ago, but no one was there."

"Did you call before you came?" asked Nikkei.

Envy sucked in her breath, refusing to allow Nikkei to send her to that not-so-pleasant place she often went when it came to her sister. "No, I just dropped by. Do you have some time today? I know how busy you are running the kids from one activity to the next."

"That's not all I do, you know."

"I wasn't insinuating that it was all you do. Look, Nikkei, I really need to talk to you about something. It's serious. Just tell me when will be a good time. I don't want to argue with you, I want to talk. There are a lot of things you need to know."

Silence infiltrated the phone for seconds.

"Okay, can you come now? Mya is at liturgical dance rehearsal and T.J. is at football practice."

"Yes, I can come now, but what about T'juan? I don't want to intrude on any hubby-and-wife private time." Envy laughed lightly into the phone.

"T'juan drove to Jackson, Mississippi on business this morning. He'll won't be back until tomorrow morning, so now is as good as it's going to get."

"Okay, I'm on my way. I'm coming from downtown, so it'll take me about thirty or forty minutes."

"See you when you get here," Nikkei said. "Bye."

"Bye," replied Envy, and ended the call. There was a lot Envy needed to say to Nikkei, starting with an apology for not being the kind of sister that Nikkei deserved. They never hung out together, rarely talked, and Envy's interaction with her ten and twelve-year old niece and nephew was practically nonexistent. With all that had happened today, Envy realized even more that there were other things she had allowed to separate her from living her best life now. Holding on to the past, and not moving forward into the future, had cost her dearly. She prayed silently that Nikkei would hear her out. Envy surmised that she had to move past the guilt if she was ever going to have a full future.

On the drive to Nikkei's, Envy tried reaching Layla again. And again, Layla's phone went straight to voice mail. She was still angry about Layla and Tyreek arranging to meet. It didn't matter that she didn't want him for more than sex, but him choosing Layla? Ugh, how could he? The time would come soon enough for her to get things straight with Tyreek, but right now her good news outweighed the unpleasant thoughts she had about the two of them. Layla would be glad to hear that she would be free to move on with her life.

Envy decided to text Layla, something that she usually didn't do while driving, but now she was just plain curious as to where Layla could be. She texted her the good news. Surely, Layla would call back.

Envy heard the chime on her cell phone and glanced at the text message on the screen. *Yaaa, hallelujah. Busy now will call u soon as I can*, the message said from Layla. Envy smiled.

On the way to her sister's, Envy couldn't quiet the mounting jealousy taking root on the inside of her. It was one area in her life that she would have to tackle next. Tyreek was her main go-to man, other than Leonard. She wasn't about to lose him to the likes of Layla. She kept her sexual lifestyle her private business.

Kacie and Layla only knew so much about it. Sure, they may have implied that she slept around, but they hadn't the faintest idea how much or with whom, except for Leonard. The men in her life were reserved for her, and only her, and it was nobody's business who they were. She decided to call Tyreek.

He answered. So much background noise filtered through his cell phone that she had to almost scream. "I want to see you tonight. Be at my house no later than ten-thirty," she demanded as usual. She knew that he couldn't say no to her. He never had. Layla may not have known about her and Tyreek, but tonight Tyreek was going to be told to keep his goods to himself—and to her.

"I can't," he answered quickly, like he hadn't given it a moment's thought.

She yelled back so loud, it was obvious that his response to her far outweighed the good news she had received from Casper earlier. "What do you mean, you can't? I know your schedule like the back of my hand, Tyreek. You do not have to close tonight; so, like I said, be here at ten-thirty."

"And like I said, I can't. I have plans." The way he came off was almost biting and cold. Envy didn't understand. From what Layla had told her and Kacie, tonight would be the first night that she and Tyreek were going out. So why would he put her off for Layla, some chick he knew nothing about? Envy was furious.

"Who is she?" She demanded to hear him say that it was someone else. She wanted him to say Layla's name. That would be her cue to roast him real good.

"Look, I know you hear all this noise in the background. You can tell it's on and popping in here. I have to go. I'll talk to you tomorrow."

"Hello," Envy said into her Bluetooth. "Hello," she said again. The phone went silent. Tyreek had hung up. "Ughh! I am so doggone mad. How dare his trifling behind hang up on me!" Envy declared to the empty car.

I don't know what he thinks is so special about Layla. I bet if he saw some of her fat pictures, he would change his mind about going out with her in a heartbeat, Envy said sourly. But why am I so worried? I didn't want to see him, anyway, plus I can call Leonard, Cedric, and any other man listed in my ladies' little red book. Your loss, Tyreek, because you'll never win this game.

She turned up the radio to the gospel station and listened to an old song playing, and sang along: "Lord, you've been so faithful, even though sometimes I didn't do what you wanted me to dewwww."

Envy let her thoughts wander back to her sister. It would be hard to tell Nikkei about everything, but Envy concluded that it was only fair that Nikkei should know; she was the only sibling she had. Certainly if she confided in Kacie and Layla, she had to give Nikkei the same courtesy.

Envy continued her drive to Nikkei's. Soon she tuned out the music playing and her thoughts about Tyreek and Layla. Maybe her life was about to make a turn for the better. Maybe a change was about to come. What would the face in the mirror have to say about that? The faint beginnings of a smile formed as she pushed her glasses up on the bridge of her nose. Life may not be fair, but she was in it to win it—at all costs.

15

Frustration is the wet nurse of violence. —David Abrahamsen

Kacie made sure all the kids had their baths before she instructed them to go to their rooms. Kyland required three stiches and the doctors did find a few small pieces of glass that they removed without any problems. The pain medicine had him knocked out, and Kacie was glad. Hopefully, he would sleep through the night.

"Kassandra, you and Keith watch the little ones. Make sure y'all are in bed by nine o'clock."

"Yes, ma'am," Kassandra and Keith answered, and then disappeared into the back of the house.

Kacie huffed audibly when she thought about the European Lit paper that was due the next day. At least she had started on it. Hopefully it wouldn't take too long for her to finish. In addition, she had to make up for the time she missed from work due to taking Kenny to court, and if that wasn't enough, to add to her list of maladies, her legs ached like "nobody's business," as her late grandmother used to say.

She crawled up into her bed and pulled out the used laptop she purchased at a good price from one of the local pawnshops. While waiting on it to power up, she got up and went to the bathroom to get some green rubbing alcohol to massage her legs. *It would be nice to have someone who loved me enough to take care of me when I'm down. Who would massage my legs when they're aching like this. Someone who would love me just for me; see the beauty that I have on the inside and not be concerned with my physical challenges.* She sat on the bed and rubbed her legs slowly, hoping that the alcohol would give her some relief. She had pain meds she could take, but then she would be out like a light, and would never finish her school paper.

Kacie picked up the phone after she finished rubbing her legs down.

"Thomas, are you on your way with my son?" she asked. "He needs to get his behind here. He still has chores to do and I'm sure he has homework too."

"I'll be there with him in a couple of hours," he told her.

"Get him home, Thomas. Two hours is too late, and you know it's a school night. I don't care if he is with you."

Thomas replied with sternness in his voice. "Yeah, okay. He'll be there. Peace out."

Kacie ended the call and looked at her computer. It had finally powered up. She was tempted to go online, but she decided to hold off on a bit of pleasure and chose to complete the 850-word paper.

Being in school helped to boost her self-esteem. To her surprise, quite a few of the students were in her age bracket. She'd met a few girls she placed in the category of associates, but none of them would be close to her like Envy and Layla. As for the men, there were certainly plenty of them walking around the campus, looking fine and smelling good, and there was temptation to be the aggressor, but so far she'd held off. After her traumatic experience and breakup with Deacon Riggs, she planned to be extra careful when it came to guarding her heart. She had seven kids now, and she was done with being used like a gas station, with men only coming to her for fill-ups.

The fact that she had cerebral palsy shouldn't matter, but it did. It weighed heavily on Kacie's mind, especially when she looked at her kids. In each of them, she was reminded of how easily she had given in to the men in her life. But what else did she have to give but her body, and she was far from being a brick house. It was sad to know that men were visual creatures, because that meant her chances of someone falling for her because of looks was even lower than the average looking females. She had a lot to contend with, and on top of being physically challenged, she was tied down with seven children. Of those seven, Kenny was already starting to give her trouble.

Kacie pushed herself to concentrate long enough to finish the last half of her paper. The doorbell rang.

"I got it," she heard Keith say.

"No, let me get it," said Kassandra, sounding as bossy as ever.

Kacie made it to the door before either of them. "Neither one of y'all are going to get it. Get back there in your room like I told you. And isn't it nine o'clock? You know you're supposed to be in the bed," she scolded.

She opened the door. Thomas stood on the other side. "Special delivery," he said sarcastically. "Here he is." He immediately lit in on Kacie. "You need to do a better job than what you're doing."

Kenny walked past her and mumbled, "Hello."

"Go in there and get those clothes off while I talk to your daddy," she ordered.

"My boy don't need to be tied down watching your rug rats, and he sho don't need to be having one of his own. So I'm giving you fair warning, right here and right now," he said while he remained at the entrance to her front door. "If I so much as think I hear a rumor, anything that he's into some more unnecessary mess because you ain't doing your job like a real mama should, he's coming to live with me."

"Are you a fool?" she yelled. "Get out of my face talking that nonsense!" Kacie used all of her strength to close the door in Thomas's face, but he positioned the palm of his hand flat on the other side. The door wouldn't budge.

"This conversation isn't over until I say it's over. Now, like I said, you better get your act together. I'm dead serious, Kacie. You got all of these kids running around here, no discipline, no rules, nothing." He pointed a threatening finger inches from her face.

Her heart beat against her chest; she was scared. Thomas could become violent if she pushed him too far. She had been the landing pad for many of his punches. Tonight she was not about to let him get to the point where he wanted to beat her down. Her body couldn't take any more beatings, no more babies, no more pain period.

"Listen, Thomas. I'm doing my best. I told you that you're going to have to start stepping up and spending more time with your son. And you got me messed up if you think he'll ever come live with you. That's a story you need to feed to some of your other baby mamas out there."

"Who do you think you're talking to? I'll slap the taste out of your mouth."

Kacie tried to regain control of a situation that could quickly spiral out of control. "Look, all I need is your support, and for you to check on him. Now, if you'll excuse me, I need to get from in front of this door. My legs are killing me, and the cold air is not good for my body. You already know that, so let's call a truce for tonight."

Thomas's bold black eyes looked her up and down. His face displayed a look of harshness and cruelty. She could see the arteries throbbing in the side of his neck. He was nearing his boiling point.

"Thomas, what do you say? Let's call it a night. I'll do better with Kenny. I promise."

Kacie saw his body deflate like air forced from a balloon. She mentally said, *Thank you, Lord.*

"Yeah, whatever. Just remember what I said about my son." He turned and walked off. This time Kacie exhaled, closed the door, and leaned her body against it. "Um, glad that's over. I can't stand that man," she said to no one. "He may be good to Kenny, but he's a hellion when it comes to me. Kenny!" she yelled. "Get your behind in here right now." Somebody was going to pay for the way Thomas had just treated her. Who better than his son?

"Ma'am," the boy answered.

"I can't believe you had the nerve to turn on me in court today. You outright lied in front of my face."

"But, Momma. . . ," he said in a sad voice.

Kacie slapped him so hard across his face that he stumbled backward and fell on the sofa. "Don't you ever in your life turn against me, boy. I'm the one that's raising you. Not your sorry daddy, not that slut who you were laying down with, nobody but me!" She continued to yell at him. "You never supposed to go against blood, especially your mama. Do you understand me?" Kacie stood over him while he remained lying back on the couch.

"Yes . . . ma'am," he answered. Tears crested in the corners of his eyes, but they remained there, almost as if they were afraid to fall.

Kacie slapped him across his face once, twice, three more times. "Here I am," she said while breathing hard, "trying to go to school to make things better for the seven of y'all. I'm trying to keep a roof over your heads. Trying to keep food on the table, and as soon as I decide to go out, just for a little while, you have the nerve to let some girl do nasty things to you, talking about oral sex. You're dumb and stupid if you think that letting a girl do that to you makes you a man. You're nothing but a punk. You're just like your daddy." Kacie was off on a tangent now. "God don't like ugly. You're going straight to hell if you don't get yourself together. Do you hear me?"

"Yes." By this time, tears were pouring from Kenny's eyes.

"If your daddy was so good like he pretends to be, he would have at least given you his last name, but did he?"

"No," Kenny whispered.

"Did he think enough of you, his own flesh and blood, and his oldest son, to at least do that?" Kacie asked, yelling again.

"No, ma'am," Kenny replied louder this time.

"Get up and get in there and get your stuff ready for school tomorrow. Then get those dishes washed and see about your sisters and brothers. My legs are hurting, and it's all because of y'all. Y'all are killing me. I'm sick of it!" she cried out. "I'm sick and tired of all of y'all."

Kacie left Kenny in the living room and she retreated to her bedroom, slamming the door closed. She fell across the bed, slammed the computer shut, and wept. Her life wasn't supposed to be like this. She wanted so bad to be normal, to be beautiful. Why? Why did it have to be her? She hated herself at that moment. She lifted her head to reach for a box of tissues on the side table, and caught her reflection in the mirror attached to the dresser. She looked at her red, swollen eyes. She lifted her crooked legs up, one by one, and felt a wave of nausea as she saw how ugly and deformed they were. "Where is the beauty in me?" she asked the person staring at her in the mirror. "What are you looking at? You're ugly. You're nothing but a slut. You're a child abuser. You will never amount to being nothing but a Section 8 hood rat." The attacks against the woman in the mirror intensified until Kacie ran out of insults. Her head fell back down on the pillow and she buried the woman in the mirror, at least for the night.

Kacie turned over and landed on top of her laptop. She must have fallen asleep. It was close to one o'clock in the morning. The house was quiet. She left the laptop in its place, got stiffly to her feet, and went to use the bathroom. When she finished, she looked in the bottom of the vanity and searched in her bag of meds until she found her pain medicine. It was late, but she didn't care. She didn't care if she missed work or school tomorrow. She was sick of everything and everybody at that moment.

More than her legs hurt. Her spirit felt like it was on fire. She leaned down over the sink until her mouth and hand were under the sink's faucet. The cold water filled her hands, which she used to swallow the strong, quick-acting pill. Back in her bedroom, she climbed underneath the covers.

"I'm sorry, God. I know I shouldn't have hit my son. I know I shouldn't have talked about myself like that either. But I need you to help me understand some things. I need to hear a word from you. I can't keep on doing this. I can't keep being like this, living like this. I need you to tell me what to do. If you don't, I don't think I can last. I feel like I'm about to break."

16

Seduction isn't making someone do what they don't want to do. Seduction is enticing someone into doing what they secretly want to do already.—Waiter Rant

Layla read Envy's text. She was thrilled that Envy would be able to put her past behind her and move on with her life.

Layla planned to do the same. She met Tyreek at Precious Cargo. He told her to keep her car parked and she got in his Dodge Challenger. He drove downtown to Tom Lee Park, named after Tom Lee, an African-American river worker who single-handedly saved the lives of thirty-two passengers on the M. E. Norman Steamboat in 1925. Luxury homes and condominiums decorated the top of the bluff that overlooked the park and the river. During the spring and summer, the park was often alive and vibrant with walkers, joggers, the famous Memphis in May Barbecue Cooking Contest, and riverfront concerts. Several cars were parked along the strip to enjoy the night view, while other couples strolled along the paved two-mile parkway or cuddled on the benches lined along the park.

The night was clear so the couple could appreciate the panoramic views of the Mississippi River, and the shores of Arkansas across the water, with the lit-up M-shaped bridge connecting the two states.

Layla listened with amusement at Tyreek telling wild stories about some of the things he encountered from customers.

"You know they say that people pour out their troubles to the bartender. It's true. One man poured out his insides all over the bar one night. I needed a drink myself after that."

Layla burst into laughter. "I can't take it anymore. You're making my jaws hurt from laughing so hard."

"I like the sound of your laughter," Tyreek said in a serious tone. "Hey, let's take a stroll along the river walk," he suggested. "I know there's a cold breeze coming off the river, but it'll be fun. And it'll be an excuse for you to cuddle up next to me."

"One thing is for sure," said Layla.

"What's that?"

"You know how to keep a girl smiling. I like that."

"I like you," Tyreek replied. "Come on, button up that jacket, sweetheart, and let's do this."

Layla said, "I'm ready."

Tyreek got out of the car and ran to the other side to open the door for Layla. He extended his hand toward hers and she placed her hand in his.

They strolled along the river walk, and Tyreek pulled her body close to his. She had to admit that it felt good, real good. It wasn't the same as being out on a date with Dennis, or going to a basketball game with Omar. There was something about being with Tyreek that felt totally different.

This brother has it going on. He has to have a lady. Prob'ly has a harem. She laughed.

"Hey!" He stopped and looked at her. "Tell me."

"Tell you what?" asked Layla.

"What you're laughing about."

"Oh, nothing really."

"Oh, it was something." He pulled her even closer to him and gave her an affectionate kiss on the cheek. "Tell me," he insisted.

"Okay, since you're going to whine about it." They both laughed. "I was thinking that a guy like you, I mean you meet all types of women in your profession."

"Yeah, and?"

"Well, you must have a lady or ladies somewhere."

"Why?"

"Because," she answered.

"Why would you think that? And if you do believe that, why are you here with me tonight?"

"Because I'm a free spirit. I got it like that."

"Oh, the lady I'm standing next to definitely has it like that. You're one fine woman. And just to be straight up with you, I don't have a girlfriend. I'm not going to lie to you and tell you that women don't come on to me at the bar, and sometimes I reciprocate, but it's nothing serious. You know what I mean?"

"I hear what you're saying. And it's all good."

"It's all good?" he repeated. "Sounds to me like you're the one who has a man. No doubt you do, because I can't imagine a man on this earth that wouldn't want to sport you on his arm."

Layla allowed his compliment to sink in. She loved it when men complimented her good looks. "I do have a friend. It used to be serious, but I can't say that I want serious anymore. I mean, look at me."

Tyreek spoke up. "Believe me, baby girl, I'm definitely looking atcha."

Layla playfully tapped him on his free arm. "I'm not talking about that kind of looking. What I mean is that if things were as serious as he wants them to be, or should I say expects them to be, then I wouldn't be here with you. He's become comfortable with having a dependent woman in his life, and that's no longer me. I don't have to depend on a man or anyone else for anything. Don't get me wrong; because he is a good man. He's kind, compassionate, a great listener."

"If he's all of that, then why are you here with me? You sound like you have a good thing at home." They approached a bench and Tyreek led the way for the two of them to sit down.

"First let me clear things up a bit. He's not at home, like at my home. I have my place and he has his. We've been friends awhile, but that's all; we are not a couple anymore. It's like going to work—it's routine. He's like a fixture in my life; that's it. I don't know if you understand where I'm coming from."

"Sure, I do. I feel you. There's been this girl that I used to want so badly. I mean, she was like someone special to me." Tyreek laid one hand over his heart. "She could have had all of me."

"What happened?" asked Layla.

"Turns out she didn't want all of me; only wanted a piece of me. Whenever she calls, I'm supposed to run. I admit it, I never turned her down. When she was finished with me, you know what she would say?"

"What?" Layla's interest was piqued.

"'Lock the door on your way out.'"

"Wow, she sounds coldhearted."

"Tell me about it. But all of my running to her and being used for her satisfaction, it has to stop. I can't do it anymore. I won't do it anymore, I should say."

"So you're still seeing her? Is that what I just heard?"

"Yeah, you heard right, but I've made a decision to put her in the past. I've never felt one hundred percent sure about it, until now."

"What makes you so sure now?" asked Layla.

"You. It may sound like a line, but all I can do is speak the truth. I don't believe in leading women on. My mother taught me better than that. She was a victim of domestic violence. I was too young to do anything about it at the time. I was just a young buck, you know. I saw her hurt too many times, not just physical abuse but mental abuse as well. She was mistreated for being a good woman, and not just once, but it seems like every man she met was on a mission to destroy the good in her, to twist the love that she had to give into something ugly and painful, until it just wore her down. I hate to say this, but I'm glad she doesn't have a man in her life now; and she hasn't had one that I know about since I turned eighteen. Now I'm a full-grown man, and I dare another man to step to her in any way except correct. However, seeing the way dudes treated her, I promised her and myself that I would never use a woman for my own gain, or just as a conquest. And I surely will never abuse a woman. If I see even an inkling that things could go in that direction, you better believe I'm out."

Dennis and his parents were reasonably close, but Layla had never heard him defend his mother's honor like Tyreek just did. Layla listened as he spoke slowly, deliberately looking in her eyes, like he was feeling his way.

"So what I'm saying to you, baby girl, is that I'm not looking for my next conquest. I don't want to be anybody's boy toy anymore. I'm looking for the real deal. Don't get uncomfortable, because it's okay if you aren't on the same page as me. But there's something about you that makes me believe that it's a lot that I'm missing by not having a relationship with someone, other than a casual hit-and-run. I'd at least like us to be friends, but something tells me that you're feeling me like I'm feeling you."

"Uh, we just met, Tyreek, so I don't know where all this seriousness is coming from. It's all about having fun, not falling in . . . well, not getting all tied up with someone, you know."

"I hear you, and I understand where you're coming from, but I'm simply speaking from my heart. I know it's our first time stepping out and all, but time rules its own course."

Tyreek's voice was like a warm fire in the chilly night, and it drew Layla to him even more.

"And, Layla," he said, "as far as being that run-to guy, that was then, and this is now." Tyreek leaned in and Layla met him halfway. He pressed his lips to hers. Suddenly she was uneasy with her sudden reciprocation of intimacy, but the sweet nectar of his lips made her shift closer to him. Tyreek's kiss was full of the passion and desire she used to feel with Dennis. The more his mouth moved over hers in sensuous exploration, the further thoughts of Dennis evaporated.

Layla pulled away.

"What's wrong?"

"Nothing." She nestled next to him as the cold wind embraced them like two star-crossed lovers. Her head rested on his shoulder for only a moment as his mouth once again moved over hers—this time he really kissed her.

17

*The real sin against life is to abuse and destroy beauty, even one's own—even more, one's own—for that has been put in our care and we are responsible for its well-being.—
Katherine Porter*

"I had a good time," Layla told Tyreek.

"Me too," he said. He was distinctively handsome, slender with a powerfully built body. He leaned his long legs and taut rear end against her car.

Layla stood next to him with her arms wrapped around her waist. "Well, I better get going. It's getting late, and I'm cold."

Tyreek stood up straight. Layla watched as he moved toward her like a sleek panther. He moved in front of her, unfolded her arms, and caught her at the waist with both hands to bring her in next to him. She rested against his chest. Layla studied his strong jawline, while she used her gloved hands to examine the bulging muscles of his arms through his wool bomber jacket.

Tyreek's phone started vibrating against Layla's side.

"Aren't you going to answer that?"

"Nope."

"She may be calling you. I wouldn't want to get you in trouble."

"I told you. I'm done with all of that. Let me handle my business, okay?" He spoke to Layla with such sincerity.

"Okay," she answered.

Tyreek's voice slowly trailed away. "I'm here, right where I want to be." He kissed her on the forehead and then allowed his thick, soft lips to travel the length of her neck, from the side to the front, until his lips meshed with hers.

Layla gasped as his tongue invaded her mouth. "This isn't right."

"Oh, it's right," he told her without releasing her mouth from his.

~

Envy couldn't sleep; she tossed and turned in bed. She clicked from channel to channel, not really searching for any one program over the other. It was one-thirty in the morning and she hadn't heard from Layla or Tyreek. She was curious to know how far he would try to take things with Layla. She didn't want to raise a stink about them, because that would make Tyreek think she had feelings for him. But the fact remained that he was her boy toy. She would never knowingly play second to any female, and definitely not Layla. As for Layla, no way was Envy going to step to her about Tyreek. Envy had to maintain her privacy, but that didn't mean that she was going to roll over and play dead.

Layla's phone was still going straight to voice mail, and Tyreek's phone rang a couple of times before it went to voice mail.

"I know one thing, he better not be in bed with her. It doesn't matter whether he knows she's my friend or not."

Her mind began to play out the best way to exact vengeance. Envy dialed the number without giving it a moment's thought.

"Hello," the man answered. The groggy sound of his voice told Envy that he must have been asleep.

"Oh, Dennis," Envy said with an innocent edge to her voice. "I'm sorry to wake you. I've been trying to reach Layla, but her phone keeps going to voice mail. I know it's late, but this is important. Do you mind waking her up? Tell her I need to talk to her."

Dennis suddenly sounded awake. "Layla isn't over here. From the last discussion we had, this is the last place she would be. She's probably at home in deep sleep and doesn't hear the phone, or maybe she's out living it up. Who knows?"

She heard a ruffling sound in the background. Dennis must have been sitting up in the bed, she imagined. "What are you talking about? Did the two of you have an argument or something?"

"That's putting it mildly. Anyway, she's not here."

"Dennis, I didn't mean to call and start problems. I assumed when she said she was going to be unavailable tonight that she was going to be with you. I had no idea y'all were having issues. Anyway, I'm going to let you get back to sleep. And, Dennis?"

"Yea?" he responded dryly.

"If you don't mind, can you keep this between us? I wouldn't want Layla to think that I was trying to stir up trouble."

"There's nothing to keep secret. Anyway, if there's trouble stirring, it's because she already put a pot on the burner."

"Look, try to get back to sleep. Sorry about waking you up. G'night, Dennis."

"Apology accepted. Good night," he replied and the call ended.

"You're going to learn not to mess with me, Tyreek." Envy paced back and forth in her apartment as Fischer followed her with his eyes. "And, Miss Layla, you're way out of your league, sweetheart. I don't care how close we are—all is fair in love and war. And since I don't do the love thing, you don't know it yet, but I just declared war."

~

Tyreek gave Layla one last lingering kiss before she got in her car and drove home with thoughts of the evening she'd spent with him replaying in her mind. He was everything Dennis wasn't; she could tell that much already.

Dennis had never been the romantic type. He was simply a nice, quiet, reserved man. His personality and caring heart were what made her fall quickly in love with him. But things had changed for her. After experiencing what it truly meant to live life, Layla was sure that the love she had for Dennis was gone.

Layla turned into the entrance of her apartment complex. She parked in her designated space and rushed inside before the coldness replaced the warmth that had surrounded her inside her car. Once inside, she removed her coat and headed to her bedroom. It was going on two-thirty in the morning, but she didn't feel the least bit tired. On the contrary, she felt exhilarated, like she could scream with pleasure. She placed her hand over her mouth and released a muffled scream as loud as she could without disturbing the neighbors on either side of her; at least she hoped she hadn't. She suddenly remembered that Tyreek had told her to be sure to turn her phone back on because he was going to call to make sure she made it home safely.

Layla had turned it off so she could enjoy a quiet night with Tyreek. She didn't know if Dennis would be calling her, begging her to forgive him for the things he'd said, or if Kacie and Envy would blow up her phone every few minutes to see how her date was going. They were known to do that. But not tonight. Tonight she wanted an undisturbed evening.

Layla ran back to the living-room closet and removed her cell phone from her coat pocket. It seemed no sooner had she turned it on, than it started ringing. It was Tyreek.

"You made it home yet?" he asked.

"Yes, I'm here. Thanks."

"No need to thank me. I told you I was going to call. I wish I could have followed you home, just to be totally sure you made it there safely, that's all."

"I don't think that would have been a good idea."

"And why not?" he asked. "Don't tell me that a self-assured woman like you is afraid of a nice guy like me," he said with a slight tease in his voice.

Layla giggled like a teen girl who had just been asked out by the star high-school athlete. "No, I'm not afraid at all. But still, a lady can't be too cautious," she told Tyreek. "By the way, have you made it home?"

"No, I still have about another ten minutes to go. I'm on the interstate."

"Oh, where did you say you live?" she asked.

"I didn't. But I have no problem showing you," he said with affection.

"You are something else. I don't want you to show me right now. Telling me will suffice."

"You like to play hardball, I see. Seriously, though, I live in Cordova."

"Wow, we're on separate ends of the city."

"That's nothing. I have a ride and so do you, so we shouldn't have a problem seeing each other."

"You sound quite sure of yourself, Mr. Tyreek Davis." She said his name with force.

"It's not that, but after what we experienced with each other tonight, I don't believe this was our last time seeing one another. I told you, there's something about you; there's a chemistry we have. Don't deny that you feel it too."

Layla sat down in her oversized living-room chair. A couple of years ago, she wouldn't have had an inch of space, now the chair almost swallowed her. She fidgeted nervously as she listened to Tyreek's seductive voice.

"What's up, baby girl? Cat got your tongue?"

"No, I'm fine. And yes, I felt something tonight, but I don't know if I would call it chemistry."

"What would you call it?" Tyreek asked.

"Like. That's it. I like you. I enjoyed spending time with you, and maybe, and I said maybe, we'll do it again sometime."

"So now that you're out of my presence, you want to play tough, huh?"

"No, I'm just being real. I don't play games, and I don't believe in filling in the blank spaces with unnecessary words just to impress the next person."

"Is that what you think I'm doing?" he asked.

Layla's phone clicked. She removed it slightly from her ear and saw Envy's number on the screen. "Tyreek, it's late and I need to get some rest." The phone clicked again. What could Envy want at this time of night—or morning? "So why don't we table this discussion to a later date and time?"

Envy's call ended, replaced by a light beeping sound that signaled she had left Layla a voice message.

"Aha, I knew it."

"Knew what?" Layla rested her head on the plush back portion of the chair.

"I knew we would meet and talk again. You just admitted it." Both of them laughed into the phone.

"Okay, you win this time, but only because I'm exhausted. You win by default," she said.

"A win is a win. Good night, Layla. I had a great time."

"Me too. Have a good night, Tyreek. Buh-bye." Right after ending the call, Layla dialed Envy's number and immediately she answered.

"Girl, you must still be pinching yourself?" Layla said to Envy. "I'm so happy that everything worked out in your favor. Now you can move forward with your life. Leave the past where it belongs–in the past."

"You're right," Envy said. Her voice was low. "I can't thank God enough for how He lifted that burden off me, girl. I've been calling and texting you, but I guess you had your phone turned off." Envy sounded frustrated, because she was.

"I know, and I'm sorry. I haven't been home that long. But, girl, tonight was marvelous, simply marvelous. That's all I can say."

"Good for you. I was worried." Envy feigned concern.

"Worried about what?" asked Layla.

"About you. I called to check on you, and you didn't answer. You can never be too careful these days, especially when you're meeting someone new."

"I know. Thanks for caring, but I wanted everything to be perfect. Me and Dennis had it out earlier, and I didn't want him blowing up my phone."

"You could have put it on silent or vibrate. Anyway, forget about all that. Tell me what made the date so marvelous. He must have really made a good impression."

"Girl, it was one of the best times I've had since I started doing the dating thing. I'm just getting home. Can you believe it?"

"Yeah, because, I told you, I've been trying to check on you all night. Is he nice? Did he try anything?" Envy asked.

"He was everything and then some." Layla laughed. Envy was silent. "And he's so good-looking, with a nice disposition. The man seems to have it together."

"Yeah, he's probably someone to have fun with. Just don't get serious because there's nothing a bartender can do for you that you can't do for yourself. So stick to what you know you have."

"Don't get started on me and Dennis."

"Did you hear me say anything about Dennis?" Envy asked.

"No, but I know you. You may not have said anything, but you sure were thinking it."

"Sounds like trouble in paradise."

"See, that's what I'm talking about. There is no paradise when it comes to me and Dennis."

"What's up with y'all?" Envy's voice sounded tired.

"I'll fill you in on everything later. Right now, I'm ready to hit the sack." Her voice dropped. "I'm going to call it a night."

"Yeah, I hear you. I'm going to turn in myself, now that I know you're at home safely. I'll talk to you tomorrow."

"All right. Good night, girl."

Envy called Tyreek next, but again she did not get an answer. "You may run, but you surely can't hide, Mr. Tyreek. Bet that."

18

Not because of who I am, but because of what you've done.
Not because of what I've done, but because of who you are. —
Casting Crowns, "Who Am I"

Envy, Layla, and Kacie arrived at church within mere minutes of each other. While Kacie parked and unloaded her kids from her 2004 Suburban, Envy and Layla had not only parked, but they were inside the church and seated in their usual spot midway in the sanctuary.

Kacie took her seat at the end of the pew, next to Layla and Envy, just as the praise team was about to start the worship service. She kept her Bible on her lap and placed her purse between her and the pew.

"You get the kids to their designated places?" asked Layla.

Kacie slowly exhaled before she replied, "Yeah. Kenny took Kassandra, Keith, Kali, and Kendra to Children's Church before going to Youth Church. I took Keshena and Kyland to the nursery. They've started assigning each child a number that they give to the parents. Look up there to the right, over the choir stand." Kacie pointed. "See that black rectangular box?"

Layla and Envy both nodded.

"When parents are needed in the nursery, the number assigned to your child flashes on and off in red."

"That's a good idea," said Layla.

"Yeah, it sure is," Kacie added.

"It is, but I hope Keshena and Kyland's numbers don't pop up."

The praise team began singing. Envy leaned forward and looked at Kacie. "Don't worry, they'll behave. They always do."

"She's right, Kacie. I don't think you've ever had to leave service because of the kids."

"Thank God for small miracles," responded Kacie. "I'll take the break any way I can get it."

"I heard that," said Layla before she turned and focused her attention on the praise team.

The three of them laid their Bibles on the pew before they stood up and started clapping their hands. They began to sing in unison with the praise team and other members of the congregation. "Emmanuel, Emmanuel, Emmanuel, Emmanuel. . . ," they sang.

The song "Emmanuel" was one of Kacie's favorite gospel tunes. Each time she heard it, it ushered her to a good, peaceful place within her spirit. Knowing that the name Emmanuel meant God with us caused Kacie to remember that God remained by her side. Yet, while the three of them picked up their Bibles, and by the time Pastor Betts stepped up in the pulpit, negative thoughts had already begun to infiltrate her mind. Feelings of guilt and shame shifted her concentration from Pastor Betts' reading of the scripture to the person she had become. What happened to the little girl who used to be so self-assured and independent? Where was the person who believed that despite her physical handicap, there was nothing she could not conquer in the world? Kacie couldn't bear to remain standing for the scripture reading. It wasn't because her legs trembled from standing too long, but it was because inside she felt weak and worthless.

"You may sit," Pastor Betts told the congregation. Layla sat down and gently nudged Kacie in the side.

"Are you all right?"

"Yes," Kacie mumbled. "I'm fine." She continued to look down; her Bible was on her lap.

Pastor Betts stood in the pulpit like the mighty man of God he was. He was an exemplary Bible scholar and teacher. Standing in a confident, but not conceited, manner, his powerful voice went forth.

"Let me read the scripture one more time. I want to make sure you heard what I just read. I'm reading from the New International Version," Pastor Betts reminded everyone. "Ezekiel chapter thirty-six, verses twenty-five and twenty-six. 'I will sprinkle clean water on you, and you will be clean; I will cleanse you from all your impurities and from all your idols. I will give you a new heart and put a new spirit in you; I will remove from you your heart of stone and give you a heart of flesh.'"

Kacie read the scripture the second time around. *Well, I don't feel clean. I don't feel like I have a new heart. I feel tainted and dirty. I feel ashamed and wretched.*

"Listen to me," Pastor Betts said. "God wants to do a new thing in you. It doesn't matter what state of despair you're in right now. It doesn't matter what you did last night or this morning before you came here. He wants to do something new in your life right now."

Kacie slowly lifted her bowed-down head and focused on what Pastor Betts was saying. How could he preach a message that sounded like he had been reading her mind? How could he know what she was dealing with?

"God says He will clean you up. He'll remove the filth and the grime in your life. Then, then, then," he repeated, "He will take all that stuff that you deem to be so important in your life. He'll take it away, yes God will do that for you because He loves you."

Kacie was in a trancelike state, totally riveted by the words pouring from Pastor Betts.

"And if cleaning you up, fixing you up, and removing the stuff that doesn't matter out of your life isn't enough, on top of all of that, God will give you a new heart. Now that's enough to make somebody shout right there."

Pastor Betts stood on his tiptoes and then took a step back from the podium with his black leather Bible in his hand. "I said, God will remove the old heart you have right now. You know the one that's unforgiving, the heart that's broken, the heart that's been used and abused. God will remove that old heart. He will take the heart that is hardened, the heart that's worldly and stubborn, and selfish and self-centered. God will take that heart and He'll give you a transplant. Only it won't be somebody else's heart that He's putting inside of you; it'll be a brand-new heart, crafted and created and made over and designed just for you by Him."

His voice boomed. Kacie could see the glistening beads of sweat that had formed on his forehead. Her heart raced. Something began to stir on the inside of her. A feeling like she hadn't felt since that day ten years ago when she gave her life to Christ, only this time it was an even stronger tug pulling at her within. Her hands began to sweat and she could feel the *beat, beat, beat,* of her heart. The more Pastor Betts preached, the more drawn Kacie was to his every word. She clung to it like paper to glue. Something was going on; something she couldn't identify or make sense of.

"Come, come on. . . ," the choir sang. Their hands were outstretched toward the congregation. Pastor Betts asked those who wanted to make a change in their lives, who wanted to be cleansed and cleaned up, to come forward.

Kacie disregarded Layla and Envy and moved past them. She felt like she was floating down the aisle, as if she was magically being drawn to a giant magnet, and it was pulling her forward. But then…each step became easier and lighter, until she was at the front of the sanctuary, along with three other people.

~

Church services ended. Layla and Envy went to find Kacie, who was led out by a team from the New Members' Ministry. Those who had walked down the aisle were taken inside a room assigned to welcome new members, those who wanted prayer or wanted to rededicate their lives to Christ.

Kacie came out after about fifteen minutes. She looked flushed. Her eyes and face were the color of cherries. "I've got to go get my kids," she said to Layla and Envy.

"What happened to you back there?" they asked as they followed her to the nursery.

"You mean in the New Members' room, or during church?" asked Kacie.

Envy spoke first. "Both."

"It's time I stop playing with God and my faith. I can't keep on living like this," she explained.

"Like what?" asked Layla. "When are you going to stop tripping about having seven children? At least you didn't abort them. It's people out there every day that do that, but you," Layla said, and stopped a few feet from the entrance of the nursery, "you kept every one of yours. I'm sure you asked God to forgive you every time you messed up."

Envy looked at Layla and rolled her eyes.

"What?" Layla asked, frowning and shrugging her shoulders at Envy.

"What Layla is trying to say is that anytime we do something or commit some sin, we know to ask God for forgiveness, and kaboom, just like that, He clears our slate and throws them somewhere, uh, I can't remember where he throws them, but wherever it is, He forgets all about 'em."

Kacie giggled. "You need to study your Bible some more, girl. How are you going to tell me something when you don't even know half of what you're talking about? You misquoting scriptures and stuff."

All three laughed.

"What you and Layla are trying to say is that if we admit our sins to God then he removes them as far apart as the east is from the west." Kacie pointed her finger toward both of them and smiled. "Now that was from two different scriptures in the Bible, but I think you get my drift."

Envy and Layla had strange looks on their faces and remained silent.

"Now it's my turn to ask. What's wrong with y'all?"

"You didn't say what they told you in there." said Layla. "You come out here trying to quote scriptures and stuff. You just sound different."

"I can vouch for that, girl," said Envy, and looked at Kacie, then Layla.

One of the nursery staff came to the entrance. Kacie saw her and immediately knew that the volunteers and staff wanted everyone to get their children. Kenny and the other kids walked up.

"Hey, Momma, we had fun in Children's Church," said Kassandra as she walked up with her sisters and stood in front of Kacie.

"We learned about, uh, about four and giving," said Kali.

"No, we didn't," said Kendra. "We learned about forgiving."

"Good, that's real good. Now, hold on just a minute," Kacie said in a gentle tone.

Envy nudged Layla.

Layla nudged Envy.

"Kenny, honey, will you go over there and sign out Kyland and Keshena from the nursery for me?"

"Yes, ma'am." Much like Layla and Envy, Kenny appeared to be shocked at his mother's calmer tone.

Kacie, Envy, and Layla held on to the kids while Kenny went to sign out Kyland and Keshena. "It's all right. I'm right here," Kacie said to the staff member standing within earshot.

The woman nodded her head and proceeded to allow Kenny inside the nursery.

Kacie returned her attention to Envy and Layla. "Like I said, things have got to change in my life. Yes, I have seven kids and seven baby daddies. I can't change that. But, y'all, I finally believe God has forgiven me for sleeping around. Shucks, I've asked Him a thousand times."

They half-smiled.

"Thing is, I have never forgiven myself. Instead, I've been taking out my resentment, my anger, my frustration, all of it, out on my children. They didn't ask to be here, but they are here, and they're mine, and I love them. But I've been angry for so long, and hurt for so long, that I dumped on them." Kacie gestured.

Envy and Layla continued to stare at Kacie, while the kids, surprisingly, played with each other in a quiet and civilized manner.

"How can I begin to be angry at Kenny, even Jackie for that matter, if I'm guilty of the same thing myself? It's not right to tell them, 'Do as I say, not as I do.' I need to be an example for my children. And if I'm going to be an example for them, it finally got through my thick skull today that"—Kacie pointed at her head, and Kali and Keith giggled. "I have to get things right between me and God, so I recommitted my life to Him. No more dropping Kenny off to Super Wednesday. No, me and all of my kids will be coming to Bible Study as a family. I'm not going through another minute, day, hour, or year being less than the woman of God I know lives inside me."

"Wow, did you get all of that from Pastor Betts' message?" asked Envy. Envy looked at Layla, who stood next to her.

Layla's mouth was open wide.

"Close your mouth, Layla," said Kacie before she started giggling. "Unless you're going to open it up and start using that amazing singing voice of yours." Immediately, before either Envy or Layla could say another word, Kacie showed the palm of her hand. "Before you think it, let me set the record straight. I am not trying to get all religious on y'all; I'm just telling you what happened in my life today." Kacie placed her hand over her chest. "I'm not one to judge y'all." She eyed the both of them. "Y'all have always been by my side, and I love you."

"Awww," said Envy.

"Ohhhh, you gonna make me cry," said Layla.

Kenny came out of the nursery with Keshena and Kyland in tow.

"Y'all are so crazy," said Kacie. "Anyway, let me go. I need to go home and cook."

Kenny came and stood next to Kacie. "Momma, you're going to cook?" asked Kenny, with a huge smile on his face.

"Yes, I sure am."

Kenny rubbed his belly and licked his lips.

"Boy, you're so silly. You act like I never cook," she said to him. "Come on, y'all." She reached her hand out toward her children, and then started to walk away from Envy and Layla.

Kacie turned, stopped, and looked over her shoulder to find Envy and Layla right behind her. "Y'all are welcome to come over. It's not like you need an invitation, you know."

"No, I believe you need this time with your children," said Envy.

"Yea, I think so. I have a feeling it's going to be totally different, but a good kind of different." Layla leaned in and hugged Kacie.

Envy copied. "I'm proud of you. What you did and what you've said today, well, I know that I have a lot of soul searching to do myself."

"As long as you know that you're welcome to come over," Kacie reiterated.

"We know," added Envy. I'll call you later."

They walked outside and said their good-byes to each other and some of the other church members who were gathered in the parking lot. The sun was shining bright, and the cold weather was slowly turning into what felt like an early spring coming on. It was a good day for Kacie and her children.

Envy went to her car and Layla went to hers. If any change was in the air for the two of them, it was hidden and not yet ready to come out.

19

Don't say you love me unless you mean it because I might do something stupid . . . like believe it! —Unknown

Tyreek pulled up in Layla's driveway. He exhaled a long sigh of contentment. Layla was different from any woman he had encountered. In the six weeks they'd been seeing each other, he had enjoyed every conversation and every moment they shared.

He was more than glad that he changed his cell phone number, and that Envy hadn't bothered to come calling on him at Precious Cargo. Maybe she'd finally gotten the message that the time was up for her pleasure-seeking games. He was fed up with allowing her to use him. It had been fun for a while, but he could bed just about any woman he wanted; and a few years ago, that's exactly what he'd done.

He used to pride himself on the number of women he seduced. But, when Envy came along, his playa card got played and quickly boomeranged when he fell hard for her. It didn't take long for him to realize that Envy Wilson was not the type of woman that a man could sweep off her feet. Instead, he was the one who succumbed to her each time she called.

Almost three years of being no more than one booty call after another, he couldn't blame anyone but himself for allowing it to happen. He felt trapped by Envy. He couldn't pinpoint what it was exactly about her, but the more he saw her the more he wanted to see her.

The day Layla walked into Precious Cargo, things changed. Tyreek spotted Layla out of a small clan of women accompanying her. Her beauty immediately pulled him in. After the server seated Layla and her friends, he continued to watch her from the bar. When she stood up and left her friends and approached the bar, he knew that he was going to do everything in his power to get to know her, unless her conversation didn't measure up to her looks. He walked to the end of the bar, where she leaned over on one elbow, waiting on the bartender, which fortunately was him. He asked her what drink she desired and smiled within when she ordered a ginger ale on the rocks. She had an air of calm and self-confidence that he liked. They carried on a conversation as he mixed drinks for other customers and then returned to her. By the time she got ready to leave, she had agreed to meet him later that night at the end of his shift. Since that time, he and Layla had hung out as much as possible.

Now here he was tonight, about to spend another evening with the woman who was swiftly capturing a portion of him. Layla made him smile and laugh. Thus far, she had refused to submit to his sexual advances, which made him respect her even more. The fact was, the more time he spent with Layla, the more he wanted to spend time with her. It had been a while since he'd taken the time to wine and dine a woman. Layla, helped him rediscover how having a woman to do things with could be fun.

Going to a Maxwell concert at the Orpheum Theatre was something Tyreek wasn't used to doing. Then again, every time he was with Layla, they did something different. Last week, they had enjoyed having a romantic dinner at the Tower Center. Earlier in the same week, they spent the evening enjoying downtown Memphis, Beale Street, and watching the entrance of the Peabody Ducks at the Peabody Hotel. Tyreek believed the two of them fit together like a hand in a glove. He walked up to Layla's door and rang the bell. She answered the door within moments. To Tyreek, she looked breathtaking.

"Hi," she said.

He couldn't contain his smile. His gaze was steady as he barely heard her tell him to come inside.

"Baby, you look uh grown and sexy." He grinned.

"Thank you," she said in a silky voice. Her beet red dress, with a V-neckline, fitted waist, and bubble hem, rested just above her knees.

Tyreek inhaled the sweet, sensuous aroma of her perfume. His eyes sent her a private message as he studied her from head to toe. She had covered every detail, from the earrings to the red peep-toe stilettos. It all enhanced the sexiness that dripped from her like nectar.

"You ready?" she asked.

"Uh, yes." He felt quite satisfied in his button-down shirt, jeans, blazer, and Cole Haan loafers. "Man, am I glad the weather turned out nice. It feels like a spring night outside."

"Yeah, I know. I'm glad too. The groundhog didn't see his shadow, so spring will be here before you know it." Layla laughed and picked up her purse and a light jacket. "I'm still taking this jacket, just in case. You know how unpredictable Memphis weather tends to be."

"Yeah, I feel you on that one."

"Oh, I didn't tell you, but you look handsome."

"Thanks, and, um, flattery will get you everything you want, and some more," Tyreek said teasingly. He escorted her outside with her hand in his and stood next to her as she locked the door.

~

"I love me some Maxwell. The man can hum," Layla said as they left the Orpheum. "I don't care how many times I see him; he gets better and better."

"Yeah, I could tell you were into him. I have to admit, it was a good concert. I had a great time. I'm glad you suggested it."

Layla blushed and glanced at his well-defined profile. She basked in the feeling of Tyreek's hand as it covered hers. He was affectionate without being overbearing. Unlike Dennis, he acted like he enjoyed doing the same things she did. There was no way she could ever convince Dennis to go to a concert, play, or anything close to having fun. Dennis reminded her of an older, settled man rather than the thirty-five-year-old that he was.

As for Tyreek, he was ready, willing, and able. Having part ownership in Precious Cargo was definitely working in his favor as far as Layla could tell, because money never seemed to be a problem when they went out. Layla liked that about him. All she had to do was mention a spot where she wanted to go, and Tyreek was all for it.

On the drive to Ruth's Chris Steak House for dinner, Tyreek reached over and rested his hand on Layla's thigh. She didn't object. They hadn't been intimate, but the time they spent together hadn't been exactly squeaky clean either.

Layla enjoyed his touch. He didn't try to go further, which pleased Layla mentally, though physically she longed to be held captive in his arms. But this time she was going to play her cards right by fighting her own battle of personal restraint. She wanted to see where their relationship was heading. No more giving up the cookies for free. She had morals and she was determined to return to exercising them. But she did admit to Kacie and Envy that she was falling for him.

Kacie seemed ecstatic, but Layla thought about Envy's negative responses just about every time she started talking about Tyreek. Either Envy told her she was moving too fast, or that she shouldn't trust him. Why couldn't Envy be happy for her instead of pressuring her to run back to Dennis?

Every moment Layla was with Tyreek assured her that she had done the right thing by putting space between herself and Dennis. Envy and Kacie would have no choice but to accept the decisions she made for her life—like it or not.

"What are you sitting over there thinking about?" asked Tyreek when he glanced over at Layla.

"About the good times we've had together," she answered, and returned his look with one of her own. "I think my two best friends are jealous," she blurted out.

"Were those your girlfriends who you were with at Precious Cargo?"

"No, those were coworkers from the salon. Remember?"

"Oh yeah, that's right. I guess we've never talked about your best friends. Are they as beautiful and sweet as you?" asked Tyreek as he continued to keep his eyes on the road.

"They're awright," Layla said, and laughed.

"Uh-huh, is that right?" Tyreek chuckled too. "I know why they're jealous. Just look at you," he said. "You've got it going on, baby girl."

"No, seriously, they're not jealous. I was just kidding. They're my girls. The three of us have each other's backs, no matter what. We've been best friends for a long time. You may get a chance to meet them one day—if you act right."

"I'm going to take that as a good sign. Whenever I meet them, I'll know that I've scored some major points with you. Am I right?" he asked.

"I guess you could say that." Layla smiled.

"Good, then I can't wait to meet 'em."

Tyreek stopped as the traffic light turned to red. He leaned over and his lips pressed against Layla's and gently covered her mouth. His kiss sent the pit of her stomach into a wild swirl, and a sound of satisfaction escaped from her lips.

Layla relaxed her head back against the car's headrest. At that moment, she admitted to herself that her vow not to become seriously involved with a man right now had been shattered. She was falling hard for Tyreek; and the more she tried to ignore the truth, the more it persisted.

They pulled up into the crowded parking lot of Ruth's Chris. Tyreek waited to get a parking space, and quickly secured one when he saw another car backing out of a space. He put the car in park and turned it off. He leaned in again and gave Layla another passionate kiss. When he pulled away this time, he touched the side of her face with the back of his hand. "Your lips feel like cotton, and they're sweet like candy," he said as he released a long, audible breath.

Layla stared at him for a second or two before she burst out in laughter.

"What's up?" Tyreek asked. He had a puzzled look on his face.

"You have to admit that sounded a little corny," she said while still giggling.

Tyreek laughed too. "Hey, I'm telling you the truth."

"I didn't say that you weren't telling the truth; I said it sounded corny."

"That's why I like you," Tyreek said.

"Why?" asked Layla.

"'Cause you're not only gorgeous, you're funny. You keep me laughing."

They kissed again.

"Come on, let's go inside before they give our reservation to somebody else," Layla said. A genuine smile was still settled across her face.

Tyreek got out of the car while Layla waited for him to come to her side and open the door. She liked the little things like this that Tyreek took the time to do. He was so considerate.

Tyreek escorted Layla inside the restaurant. He gave the maître d' his name and they were quickly escorted to their table.

Tonight Tyreek couldn't deny the obvious any longer. He really liked Layla, and he wanted to get to know as much as possible about her.

20

People have a hard time letting go of their suffering. Out of a fear of the unknown, they prefer suffering that is familiar.—Thich Nhat Hanh

The morning sun shone bright like a crystal on what was a clear, spring day and Envy's favorite season. She opened her eyes barely an inch so as not to allow the sun's brightness to pull her out of her second round of sleep prematurely. Instead, she threw her right hand out and hit snooze on the alarm clock before falling back on her pillow and closing her eyes. Five minutes later, the alarm went off again. This time she stretched, yawned, and forced herself out of bed.

She ambled toward the bathroom with the brightness of the sun providing God's natural light to most of her bedroom.

"Oh, thank you, Lord." Fischer barked, wagged his tail, and jumped up and down. "Fisch-errrr," she sang. "Let me go pee, and then I'll put on my gear and take you out. You would think by now, you would know the routine." She stepped inside the bathroom. Before closing the door, she told Fischer, "You're just like a man. You always want what you want, when you want it. Well, you should know me by now. I'm in charge. Now be patient, I'll be out in a minute."

Fischer cocked his head to the side and plopped down on his butt as Envy closed the bathroom door.

~

"It feels good out here, doesn't it, boy?" Envy jogged with Fischer on his leash. The thirty-minute morning ritual through the neighborhood was part of Envy's way of preparing for whatever the day might bring. It had been going on two weeks since she last talked to Casper. The criminal trial he was trying took up a great deal of his time. He was out of the office all day, almost every day. His assistant informed Envy that the closing arguments were supposed to start today. Envy had mixed emotions about it. The longer Casper put her case off, the more she wrestled with thoughts of going to jail. It didn't matter that Casper told her about the odds of her going to jail were slim to none, or about the expired statute of limitations. Envy still refused to erase the possibility.

Envy understood her company's policies and procedures and was well versed in what would happen, other than losing her job, if she was imprisoned. She had a nice, hefty nest egg that would carry her for a couple of years easily.

On her way to the office, her thoughts gelled even more. She would rent out her part of the duplex, which would give her extra ongoing income. Layla, maybe even Nikkei, could look after Fischer. Perhaps, if push came to shove, Leonard would do it.

Leonard, I haven't talked to him and he hasn't called lately, she thought like it had just dawned on her. And Tyreek, oh, Mr. Tyreek. I will see you today. Bet you think I let you off the hook. Not.

At work, Envy spent most of the morning working on several regulatory projects for one of her company's offices based in the United Kingdom. She didn't have a designated lunchtime, but she usually tried to leave the office for at least an hour every day. Today she was going to make a surprise visit to Tyreek. She still had a hard time believing that he had changed his phone number. It only added fuel to the fire, and Envy was determined to let him know that she was the one who did the walking away, not him.

As for Leonard, she was somewhat concerned about not hearing from him. She made a note on her phone notes to give him a call. It was time she gave him a little attention. He was probably somewhere nursing his wounds because she didn't want to make a commitment to being his lady.

"Darcy," she said to her new administrative assistant, "I'm going to run an errand."

"Yes, Miss Wilson."

"You can reach me on my work cell phone, but only if it's a dire emergency."

"Yes, ma'am, I know."

"Fine. I'll see you later this afternoon."

Bobbie, Envy's former administrative assistant had been with her for several years. It was a surprise when she told Envy she bidded on a lateral position in another department.

"Do what you feel you have to do," she coldly told the administrative assistant, and the woman did just that. Within two weeks of bidding on the position, Bobbie was gone, and Envy was assigned a temporary administrative assistant, until HR gathered potential qualified candidates. Darcy, who already worked for the company, got the position. Working for Envy was a promotion for her; so things had worked out really well. Darcy was easygoing and eager to please. Envy had no problem keeping her just where she wanted—under her thumb.

The lunch crowd at Precious Cargo was a different clientele from the evenings and weekends. The restaurant presented a relaxing aura, with delicious food.

Envy walked inside with bold steps. She was professionally dressed in a dark-navy-and-white short-sleeved boatneck blouse with contrasting stripes, a dark navy pencil skirt, finished off with a pair of dark navy patent pumps.

Much like always, Envy made a statement wherever she went, and today was no different. She knew it when she looked toward the bar and caught Tyreek's eyes fixated on her. For a moment, he stopped staring like he was a deer caught in headlights. A smile of conquest formed on her perfectly polished lips.

Envy walked past several tables already filled with customers. She did not stop until she was leaning on the bar with both elbows; her hands cupped her head.

"When are you going to realize that you cannot avoid me, Tyreek? Did you honestly think that wasting valuable money to change your number, would keep me away?"

"Look, Envy, I don't understand you. We don't have anything together, so why are you here? I need you to leave me alone. You know what I'm saying?" Tyreek continued to serve customers and supervise the wait staff too.

The restaurant was busy, like Envy knew it would be. It was the perfect time for her to make him uneasy. While he didn't have time to spend talking to her, she forced him to. Envy could put on a show if she wanted, if that's what it took to get her point across, something she was sure Tyreek wouldn't want her to do.

"Why don't you leave. You see I'm busy. This is the rush crowd. I don't have time to waste trying to get you to—"

Envy put a polished finger up to his kissable lips. "I don't think you want to go there," she said. "Not here." She looked around the restaurant and then looked back at him. "Do you?"

"All I'm saying to you, Envy, is that I've moved on. I'm looking for something serious, you know. You." He pointed at her, "and me, it was all good while it lasted, but it's over. So before you start trying to clown up in here, I suggest you take your finger out of my face." He used his hand and gently removed her finger aside. "And go find yourself another toy."

Envy turned a shade darker. "Do you think that Layla is serious about you? Is that what you think? Well, I have news for you. She may be my best friend but she's still a wannabe version of moi."

"What did you say?" He quickly told one of the wait staff to do something for him, so he could turn back to hear what Envy knew about his and Layla's relationship.

Envy laughed rather loudly. "See, that's what I mean about men like you. You have no idea about women. You think that just because you have the goods to pleasure a woman physically, that it's all good."

"Irrespective of what you say, and what I've shown you in the past, I'm not the guy you want to make me out to be."

"I can't tell. You come every time I call for how long?" Tyreek's cream-colored face turned pale. "Let's see—two, two and a half, three years?" Envy chuckled and watched the play of emotions on his face.

"Look," Tyreek leaned in toward her until he was mere inches from her face. "I don't care how long it's been; it's over," he said with brute force. "Now tell me what you know about Layla," he demanded.

Envy didn't move back one bit. "So Layla hasn't told you that we're best friends, huh?"

"You are really a piece of work. You've gone so far as to track down someone I'm seeing? What are you? A psycho?"

"Didn't you hear what I said? Layla is one of my best friends. I can't believe she hasn't talked about me and Kacie. You see, that's where your weakness lies. You don't think, Tyreek. You don't know how to think. Maybe I need to write a book, Act Like A Man, Think Like a Woman."

"You and Layla?" His voice lost its steely edge.

"Now you get it. Makes you wonder why she hasn't mentioned me, doesn't it? Well, she's been asking me how she can step up her game on this player's field. I told her you would be the perfect practice target, and I have to give you your props, Tyreek. You're living up to everything I told her about you."

"What did you tell her? I know you aren't telling me that the two of you been messing with my head. Don't be a fool, girl. You need to stay up out of my business."

"The fool is gonna be played by you, boy. You don't mess me around. You and no other man will ever have that kind of power." Envy looked at the fashionable timepiece she wore. "I guess I might as well have a bite to eat while I'm here. Fix me a turkey club with a Caesar salad on the side. You know how I like it. Oh, and I will eat it here at the bar. I haven't seen you in a while. And you know how much I like watching you."

Tyreek turned and said something to one of the servers going into the kitchen. He came back, waited on two other customers seated at the bar, and then did a quick walk through the restaurant to make small talk with the customers. The people who came to Precious Cargo loved Tyreek's charm and personality.

"I don't believe what you said about Layla. I don't trust anything you say," he told Envy when he returned to the bar.

"You better trust me if you don't trust anybody else," Envy responded without cracking so much as a smile.

Tyreek snapped back, but in a low voice to make sure the customers could not hear, "I don't trust anybody but the man upstairs."

Envy laughed again. This time she laughed so hard, her head bobbled back and forth. She pointed at Tyreek. "You are really, really funny." She touched a man who was seated two stools down from her. "Did you know this guy is really funny?" she asked the stranger.

"No, I didn't know that. Must be true what they say: 'You learn something new every day.'" He returned to nursing his drink.

"You—and the man upstairs? I know you are not talking about God."

"That's exactly who I'm talking about."

"Hold on, there. You mean to tell me that you"—she stopped talking and started laughing again—"are a church boy? Now that's something serious you got going on there, Tyreek. You might have a little something-something after all." She continued to mock him.

The server presented her plate of food and Caesar salad. "Thank you," she said.

"You're welcome," he said, and then winked at Envy.

"Not in your wildest dreams," she replied.

The server turned and left with a look of total embarrassment on his face.

"Be gone now, Tyreek. I want to enjoy my lunch. I'll watch you from afar. I'll be sure to give Layla a few extra pointers about you."

"You can tell Layla whatever you want. If she's anything like you, then I'm glad I found out now. I'm telling you for the last time, Envy, leave me alone, and you can tell that to your little protégée too."

Tyreek walked away and disappeared in the back of the restaurant. The server who had waited on her took his place. Envy took a couple of bites of her sandwich, then pushed it away, got up, and left the restaurant without bothering to pay. *Let him take up my slack.* She strolled out of the restaurant furious, but she would never give Tyreek an opportunity to see her sweat.

Envy got in her car and headed back to work. Once she arrived and parked in her designated parking space, she sat in the car for a few minutes. She called Layla. Layla didn't work on Mondays, so either she was at home or at the Y working out.

After several rings, Layla's voice mail came on. "Hi, this is Layla. If you're calling to schedule an appointment for beauty services, please call 901-555-5555, and the receptionist will be able to assist you. If this is personal, leave a message and I'll return your call as time permits."

"Layla, girl, I went to Precious Cargo for lunch. Guess who I happened to run into? Give me a call as soon as you can. Bye." Envy ended the call and stepped out of her car with a look of satisfaction on her face. "I bet she'll be calling me as soon as she hears my message."

Envy got on the elevator and punched the button for the eighth floor. She got off and walked down the corridor to Regulatory Affairs.

Darcy approached Envy with a wide, open smile. "Miss Wilson."

"Darcy, what is it? I've barely stepped in the office and you're calling my name."

"I'm sorry, but you have a call on line one."

"Take a message." Envy waved her off and walked into her office. She was still plotting and planning in her head payback for Tyreek. Darcy followed right behind her footsteps. "What is it?"

"I'm sorry, Miss Wilson, but I think you might want to take this call. It's an attorney, Casper Step—"

Envy's head snapped around and she gave Darcy an evil look. "Why didn't you just come out and say that?" She shooed Darcy off. "Go, and close the door behind you. I do not want to be disturbed by anyone. I don't care if President Barack Obama calls. Do you understand?"

"Yes, ma'am." Darcy hurried out of Envy's office and closed the door behind her.

She picked up the phone. "Casper, I'm sorry to keep you holding. I have a new administrative assistant and, well, let's just say she's still in the learning stages of what calls need screening. I'm sure you know what I'm talking about."

"She actually sounded professional and handled my call efficiently."

Envy quickly changed her opinion. "Oh yes. She is a great assistant. I'm glad she was able to keep you on the line. I had a meeting and I was just coming back to my office, so your timing is perfect. I hope you're calling with some good news."

"When can you come to my office?" asked Casper. "We need to talk." He sounded serious.

Envy's sensual voice changed to an empty tone. "Please tell me if it's good news or not, Casper."

"How soon can you get here?" he asked without acknowledging her request.

"I'm on my way." Envy hung up the phone and then gathered her purse and jacket. "Darcy, I have an outside appointment that I have to go to unexpectedly. I may or may not be back this afternoon; it depends on what evolves during this meeting."

"You look a little on edge, Miss Wilson. Is everything all right?"

"Yes. Everything is fine. I'll be in touch with you as soon as possible. Good afternoon."

"Okay, good afternoon, Miss Wilson."

Envy zoomed past her assistant's cubicle and dashed to the elevator. What could it be? Casper sounded far too serious. Maybe I'm going to be charged after all. The elevator stopped on the next floor, and Envy huddled closer to the back corner after nodding to the three men who stepped inside. They were chatting about politics. Each one of them carried black leather cases and their suits matched their cases. If she hadn't been familiar with most of the departments in her building, and people's faces, she would have pegged them for Secret Service agents. Envy half-smiled at the thought.

The elevator didn't stop until it reached the main lobby. One of the men stepped aside and allowed Envy to walk out of the elevator ahead of them.

"Thank you," she said to the man.

"My pleasure," he replied.

The drive to Casper's downtown office was long and exasperating. The streets seemed stockpiled with cars. Where could all of you be going? She maneuvered down several side streets so she could avoid the traffic on Union Avenue. Arriving at Casper's office twenty-two minutes later was a relief. She parked in the underground garage and hurried to the elevator.

"Miss Wilson," his gray-haired assistant said when Envy walked into his office. "Attorney Stephens stepped out for a moment. He'd like you to wait in his office."

Envy nodded slowly. "Oh, okay. Do you know how long he'll be gone?"

"Not long, ma'am." The assistant walked in front of Envy and opened the door to Casper's inviting office. "Please have a seat on the sofa, or"—the assistant pointed to the round mahogany table and chairs—"you may sit here."

"Thank you."

"Would you care for coffee, soda, water?" the assistant offered.

"Yes, may I have a cup of coffee with two packets of artificial sweetener and three packets of cream?"

"Of course. I'll be back shortly," the stout, broad-shouldered woman told Envy.

Envy looked around nervously at the various art pieces that hung on Casper's wall. She chose to sit at the table. Several magazines were neatly arranged on a nearby table, and Envy got up to retrieve one. Without taking a moment to read any of the articles, she nervously flipped page after page; then she stopped and began to twiddle her fingers.

"Here you go," the assistant said, startling Envy, who had not heard her return.

She placed a hand over her racing heart. "Thank you."

"You're welcome. If there's anything else you need, please just peek your head out the door."

"Thank you." Envy added the artificial sweeteners and all three packets of cream to her coffee and stirred the mixture. "Ahhh," she said after taking the first sip of the piping hot, strong brew.

Ten minutes, then fifteen minutes passed, and Casper had not returned. Envy was becoming fidgety. She walked to the door and stuck her head out, but there was no sign of his assistant. Rubbing both of her hands together and then using them to press down her skirt, she retreated to the table, pulled out her cell phone, and called Kacie, but there was no answer.

After her confrontation with Tyreek, she was not about to call Layla again. She would handle that unnecessary problem later on. The last person who came to her mind was Leonard. Maybe he'll come and sit with me. No, I can't have him looking at me like I'm evil, especially when he knows nothing about my past. But, Lord, I need someone here. I can't go through this alone. Nikkei, I can call Nikkei, but I haven't told her about any of this. It'll be too much for her to take.

Casper Stephens walked in. "I'm so sorry, Envy. I had to go back to the courthouse and meet with the judge about a case. I didn't expect it to take this long." He walked over to where Envy sat and extended his hand for her to shake. "How are you?"

She reciprocated by shaking his hand. "Not good," she said. She put her phone on vibrate and tucked it away. "I'm terrified."

"There's no need to be. Excuse me for a moment while I get your file folder."

"Okay."

Casper walked to a two-drawer black file cabinet located next to his desk. He retrieved the file folder from the cabinet and went to sit across from Envy at the table.

"I've spoken to law enforcement, several lawyers in my group, and one of the criminal court judges. I don't have to tell you how surprised everyone was when I told them that the mother has turned herself in—only she's no teenager anymore.

I listened to everything you told me that took place that day and compared it with the evidence that was in the file. You probably aren't aware of this, but the police always hold back some essential facts and information about a case so that they can check out the stories of suspects or confessors."

"I don't understand. I told you everything. Everything I can remember."

"I believe you did. You also gave me some missing pieces that were needed to solve this case, which gave me additional cause to believe you. Since I have been investigating this case, I have, thanks to you coming forth, been able to fill in the missing blanks."

"What missing blanks?" asked Envy.

"For instance," said Casper, "what was used to cut the baby's umbilical cord? What happened before and immediately after the birth? What happened to the placenta, and the fact that no one suspected you were pregnant, not even your mother? I was also able to locate the baby's reported father, Stanton Hall."

"You what?" Alarm filled Envy's voice. "Why didn't you let me know? Where is he?"

"Hold up, remain calm." Casper reached over and patted her on the shoulder. "He lives in D.C. with his wife and two kids. At first, he refused to cooperate with the DCPD, but after I told them to mention that he could either talk to them or come to Memphis and talk to me, he opened up. He corroborated what you told him, which was, you lost the baby. He denied any prior knowledge of you giving birth or saying that you were about to give birth. He also said when he heard about the deceased infant, he thought about you, but he didn't want to believe you could do something like that; yet part of him was relieved because he was not ready for a child."

"How could he be so heartless? He's still the same selfish, self-centered dog he was back then."

"Envy, I do not have a reason, nor do I have evidence that you planned the events that followed the birth of your child. The medical examiner ruled it as a stillbirth, not a homicide. And, like I told you previously, the only possible charges they may have considered placing against you back then would have been desecration of a corpse, or possibly failure to report the incident."

Envy leaned over on the table. She felt a mixture of joy and sadness. "What happens next?"

"The DA analyzed the evidence and determined there were no grounds to prosecute. You're free."

The bottom of Envy's stomach felt like it was about to burst.

"Envy, this is great news for you. But I want to share some statistics with you that might help you to understand that what happened with you is not all that uncommon."

"Okay," she responded.

"First of all, research shows mothers who suffer a stillbirth don't even receive recognition in thirty-nine out of fifty states. There is no certificate of birth, which makes these births 'invisible.' So what would be the need in bringing charges against, in your case, a fifteen-year-old child, who was frightened and terribly alone? Add to that, you had an older boyfriend, who could have been charged with statutory rape. You had no prenatal care and no knowledge that when you went to the bathroom that day, you were going to deliver a child."

Envy trembled and gathered her arms together.

"I don't know if you've confided in anyone, other than me, but I suggest that if you have not, that now is the time. If you don't have anyone you can talk to, let me know. I have a colleague who is a licensed clinical psychologist. You need to talk to somebody."

"I have friends," Envy replied.

"Good. I'm glad to hear that." Casper stood up. "Well, I've got to get back to the courthouse. The trial I'm handling reconvenes at four o'clock. If you need to reach me, call and leave me a message and I'll get back to you just as soon as I can. Oh, before I forget, the DA wants to talk to you to go over everything before he closes the case. Soon as he says he can meet with us, I'll call you."

Envy stood up too. Casper placed the flat of his hand at the small of her back and walked with her to his door. Envy turned around. "Thank you." Tears streamed down her face.

Before he opened the door, Casper gathered her slender body inside his and held her for fifteen seconds or so until she regained enough composure to leave.

"I'm sorry about that," she told him.

"No," he shooed her off with the slight wave of his hand. "You're going through a traumatic experience. It isn't easy reliving the memories of the past, especially when those memories are nowhere near being pleasant. Take care of yourself, Envy. Okay?"

"I will, Casper. Thank you."

Casper opened the door. Envy, without looking back, or acknowledging Casper's assistant, walked off.

Envy sat inside her car and thought about what Casper Stephens had told her.

Envy began to think about Kacie and the decision she'd made to recommit her life to God. Since her decision that Sunday, Kacie appeared to be different. She was trying to be a better mother and a more loyal church member. But most of all, Envy believed Kacie had learned something she hoped one day she would learn—how to forgive herself.

Envy believed she should be happy now that she could move forward and stop hanging on to her past. Yet, she still felt a sense of lingering fear and she could not understand why.

She ruled against calling Kacie, and Layla was no one she wanted to confide in right now, for obvious reasons. She wanted to avoid talking to Layla as much as possible, because all Layla talked about was Tyreek.

She called her sister. "Nikkei," she said in a humble voice, "I need to see you." Envy waited for Nikkei's response. If Nikkei didn't want her crying on her shoulder, Envy was prepared to accept it. The way she had avoided a close relationship with Nikkei there was no way Envy could see herself being presented "a good sister award" by Nikkei.

"If you can come now, it'll be fine. I don't have to pick up the kids; they're carpooling with one of the other mothers and won't be here until after they finish soccer and dance practice." Nikkei sounded upbeat and almost excited, which made Envy smile.

"Thanks, sis. I'm on my way."

Envy arrived twenty minutes later and parked in Nikkei's driveway. Before she could ring the doorbell or knock on the door, Nikkei opened it.

"Come in. You didn't sound right on the phone." Nikkei greeted her sister with a look of concern. When Envy stepped inside the foyer, Nikkei hugged her. Envy returned the show of affection. "Let's go in the kitchen. I put on a pot of water so you can have a cup of coffee or hot tea, your choice."

"Thanks. Tea sounds good." Envy removed her jacket and hung it on the back of her chair, and then sat down. Nikkei had two cups, tea bags, instant decaf, cream, and stirrers on the table.

Envy didn't wait to start talking. She believed if she didn't tell Nikkei now, she would never have the courage to tell her about her past.

Nikkei remained quiet while Envy talked.

"You could have told me," Nikkei said after Envy finished. "I'm your sister. Your only sister, at that. I don't know why we never could really connect like sisters. I guess it was because I always felt like I had to compete against you for Momma's affection, and to get friends. I couldn't get the attention of boys because most of them only came to me to get advice on how to get next to you. I would have thought you were far too smart to get pregnant. But, hey, mistakes happen. I can't say that I understand what was going on in your life. I mean, I couldn't see myself leaving either one of my babies in a toilet, and never telling anyone."

Nikkei poured her sister a cup of hot water and hung the raspberry tea bag on the inside to steep, and then sat down at the table across from her sister.

Envy felt miserable when Nikkei said what she said, but Nikkei quickly cleared it up with positive words.

"I'm sorry that you felt like you didn't have anyone you could talk to back then, Envy. I wish you would have let me help you. I always idolized you, your beauty, your popularity, everything. I would have done anything to help you."

"Nikkei, I never knew you felt like that about me," Envy said, with a surprised look on her face.

"I'm just telling you what God loves—the truth."

"You don't know how much better I feel after confiding in you. I did tell Kacie and Layla, but just recently. And I hope you don't get upset about that, but I was too ashamed to tell my baby sister how badly I messed up my life. I've been dealing with this for so long, Nikkei. I've felt so ashamed, so ugly, so evil, all of these years. Now that the attorney has told me that it's all basically at an end, I don't know what to do. Part of me feels like I don't deserve to walk away scot-free. I should be behind bars."

"Stop it, Envy. You don't deserve any such thing. Was it a terrible thing that happened? Yes, it was. But it wasn't your fault. Your child was not born alive. God allows things for a reason, Envy. His ways are not our ways, and His thoughts are not our thoughts."

"The years of fear and terror over my secret keep tormenting me, Nikkei. And now to hear the lawyer say that I'm free. I don't know how to handle being set free."

"Only God can help you, sis. Only God can give you the peace you desire. I'm here for you, but you need to be healed from the inside. His mercy and grace will never let you go. He won't let you slip away. You don't have to be afraid. Place your trust in Him. Ask Him to help you and give you what you need to move ahead with your life."

Tears blinded Envy's eyes. She wept aloud, rocking back and forth.

Nikkei got up and walked over to her sister. "Shh, it's going to be all right," she whispered as she knelt beside her. She wiped the tears from Envy's face and stroked Envy's hair and continued to reassure her.

Envy finally stopped weeping. She looked at Nikkei. "I love you, Nikkei. I'm glad I came here."

"I'm glad you came too." Nikkei hugged her. "God knows what He's doing, Envy." Nikkei returned to her seat. "You're my sister, and I'm sorry for the way I've snubbed you most of our life. I had no idea the pain you were carrying. Hearing what happened to you back then hurts me now. And Stanton, whatever his name, walked out on you. I believe I understand why you didn't confide in Momma."

"You do?"

"Yes, I do," answered Nikkei.

Envy was surprised to hear Nikkei say that she understood, but she was glad that she did. "I'm still afraid, Nikkei. I walk around pretending like my life is all put together, when it's imploding. I can't shake the awful memories. They keep crowding my mind. It's like a door opens and no matter how hard I try to close it, the torment of what I did always kicks it back open, and I can't get rid of all of the thoughts." Envy wrapped her arms on the table and placed her head inside them.

"Let it go, Envy. I told you, you have to give this problem to God. It's the only way, and I mean the only way you're ever going to get through this. I'm sure you've heard or read the scripture that says, 'Brethren, I count not myself to have apprehended: but this one thing I do, forgetting those things, which are behind, and reaching forth unto those things, which are before.' That's what you're going to have to do."

Envy lifted her tear-filled eyes and looked at her sister. "I don't know how to forget. My mind won't let me. I should have kept it to myself. I shouldn't have gone to a lawyer. I shouldn't have told you, or Kacie, or Layla. I should have just kept it inside, like I've done all this time."

"No, that's what the enemy wanted you to do, so he could make you feel a little bit worse every day that you kept it bottled up inside. Don't you see? Look where it's gotten you. You're a wreck about a mistake you made in the past. It took a strong person to step up and admit what you did. I admire you."

"You? You admire me. Why?"

"For your strength. Now take that strength and mix it with the faith you know you have in God. It's inside of you, Envy. God is ordering your steps. Stop trying to step to the other side. Let God be God. And another thing," added Nikkei.

"What?"

"If there is any bitterness, anger, jealousy, anything you're carrying that isn't of God, now is the time to let it all go, so He can work in every area of your life. Look at the two of us." Nikkei reached across the table and laid her hands on top of Envy's. "Who would have thought that we would finally connect like we have? What the devil meant for bad, God is using it for your good, and mine too. You don't know how much I've prayed to have a close relationship with you. I didn't think it would come out of something that we deem as bad, but God doesn't see it that way. Now that you've admitted what happened, don't you know that healing is taking place?"

"You really think so?"

"I know so," Nikkei said with total confidence ringing in her voice as tears streamed down her face.

Envy's phone rang. She looked up at Nikkei. "It's my lawyer." Her hands shook when she pushed the talk button. "He-hello, Casper. I wasn't expecting you to call this quickly. I thought it would be days, maybe weeks."

Nikkei stared at Envy. Her hands were clasped together while her elbows rested on the table. Envy nodded and said, "Yes, uh-huh. No. Oh, I see. Yes. And thank you, Casper." Envy uttered an inward gasp.

"Thank you so much. I'll see you tomorrow morning at ten. Buh-bye." She bounced up from the chair. With a look like the breath had left her body, Envy screamed with shock and excitement. "He wants me to meet with him and the DA tomorrow! Everything should be completely over after that. Can you, will you, go with me, Nikkei? Please—"

"Girl, yes. That's what sisters are for."

They stood up and joined hands; like a carousel, they went around and around in circles in the middle of the kitchen floor.

~

The following rainy morning, Envy drove to Nikkei's house and called her when she was in her driveway. "I'm outside," she told her.

"Okay, I'm on my way out." Nikkei came out the door and opened up her yellow ducky umbrella. The puddles of water forming on the walkway were no match for her pair of multicolor rain boots.

Envy leaned over to the passenger side and opened the door for Nikkei.

"Good morning," Envy said.

"Hey, sis. How are you? Do you want me to drive?" Nikkei asked.

Envy paused a moment before she answered. "You know what? That may not be such a bad idea. I'm so nervous and it's raining out here too. People drive crazy in the rain. Do you mind?"

"Get out and let's change places right quick," ordered Nikkei.

"All right," said Envy, and the sisters exchanged seats.

"I want us to pray before we leave."

"Thanks. I can use all the prayer I can get."

Nikkei sent up a powerful petition to God, and the sisters headed downtown.

The hearing lasted all of half an hour. They went inside one of the courtrooms where the DA and presiding judge over that courtroom listened to Casper Stephen tell the events of what happened, including how Envy Wilson turned herself in.

At the end of the hearing, it was determined that based on the medical examiner's autopsy report, along with the fact that Envy came forth, even if it was eighteen years later, there was no evidence that a homicide had been committed. It was also in the medical examiner's report that there was no trauma to the stillborn. The judge did give Envy a strict tongue-lashing about the alternative she had after giving birth. Charges of desecration of a corpse or failure to report an incident were not brought up.

Envy hugged Casper Stephens and thanked him continuously for all he had done to help her through the ordeal that had tormented her all of her life.

"It's time to release the self-guilt, self-condemnation, and the blame you've placed on yourself. I wish you the very best," Casper told Envy.

"You too, Casper." She hugged him tightly.

"May God bless you, Attorney Stephens," commented Nikkei. "It was nice meeting you."

Casper nodded. "And you as well. Now, ladies, if you'll excuse me, I have a case about to reconvene in Criminal Division VII. Envy, have a great day and an even better life."

"Oh, I will. Buh-bye, Casper."

"Keep in touch," he said. "Good-bye."

~

Casper Stephens disappeared in the sea of people. For a long time, he would remember the day Envy Wilson had walked into his office. She didn't know it, but she had changed the course of his life. She made him want to put behind the issues with his own past and move forward in his life. Perhaps if they had met under a different set of circumstances, at a different time and place, he would have tried to make something happen between him and Envy. But the timing was way off. He still had too much of his own baggage that needed clearing out. At least, she'd shown him that he still had feelings and emotions.

In a weird sort of way, Envy reminded him of himself. He was so busy focusing on his past that he couldn't move into his future, so he kept himself buried deep into his law practice. But no matter how many hours he worked, there were still those moments he felt himself alone, lonely and afraid of loving again. He couldn't bare the anguish of lost love, or of hurting another human being the way he had hurt Lillie.

Then Envy Wilson came along. He'd long stopped being a religious man, but maybe, just maybe God brought her into his life for a reason. She was more than just another client. It was Envy who caused his eyes to open and see what he was doing to himself. He wasn't living; he merely existed, going through the motions of life. When she walked into his office for the first time, his body and mind betrayed him. He did not know it at the time, but it was the dose of reality that he needed.

There was hope for him after all. Hope to have someone in his life again. It wouldn't be with Envy, but it would be with someone—someone who would love him for the man he was. It was time for him to live and love again.

With each step Casper took toward the courtroom, he walked more confidently. There was someone out there just for him. For the first time in years, he believed it. It was just a matter of time. Casper was willing to open his eyes, his heart, and his mind. God had spoken to his heart through an unlikely source, and he had finally listened.

21

. . . And there is a time for every event under heaven. . . . A time to throw stones, and a time to gather stones; A time to embrace, and a time to shun embracing. —Ecclesiastes 3:1a, 5

Layla had been trying to reach Envy for two days, but Envy hadn't returned her phone call or answered her text messages, so Layla called Kacie to see if she had talked to Envy.

"Kacie, have you talked to our wayward friend?"

"Girl, naw. Not in a few days. Why?"

"She called me the other day and left me a message. She said she went to Precious Cargo and she met Tyreek. I've been trying to reach her, but I keep getting her voice mail, and she's not responding to my texts. I wanted to know what happened."

"You know Envy, girl. It isn't unusual for her to go ghost for a few days. She's probably somewhere doing her thing with somebody."

"I know, but I wish she hadn't called and told me she talked to Tyreek. Now I'm anxious to know what happened."

"You know Envy. She probably grilled the poor man. Have you talked to him? Has he said anything about talking to her?"

"No, I haven't talked to him today. And yesterday I talked to him for a few minutes, but he was extremely busy. I'm sure he'll call tonight and tell me what she said, but I wanted to hear from her first."

"Sounds like you're just going to have to exercise some patience. She'll call, or he'll tell you about it. Either way, you'll probably know something later today."

"Yea. Anyway, how are you?"

"Girl, I'm wonderful. I feel great. The kids are good."

"I'm glad, Kacie. You are really making a one hundred and eighty degree turn in your life. It's amazing."

"It is. And I plan on not looking back."

"Good for you. Well, I'm going to let you go. I'm going to straighten up my kitchen and then chill."

"All right. I'll talk to you later. Oh, and be sure you let me know when you hear something." Kacie laughed into the phone.

"You know I will. Buh-bye."

"Bye," replied Kacie.

Layla hung up the phone. She texted Envy instead of calling this time and asked Envy to call ASAP. Several minutes later, Envy texted back and said she was with Nikkei, which was surprising to Layla, and that she would call her as soon as she could.

Layla washed her glass, plate, and fork. Afterward, she retreated to the den, pulled off her shoes, and lay back on her modern sea blue sofa. She propped both her feet on the matching ottoman. With her head resting comfortably against the soft fabric, she dozed off, only to be awakened by the sound of her cell phone ringing. Still in a half-sleep state, by the time she got up to follow the sound of the phone, it had stopped. Layla walked to the kitchen and found the phone on the countertop next to the stainless-steel microwave. Dennis's name and number were on the screen as a Missed Call. "Lord, I hope he's not calling to try to get back with me."

Layla hit the Talk button on her phone. After five rings, Dennis answered.

"Hello."

"Dennis, it's Layla. What's up?" she asked nonchalantly.

"Whaddaya mean, whuzzup? Why don't you care about me anymore, Layla?" His speech was slurred. It was unusual to hear his words jumbled because Dennis wasn't a drinker. He may have had a glass of wine every blue moon. But the way his words were coming out, it was obvious that he'd had more than a glass or two of alcohol.

"Dennis, what are you talking about? Have you been drinking?" Layla asked.

"If you were so concerned about me, then we would still be together. You wouldn't be running around with other men. I know that you've been cheating on me."

"First of all, I haven't the slightest idea what you're talking about. I have not cheated on you, because I am not your woman and you are not my man. I have told you that. I've tried to be as truthful as I could without hurting you. You are special to me, and you always will be."

"'Special'? I don't wanna hear that."

"All I can say is that I didn't mean to hurt you, but it was unfair to you and to me to keep seeing each other, when I knew I didn't want the same kind of relationship you wanted."

"You used to want it. You used to love me. Now you're running round, God knows where, sleeping with somebody else," he accused her in a drunken tone. "Envy calling here at two, three o'clock in the morning, looking for you. You think I'm stupid? You think I'm dumb, Layla? Well, I'm nobody's fool, not even yours."

"What are you talking about? What does Envy have to do with us? And why would she call you looking for me?"

"You ask your girl why she called. I guess your game ain't as smooth as hers. But you tell her to call whoever you were with from now on. Leave me alone," he said in a harsh voice.

"When did Envy call you, Dennis?" Layla tried to make some sense of what he was saying.

"I don't know. A week, two weeks, yesterday, a month, I don't know. She's your friend. Hey, why don't you ask her? And tell her not to call me ever again."

"Look, don't accuse me of something that you heard from somebody else. I don't know what's up with you, and I don't know what's up with Envy. But I'm a grown woman. I do what I want, when I want. I don't answer to you, Envy, and nobody else, but God!" Layla yelled.

"Don't you bring God up in this. You need to take a look at yourself in the mirror for real. You fooling yourself." His speech was warped by the liquor, but Layla still understood every cutting word.

"Right now, I'm trying hard to excuse what you're saying, Dennis, because you're intoxicated. But I do have respect for myself, and no matter what you may think, I also have reverence for God. I'm sorry that you believe I've committed some adulterous act against you, whatever you want to call it, but that's you and your assumptions," she responded sharply.

"What do you expect me to think, when you've been going behind my back seeing other men? We were supposed to be committed to one another. Since our relationship started, not one time have I ever entertained the thought of going out or spending time with another woman. And don't think I haven't had offers either, because I have. But I was committed to you and the relationship I thought we had. I never did anything to jeopardize it."

Layla sighed into the phone and returned to sit down. This time she sat in her recliner, which she usually reserved for reading. Her nerves tensed immediately. "I told you that I'm sorry for hurting you. You really are a good man."

"Oh, I know that I'm a good man," he said in a tough, raw voice. "See, unlike you, I don't need to have my ego stroked in order to feel good about myself. I know that I am a God-fearing man. I loved you. I wanted to marry you. But like you told me, we don't have anything anymore. You wanted out, so that's the way it is. I can accept it. But I needed to let you know what was on my mind."

"Good, then you've let me know, so I don't see that we have anything else to discuss. And if Envy or anybody ever calls you again looking for me, do me a favor and don't call me whining about it. I'm sick of all of this mess."

"You talk a good talk, but until you can come to terms with who you are on the inside, until you can learn what true beauty is, then there's nothing I can do or say that'll change anything." After an insulting pause, he came back with more angry, verbal attacks. "All I can do is pray that one day you'll look in the mirror and see that it's not what you look like on the outside that made me fall in love with you. And any other man that you meet out there, I hope he isn't superficial and vain, because if he is, then he'll miss out on the Layla I used to know. I pity you. . . ." His voice trailed away, like he'd said enough.

"Dennis, let me tell you some . . . Hello? Hello? Dennis?" The only reply she got was a dial tone. Dennis had hung up.

Layla called Envy repeatedly. She was going to get some answers. She didn't care if it took her calling Envy all night long. If she had to camp out on her doorstep, she was ready to do that too. Whatever Envy was up to, Layla was going to find out— and she was going to find out before the sun came up.

22

Jealous people poison their own banquet and then eat it. —
Unknown

Layla pushed aside her thoughts about Envy meeting
Tyreek and exchanged them for thoughts about why
Envy called Dennis. For the sixth or seventh time, she
called Envy's number. No answer. It wasn't until eight-
thirty in the evening that Envy answered her phone.

"Hey, girl," Envy immediately said before Layla
could say a word. "I know you want to know what your
boy said about you, but I've been busy all day long, and
now I have company. I'll have to tell you about
everything tomorrow."

"No, we won't talk tomorrow. We're going to talk
now," Layla said with tremendous force and anger. "I
don't want to hear about Tyreek or what your lawyer
said."

"What is your problem?" Envy asked.

"Naw, honey, what is your problem?" Layla jumped
in with a voice full of attitude.

"What are you talking about?"

"You know good and well what I'm talking about.
You had no right whatsoever to call Dennis at two
o'clock in the morning, lying on me. What is wrong with
you? It's beginning to sound like you can't handle
someone who's got it going on besides you."

"Look, Layla, I don't have time to listen to you
tripping about whatever it is you're talking about. Like I
said, I have company, so whatever you're bellyaching

about, why don't you go get you a hot box of Church's fried chicken and an apple pie. That ought to calm you down. 'Cause right now, you're flat-foot trippin'."

"How dare you. That's what you'd like, isn't it, Envy? You want to see me fat and out of shape again. But to stoop so low as to call and hurt Dennis with your lies. That's low for even someone like you." Layla seethed with anger.

"I called Dennis one time, Layla. It was because I needed to talk to you. I had something on my mind and I panicked when I couldn't reach you, so I called him because I knew if you weren't at home at two in the morning, then you had to have been with him. But I was mistaken and surprised."

"That's a bold-faced lie, and you know it!" Layla yelled into the phone. She was heated. "You never bothered to tell me you even talked to Dennis. You tried to put doubt in Dennis's mind, and you did. But you didn't hurt me; you hurt him."

"Girl, please. I talked to you that same night I talked to Dennis."

"Why didn't you tell me that you called him then, if you were straight up? I'll tell you why, 'cause you wanted to be messy for whatever reason."

"Look, I didn't think you were out with some buster you'd just met. I was just being concerned about you. But, oh, well; I guess I was wrong. Anyway, don't call here trying to go off on me because you and your man are having issues."

"All these years that we've been friends and you turn out to be a backstabbing, lying . . . Dang, I wish I could call you what I want to call you. Thank God for the Christ in me."

Envy laughed so loud in the phone that Layla pulled her cell phone away from her ear.

"I am busy, Layla. I refuse to entertain your immature behavior. Why don't you sleep on whatever it is that's got you whining like a little girl, and tomorrow maybe the two of us can talk about this like real women. Bye." The call ended.

Layla held the phone back and inspected it. "She has some nerve. Oh, but she's going to get hers. I'm going to make sure of that," she muttered aloud.

Layla marched to the bathroom, undressed, and took a shower. After that, she went into her bedroom, put on her favorite pink pajamas, which her dear mother had given her for Christmas, and lay back on the bed. She wanted to call her mother, but it was too late. Her parents were usually in bed by eight-thirty every night and up by five every morning. She never could understand why they did that, but it worked for them. She called Kacie again and told her what Envy had said.

"I'm sorry, but I had to call and tell you about your friend," Layla said.

"She's our friend, Layla, not just mine. What happened?"

"Do you know she had the audacity to call and give Dennis the impression that I'm cheating on him?"

"What? Why would she do something like that? It doesn't make sense. Who told you this, anyway? And I thought you and Dennis were a done deal?"

"We are, but he just called and we got into it bad. Anyway, while we're arguing, he brings up Envy. Said that she called his house looking for me."

"Wait a minute. I'm getting confused here. Why didn't she call you? When was this?"

"Kacie, listen. It doesn't matter when she did it, the thing is she did, and that was foul. Anyway, she called him at two o'clock in the morning, pretending like she was looking for me. She flat-out lied, talking about how she thought since I didn't answer my cell phone that I must have been at his house, when she knew good and well that I wasn't. I haven't spent the night at Dennis's in I don't know how long. You and Envy both know that."

"I know, but when did she do this?" asked Kacie.

"I said I don't know. Dennis was drunk. I couldn't get much sense out of him."

"Dennis? Drunk? This is starting to sound crazy. I've never known him to drink, let alone to get drunk. That's not the Dennis I know."

"I guess he's still hurt 'cause I told him I don't want to be with him. I care about him, Kacie, but I am not in love with the man. Maybe I never was in love with him. He was there when I needed someone, and maybe I mistook it for love."

"But what does any of this have to do with Envy? Why would she try to throw salt on you like that? Something else has to be going on, Layla. Envy is not like that."

"Yeah, I thought so too, until me and her got into it when I called her out on it."

"But I thought you hadn't talked to Envy?"

"I called her after I talked to Dennis, and this time she answered the phone. But you are not going to believe how she talked to me."

"What did she say?" Kacie asked.

"She had the nerve to say that I was jealous of her and that maybe I needed to go and get some Church's fried chicken to calm my nerves. Talking about I'm acting like a child. Then she had the audacity to hang up in my face. Kacie, girl, you just don't know. I wish I could have reached through that phone and knocked every tooth out of her mouth."

"Oh, my goodness. I can't believe this. I need to call and talk to her. Something doesn't sound right," said Kacie.

"No, don't call her, especially not on my behalf. When I see her in person, I plan on showing her exactly how I feel."

"Look, there is going to be no fighting between the two of you. We have been friends too long for something like this to come between us. This is straight from the devil. He's just trying to cause dissension."

"Well, he's sure doing a good job of it. I'm not going to be talked down to by anyone ever again. I've lived my life far too long with people making fun of me, laughing and pointing at me, and you think I'm going to let someone who is supposed to be my friend betray me and talk down to me? No, no, no. I'm not taking it, Kacie. She can go right on about her way."

"Layla, will you shut up and listen for a minute? Let me talk to her. There has to be a reasonable explanation for her actions. You know for yourself that she's been stressed out trying to deal with rectifying her past. It's taken a lot out of her. So let me talk to her and I'll get with you tomorrow, okay?"

"I don't know, Kacie."

"Please, will you at least do it for me? We all have gone through some tough times, but it's a new season and great things are in store for all of us. I truly believe that."

Layla hesitated before speaking. "Ummm, allright."

Kacie exhaled. "Great. Now, last question."

"What?"

"Are you sure there's no chance of you and Dennis patching things up?"

"Honestly, Kacie, I don't want to patch things up with him. Talking to him again just made me that more certain that it is over for good. And I really like Tyreek. I want to see where things can go with him."

"But you haven't known him long, Layla. I'm not saying anything negative about him, because I don't know the man. I can only go by what you say about him, and you say that he's a really nice guy. But you know Dennis loves you, and I just don't want to see your relationship fall apart."

"Our relationship has already fallen apart. All I know is that Dennis came into my life when I was vulnerable, not feeling good about myself at all, and in a bad place mentally and emotionally. He is a great man. He's been nothing but good to me. However, it's not about Dennis loving me, Kacie. It's about me. For the first time in my life, I'm thinking of me, how I feel, and what I want." Layla spoke with force.

"And what you want is Tyreek?"

"Not necessarily. I'm just saying that I like Tyreek. And I want to see what's up with him."

"I see. Well, seems like I have a lot of praying to do. I'm not about to sit back and allow the enemy to destroy you and Envy's friendship. The devil is a liar," Kacie said in an elevated voice.

"Yeah, and so is Envy. I wish you could have heard her. I'm still in shock. I can't even go to sleep."

"Pray, and I'll pray too."

"I already prayed," replied Layla. "But I'll talk to you tomorrow. Maybe by then, you would have talked some sense into that dimwitted friend of yours. I can't stomach her anymore right now."

"Pray some more. Lay yourself down and ask God to rock you to sleep. This stuff that's going on now isn't worth losing sleep over. Do not give in to the devil's tactics. You hear me?"

"Yeah, I hear you. Thanks for listening. I'll talk to you tomorrow."

"Good night, Layla. I'm going to call Envy. Buh-bye."

"Good luck with that phone call. Anyway, nighty-night." Layla ended the call.

After Layla finished talking to Kacie she thought about the relationship her parents had. Would she ever have a divine mate like her mother and daddy were to each other? Forty-two years of marriage and they still acted madly in love. They still held hands when they went out together. They still, as her father often said, courted each other. Her mother never worked outside of the home, except on a few occasions, and that was because she wanted to have something to do when all the kids were in school. It wasn't because of money, because Daddy made sure he was the breadwinner of the family. Everything they did was based on the Word of God. If there was a problem, they prayed about it. If there was a need, they prayed about it. If there was sickness, they prayed about it. And they still remained like that today.

Layla had never heard them angrily disagree with each other, and there was not a time she could remember where either one of them ever walked out in anger. Maybe those times did exist, but Layla could never attest to seeing or hearing it.

She would call and talk to her mother tomorrow. She wouldn't tell her all of the details, but Layla planned to tell her just enough for her mother to give her some much-needed godly and woman-to-woman advice.

Layla got out of the bed and knelt beside it to say her nightly prayers. By habit, she started by reciting, "Our Father, who art in heaven, hallowed be thy name. . . ."

When she finished praying, she got in bed and tried to sleep, but she was still too furious with Envy. She sat up on the side of the bed and thought of the reason Envy had turned on her. Whatever it was, she was ready to fight fire with fire, if that was the way Envy wanted it.

The phone startled her. It was Tyreek's ringtone. Layla smiled while she pushed the talk button. "Hello," she said.

"Hey, whatcha doing?"

"Seething."

"What's got you upset?"

"I heard you met one of my used-to-be best friends."

Silence infiltrated the phone line for several seconds.

"Hello? Hello?" Layla asked into the phone.

"I'm here. Yeah, I did. And that's why I'm calling. We need to talk."

"Talk about what? And when?"

"Your friend. And you. Tonight."

"Tonight? Okay, go for it. What happened? I already know the girl been trippin'. I don't know what's up with her."

"I'll be there in fifteen or twenty minutes. I'm getting ready to leave work now."

"Oh, you want to come over here? I don't know about that, Tyreek. It's late. And you know—"

"Layla, believe me. I cannot talk about this over the phone. Please, I need to see you face-to-face."

"Tyreek, you're scaring me. What is it?"

"Can I come over?" he asked again.

"Yeah, I guess, come on. I'll be waiting."

Layla got up from bed and went to find something to put on. Tyreek sounded serious, even worried. What had Envy done? If she told him about Dennis or led him to believe that she was involved with Dennis, she would never speak to her again. She had already caused enough damage as it was, but telling Tyreek her personal business was way off base.

Layla slipped on a pair of chocolate leggings and an oversized thigh-length white shirt, with chocolate abstract designs. She put on a pair of slides, then brushed her teeth and rinsed out her mouth. *What could he have to tell me?* She didn't know how to sort out her feelings. She called Kacie again.

As soon as Kacie said, "Hello," Layla let loose.

"Girl, Tyreek just called. He's on his way over here."

"Whaaat? Girl, do you think that's a good idea? You don't want to put yourself in a position to fall weak to him. What can he possibly want at this time of night anyway other than some booty?"

"Naw, listen. He said he has to tell me something about him meeting Envy. He said he needs to see me face-to-face, that it's not something that can be talked about over the phone. So I told him he could come. I need to hear what he has to say, Kacie. Believe me, nothing else is going to happen. But Envy is messing with my life for some reason or other, and I need to know what she said to Tyreek. It's like she's gone loco."

"I don't know what's going on. Look, still be cautious. I have to get in touch with Envy. She must really be flipping out. I already tried calling her when I hung up from talking to you the first time, but she didn't answer. She probably knows that you called and told me what she said."

"Yeah, she probably does." Layla spoke with light bitterness resonating in her voice. "But, Kacie, if she's said anything, and I mean anything to him about my personal business, or told this man something that can mess things up for me, I'm telling you now that I'm not going to have anything else to do with her ever again."

"Hold up, Layla. Wait to see what he has to say before you start talking like that."

"I'm just telling you. She's going to make me hurt her."

"Call me after—"

"Kacie, the doorbell is ringing. That's him. I'll talk to you later. Bye." Layla hung up the phone and went to answer the door.

"Hi, Tyreek," Layla said. He looked tired, and a frown was on his face.

"What's up, baby?" Layla asked as she stepped aside to let him in and then closed the door behind him.

Tyreek walked up behind her and swallowed her in his arms. He spoke slowly in her ear. "You smell sweet. But I am not going to let your sweetness be my weakness."

Layla clung to his arms and rested her head against his chest. Suddenly her head popped up. "What do you mean?"

Tyreek took a deep breath; his body stiffened; he released his grip on Layla. "We need to talk. We need to talk now."

Layla turned around and faced him. "Why do you look so . . . well, so tense all of a sudden?"

He took hold of Layla's hand and led her to the sofa; they sat down. Tyreek looked directly into her eyes. "Why didn't you tell me that you're Envy's best friend?"

Layla drew back her neck. "What?"

"You heard me. Why did I have to find out from her that y'all are best friends?" Tyreek jumped up off the sofa. His composure disappeared without warning and he blew up. "I should have known you were too good to be true. All of this time, I'm believing you're different, when you're another Envy. What did y'all do? Sit around and scheme on me?"

A confused look washed over Layla's face. "I have no idea what you're talking about."

"Y'all trying to see which one could make the bigger fool out of me?"

He was beginning to make her mad too with his false accusations against her. What in the world had Envy said?

Layla stood up. "Look, I have had just about enough of people coming to me with one lie after another. I do not appreciate you coming to my house accusing me of something that I know nothing about. If anything, I should be the one asking the questions, because why would you believe anything someone has told you— especially someone you don't know, over me?"

"I do know her, but you already know that."

"What?" Layla placed both hands on her hips and bit on her lip. "Tyreek, I do not, and let me repeat this to you, I do not have time for your games. If you have something to say, say it, because what you've said so far doesn't mean a thing to me. Envy is my best friend, which is all she could have told you."

"See, I knew it. You know she came and showed out, huh? She told me that you knew about me and her."

"You? And Envy?" She felt her fists forming. Her chest felt like it was about to explode. Anger lit up in her eyes. "Are you saying that you've been dipping and dabbing around with my best friend? Is that what you're saying? And now you're up in here trying to make this my fault?"

"Look, don't pretend you didn't know about me and Envy," he retaliated.

"Get out of here!" Layla pointed toward her door. "Beat it!" she screamed again. "No wonder she's been acting like a darn fool. It's because the two of you have something going on."

Tyreek stared at her, baffled. "You really don't know, do you?" His voice dropped. "What has she done?"

"What has who done?" Layla asked, standing with one hand on her hip and the other hand on the doorknob. "You better start making some sense, brother. And you better do it now."

"I'm—I'm sorry, Layla. When she came to Precious Cargo, she told me that—that." Tyreek mumbled. His head hung down and his shoulders slouched. "I should have known."

Layla turned the doorknob loose. "Look, I'm going to ask you one more time to talk to me like you got some sense or you better get to stepping. I don't have time for your dramatics, and I've had enough of Envy's foolishness."

"Layla, I didn't know that you and Envy knew each other until the other day. I promise I didn't. But right now, I need you to listen. I'll make this right. Please."

Layla remained silent. She felt numb like she was afraid to question what was written on his face.

"Layla." He walked over to her. "I'm sorry." He spoke slow and deliberate. "I had no right to come in here the way I did. I didn't give you a chance. I just assumed you were part of Envy's sick mind games."

"Well, I'm not." Layla folded her arms and stared at Tyreek. "Keep talking," she said, hoping her voice didn't reveal the hurt forming on the inside.

"Remember when I told you that I was involved with a woman that I really liked but she used me?"

Layla placed her hands over her ears. "I do not want to hear it. I do not want to hear it," she repeated. A bevy of tears immediately formed in her eyes before they poured down her face like a raging river.

"You waltz in here and go off on me without telling me what this was all about, and it turns out that you and Envy are the ones that are diabolical and—and plain, plain ole . . . get out." Layla opened the door.

Tyreek closed the door. "I can't leave until I tell you everything. I knew Envy was jealous and controlling, but I had no idea she would try to hurt her own best friend." Tyreek reached out toward Layla, but she moved back.

"Do not touch me. And don't you dare stand here and tell me the woman was Envy."

Tyreek was silent.

"It really *is* her, isn't it?" Layla asked like a light bulb had been turned on in her head.

Tyreek nodded.

"Wow, how crazy is this? Now I understand why she's been acting the way she has." Layla paused. Suddenly like an epiphany had hit her upside the head she said, "It all makes sense, now that I think about it. When I first mentioned your name, that's when her attitude changed. Instead of acting like she was happy for me, she didn't show much emotion at all. And Dennis, she wanted Dennis to know. She wanted to hurt me."

"Who's Dennis? Now I'm lost."

"Dennis is the man I was seeing when I met you."

"So you've been involved with another man all along? Is it the guy you said was only a friend? Because you made it clear that the two of you were not an item."

Layla nodded. "He is a friend, except he . . . he used to be more than a friend."

Tyreek hit the top of his head and looked away from Layla. "How did I fall for all of this? Man, you and Envy are a piece of work—a real piece of work. I've been used all of this time. What is it like, Layla?"

Layla continued to cry. Her voice quavered as she tried to speak. "Don't you dare try to put this on me. I had no idea you and Envy had anything going on—until now. Yes, I was seeing Dennis, but when I met you, I realized that I was not in love with him. And I hadn't been in some time. So I fessed up; I told him that I wasn't in love with him. But the man was there for me when I really needed someone in my life, besides my girlfriends. There was no need to tell you any more than what I told you about Dennis, because I didn't know how things were going to turn out between us. I've been a fool too many times, Tyreek, and I wasn't about to be a fool again, no matter how much I was starting to care about you. And I'm glad I know now what kind of man you are—you're nothing but a deceiver."

"Me?" he hollered. "How can you stand here and call me a deceiver?" Both of his hands flew up in the air. "I was straight with you. I told you in the very beginning how I felt about you. I told you that there had been another woman in my life. I've never lied once during the time we've been seeing each other. No, I didn't tell you her name because I didn't think it was necessary. Boy, was I wrong, especially after Envy came to the restaurant and told me about you being her best friend, and that she had been giving you pointers about how to nab me. She had me going. After listening to her, I really thought she plotted with you to make a fool out of me. Can you imagine how stupid I feel?"

"No, I can't, Tyreek. Can you imagine how you've made me feel?"

"I imagine that we've hurt each other, baby. I imagine that Envy has lived up to her name. That's what I imagine. She's been so used to me being at her every beck and call, but that was before you came into my life. Sounds like we've both been had." Tyreek inched toward Layla. This time she didn't move away.

Tyreek embraced her. "I'm sorry, baby." He held her against his chest while he stroked her hair. "I'm so sorry. I'm so sorry."

Layla slowly lifted her head and their eyes locked. "Envy has some serious problems going on in her life. I didn't really understand the depth of them until now. Part of me is to blame for what happened too."

Tyreek wiped her tears with the back of his hand. "We've both made mistakes. I should have left Envy alone when she made it clear to me that I was only good for one thing in her life. I used to fool myself into believing that one day she'd realize that she was in love with me. But it never happened. It was just a pipe dream." Tyreek continued to stroke Layla's hair. "Then something amazing happened."

"What?" she whispered.

"You came along and changed my life. You're beautiful, so easy to talk to, so kind, so sweet, and so compassionate. You're special to me. You make me laugh. You make me believe that I can be a better person and a better man."

"What! I do all of that?" Layla stepped out of his arms and squinted her eyes. "I must really have it going on," she said with a mixture of laughter replacing tears.

"See, that's exactly what I'm talking about." Tyreek laughed. "Come on, woman, will you let me be serious?"

"Yes, I'll let you be serious." She took a deep breath and prepared herself to listen.

"Layla, what I want to say is . . . I know it hasn't been a long time, but it doesn't matter to me. I got some feelings for you. I mean some real deep feelings, girl." He kissed Layla with passion and desire. When he pulled away, he said, "I just want you to tell me you feel the same."

"I do."

"You—you do?" His eyes scanned her face like he was searching for the truth.

"Yes, I really like you." They kissed again and embraced each other tightly.

23

Jealousy contains more of self-love than of love. —*Francois de La Rochefoucauld*

Envy turned off her cell phone and rested back in the crook of Leonard's biceps.

"Wasn't that Layla?" Leonard asked.

"Yep."

"What was that all about? Is everything all right?" asked Leonard. "Sounds like that was a nasty catfight."

Envy remained quiet for several minutes. She was breathing a little heavy and her face was flushed.

Leonard asked. "You all right?"

Envy nodded.

"Can I get you something?"

Envy shook her head. "Naw, I'm good," she finally said. "It's just that I'm so mad right now. Layla's been tripping a lot lately. She and Dennis have been having problems because she's stepping out on him, and I guess he found out. And in that warped mind of hers, she's blaming me."

"Y'all have been tight too long to let some he said, she said mess come between your friendship."

"I know. And it's nothing that won't work itself out eventually." Envy turned over in the bed until she was face-to-face with Leonard. "No need to talk about it now. I'll tell you all about that another time. But I have to admit, I am furious that Layla had the audacity to call me and call herself going off on me. She's so uppity, and all of a sudden, she has this thing."

"What do you mean?"

"Like she's better than me and Kacie or something."
She gave him a quick glance. "The girl has brain damage
if you ask me. Maybe when Mike shot her, it affected her
mind or something. All I know is she got some serious
issues."

"Well, there's one thing you don't have to worry
about." Leonard lowered his head and his mouth touched
hers.

"What was that for?" Envy smiled.

"Because."

"Because what?"

"Because." He kissed her. "You're beautiful. Let me
reassure you there's nothing, absolutely nothing, Layla
can do to change that. And you can't blame her for being
jealous. I mean, she's lost a lot of weight, a whole lot, but
she'll never be as beautiful as you."

"Leonard, you're so sweet."

"I'm only speaking the truth," he said, and picked up
where he left off with feathery kisses over her body.

Envy smiled. Leonard was right. Why was she
allowing the likes of Layla to get under her skin? So
what if Tyreek was smitten by Layla? She still had him
first, and if she really wanted him, she could have him
back in her bed before either he or Layla saw it coming.
Layla probably wasn't giving him what he craved, and
that was sex. And even if she was giving it up, Layla
couldn't compare to her in the bedroom. Either way,
Tyreek would soon grow tired of Layla's goody two
shoes fake attitude, and then he would want to come
crawling back. But Envy made up her mind, while
Leonard was doing all he could to satisfy her that
Tyreek was a has-been.

He'd lost out on her goodness. No way did she go
behind any female. She sighed, and Leonard took it as a

sign that he was pleasing her. But Envy knew it was because she had won the game; it was only a matter of time before Tyreek and Layla realized it.

Envy focused back on Leonard. His touch brought her mind and body back to the bedroom. He lifted her hands to his shoulders, and Envy clung to him. His eyes met hers, filled with desire. It seemed as if fire was racing through every nerve of her body. Only if she could experience true love and not purely sexual gratification, but she could not. She had far too much baggage.

In the privacy of her own heart, Envy did admit one thing: if she could ever love anyone, that man would be Leonard. But falling in love was never part of her game plan in her adult life. She was fascinated by having fun and satisfying her sexual craving.

She understood the Bible said it was better to marry than to burn with passion, but she couldn't see herself walking down the aisle. No way was she going to give a man the chance to desert her the way her father deserted her mother. She was not going to chance having another man leave her the way Stanton had done. That kind of pain was unbearable and undeserved. Better to be safe than sorry. This was an issue God, Himself, would have to come down, knock on her door, and tell her that He wanted her to stop what she was doing. Until that happened, she would do what she had to do, which was repent, ask God for forgiveness—until the next time.

Envy lay spent in Leonard's arms. She listened to his labored breathing. She began to pray the prayer that only she and God knew word for word. "Lord, you said if I confess my sins, you were faithful and just to forgive me of my sins, and to cleanse me of all unrighteousness. Well, I confess to you right now the sinful act I have just committed. I can't stop unless you help me, Father. I need you to intervene if you truly want me to make a change in my life. Until that time comes, forgive me, for I have sinned again. Amen.

Envy nestled closer to Leonard. Without opening his eyes, he turned back toward her and kissed her on her forehead. He gathered and squeezed her in his arms and they went for round two.

24

Don't worry that children never listen to you; worry that they are always watching you. —*Robert Fulghum*

The past weeks since she had rededicated her life to God, there was a remarkable improvement in the lives of Kacie and her children.

Kenny's attitude could have led him down a road of trouble and perhaps destruction, but God had heard the prayer of His children. The youth group Kenny was involved in at church was something he loved being part of. He had learned a lot about being a young man in Christ. It was during the midweek youth ministry's Bible Study that Kenny gave his life to Christ, accepted God as his Lord and Savior, and was baptized.

Kacie was more patient and had not laid a hand on any of her children in an abusive manner. She still believed spare the rod, spoil the child, but she didn't discipline them in the harsh manner she used to do. If she thought about it, she hadn't had to use disciplinary tactics lately because now she and her kids spent more time talking and being together.

Kacie attended weekly Bible Study too, and also became involved in a separate singles' ministry called "You're Not in It Alone: Being a Single Christian Parent." Kacie began to understand about her frustration and stress from listening to some of the other single parents in the group. It gave her a new insight into her life, and provided tools to help her cope during stressful times.

While the younger kids were in the nursery and at children's Bible Study, Kacie thrived in her classes. She met new people and other parents who shared some of the same feelings she experienced from raising their kids alone.

Youth group leader, Minister Cecil Brunson, often spent extra time talking to Kacie about ways to improve communication with Kenny now that he was a teenager. Kacie was encouraged by his advice, because everything he told her, thus far, had worked just as he said.

Praying with her children rather than depending on them to pray by themselves, left Kacie with her spirit high and her heart light. There were times she asked Kenny to lead them in prayer, and other times she would ask one of the other kids, including little Keshena and Kyland. It was exciting to Kacie watching the spiritual transformation take place in her household and in her life.

One particular Wednesday night, Kacie and her children were piled in the Suburban on their way home from Bible Study.

"Mom."

"Yes, Kenny."

"Can I ask you something?"

She looked at the growing young man sitting on the passenger side. He had the makings of a thin mustache. A small, but noticeable, patch of hair was evident underneath his chin. *He is so handsome.*

"You know you can talk to me. I don't want you to ever doubt that again. You hear me, son?"

"Yes, ma'am." Kenny smiled. "I was thinking…" and then he looked over his shoulder and saw some of his siblings staring directly at him. "Maybe we should wait until we get home, if that's okay with you."

"Of course." Kacie continued to drive while the children engaged in conversations among themselves.

The smaller kids were quiet and in a car-induced hypnotic state and were about to fall asleep. It happened almost every time they rode in a car.

Since church was less than fifteen minutes away, they made it to the house quickly. Kenny helped get all of the children out of the car, along with emergency bags that contained snacks, pull-ups, juice cups, and loads of other items for the little ones.

Kacie was glad they had three bathrooms. It was another reason she loved her house so much. She divided the girls up to share one of the bathrooms, and the boys shared another bathroom, and Kacie had an on-suite bathroom.

Kenny helped get the boys prepared for bed, while Kacie and Kassandra helped get the girls ready. After everyone had their baths and was prepared for bed, they gathered together and prayed.

Once everyone was in bed, Kenny came into his mother's room. "Do you still feel like talking, Momma?"

"Yes." She patted her hand on the bed. Kenny sat down on the bed next to her. "What is it? Girl problems?" She smiled.

"No, I know how to handle that now."

Kacie pulled her head back, bucked her eyes, and smiled. "Ah, so you do, huh? Well, that's good news. At least I think it is."

"It is. Minister Cecil has been talking to some of us older boys." He said "older boys" proudly.

"And what did Minister Cecil have to say?" she asked. *With his good-looking self.*

"You remember what happened between me and Jackie?"

"Ugh, will I ever forget? I don't think I will. What about it?"

"During one Super Wednesday, Minister Cecil and Minister Isaac, divided us up in two groups. One was for the teenage boys and another one was for the teen-age girls. We talked about things that were pleasing to God and the stuff that wasn't pleasing to God."

"Like what you and Jackie did?" asked Kacie, but without sounding like she was fussing.

"Yes, ma'am. Mom, lots of teens at school talk about sex."

"Honey . . ." Kacie raised her hand to stop Kenny.

"Mom, please, just listen. I really need to talk to you about this."

Kacie nodded. "I'm sorry, go ahead, baby."

"Anyway, my friends talk about having sex all of the time. And not just my friends, but kids all over the school. They say the safest way not to get a disease or to get a girl pregnant is by . . . well, by," he stammered, "by . . . you know."

"What? By what, Kenny?"

"Oral . . . sex."

"Oh, I see. What did Minister Cecil say about it? I really can't believe y'all talked about something like that."

"Mom, you signed the papers giving your permission. I hope you won't stop me from going to Super Wednesday." A look of fear and disappointment attacked Kenny's young face.

"No, I wasn't thinking that. Go on, I want to know what he said."

"He told us that anything we do outside of marriage is fornication or adultery. He said that sex was invented by God to procreate. Do you know what procreate means, Momma?" Kenny asked, like he was eager to give her the definition.

"Oh, yes, I know what it means." Kacie smiled. "I think I have that down pat. I have seven of y'all running around, and I believe it's because of procreation." She laughed.

Kenny laughed along with his mother. "That's right, but the bad thing about having all of us is that you had us without being married. People who aren't married are not supposed to have sex.

"You're right, son. But I don't regret having each of you in my life. "

"Mom, I never told you that I was sorry for going against you in court that day. But, I was already the laughing stock of the school, in the neighborhood and even at church. Guys were teasing me and calling me sissy because my momma took a girl to court. I know I should have taken your side, but I couldn't. Even though I'm thirteen, I know what me and Jackie did was wrong. Just because she can't get pregnant from oral sex still doesn't make it right. Did you know that a person can still get sexually transmitted diseases from doing that?"

"Uh, yes," answered Kacie. She used one hand to move her weaker leg onto the bed. She felt a little uncomfortable about the conversation, but she hoped Kenny didn't pick up on it.

"Kids say, 'If you don't put it in, it ain't no sin.'"

"What? I never heard that before."

"That's because you're, well, you're old, Mom."

Kacie tried not to giggle. But it was funny that Kenny considered her as old.

"Having sex in any form is wrong, Mom. Minister Cecil says that sex is meant to take place between a man and a woman who are married to each other. You see?" explained Kenny with a look of pride on his handsome face.

"Seems like Minister Cecil knows his stuff."

"He does, Momma. And, oh yeah. I almost forgot. He wants to talk to you about a weekend youth trip next month. He wants me to go."

"Honey." Kacie looked concerned. "First, I want to tell you that I'm sorry about the way I behaved when the incident occurred between you and Jackie. I should never have hit you like I did. Will you forgive me?"

"You're my momma. Of course I forgive you."

Kacie reached out to hug her son. "Now, about this church outing. Is the church sponsoring it? How many other kids are going?" She shot off one question after another. "And it depends on the cost as to whether I can afford to send you. What is it about, and when is it, anyway?"

"It's in Chattanooga, Tennessee. It's a weekend retreat with other youths coming from several churches. I'll learn how to become a junior youth counselor. I'll get a certificate at the end of the course; then when summer camp starts, I can get a job at one of the church retreats and work as a junior counselor. Minister Cecil said once I get my certification, I can get a stipend when I work with the younger kids. I could help you out with bills and stuff. It'll be great." Kenny jumped up and turned around, then smacked his hands together.

"Kenny, honey calm down. It sounds good, but it still depends on the cost." Kacie got up out of the bed. "And bills are not for you to worry about," she reassured him.

"I guess that's why Minister Cecil wants to talk to you. He was going to say something to you tonight, but Minister Briars called him and the other youth ministers into a meeting. But I gave him your phone number."

Kacie had gotten up and was about to walk toward the kitchen, but she whipped around and stood still at the bedpost. "You did what? Kenny, why did you do that?"

"He already has my cell phone number, so I didn't think it would do any harm if I gave him yours. It's listed in the Members' Directory, anyway, isn't it?"

"Well, we'll see. That's all I can promise."

Kenny ran beside his mother, picked her up off her feet, and twirled her around.

"Ahhh, boy, put me down." Kacie laughed and lightly pounded her son on his shoulders.

Kenny put her down and then hugged her and kissed her on the cheek.

"Momma, I'm so glad God saved our family."

"Me too, Kenny. Me too." She hugged him. "I think it's about time you double-check your homework and get ready for bed. Okay?"

"Yes, ma'am. Good night, Momma. See you in the morning."

"G'night, son. I love you."

"Love you too." Kenny disappeared down the hall, while Kacie went into the kitchen to fix a cup of hot chocolate.

Sipping on her hot drink, she sat at the kitchen table. Then she bowed her head in prayer on behalf of her friends. The phone rang almost as soon as she finished praying.

"Miss Mayweather, please."

"This is Miss Mayweather," Kacie replied.

"Miss Mayweather, this is Minister Cecil from Cummings Street."

"Hello, Minister Cecil. I was expecting your call. Kenny told me he gave you my phone number."

"Yes, he did. I hope you don't mind, but I wanted to talk to you about Kenny."

Kacie's smile line formed. "No, I—I don't mind at all," she stammered nervously after hearing his baritone voice. It sounded even more engaging than when he talked face-to-face with her.

"Let me apologize because I know it's late, but I just made it home from church. I hoped I could talk to you before you left Bible Study tonight, but I ended up having to meet with some of the other ministers."

"It's no problem."

"First let me tell you how proud I am of your son. Since he's been attending Super Wednesday, I've seen a new boy materialize. He's more confident, eager to learn about God's Word, and he enjoys participating in youth group activities. Which is the reason I called," explained Minister Cecil.

Kacie smiled. "Kenny told me about a trip y'all have planned for some of the youths."

"Right. We're going to the Youth Ministry Conclave in Chattanooga."

"What does it involve?" asked Kacie as she took a sip of hot chocolate.

"It's for youth ministers such as myself and core student leaders. I highly recommend Kenny to become one of the core student leaders. He'll receive over sixty hours of quality training from some of the best youth ministry leaders around. I believe God has purposely designed this for Kenny. He's thirteen years old and in the ninth grade, which means he's an exceptionally bright young man. And though he's too young to actually be employed by the church, he'll be able to receive a stipend by working with some of the older counselors as a Core Student Leader-in-training, or junior counselor is what they call it. When he turns fifteen, and if he continues to remain in the program, he'll automatically become part of the youth staff during camp season."

"Oh, this is such a blessing for Kenny. Thank you, Minister Cecil. One thing about Kenny is that he's always been smart. Since he started school, he's been involved in CLUE, tested and moved twice to a higher grade; first from second grade to third grade, and this past year he tested again and skipped eighth grade."

"Yes, Miss Mayweather, God is awesome."

"You can call me Kacie."

"Kacie, God proves His love for us all the time. If it wasn't for Kenny being in the ninth grade, he wouldn't be able to participate."

"Oh, this is a blessing. Tell me, Minister Cecil, what will he learn and is there a cost?"

"Well, the good thing about this retreat is that youth ministers and church leaders can invite some of their key students to be a part of the retreat. The goal is to develop student leaders by teaching them biblical principles, show them how God can use them to be an agent of change in their generation. After spending time talking to Kenny, I find him to be a remarkable young man. He's eager to learn about the Word of God. He and the other youth we chose will be able to come back to the church, their schools, and their neighborhoods and have a plan of attack against the enemy."

"Everything you've said sounds good, but I still haven't heard you mention the cost?"

"The cost is two hundred and twenty-five dollars. That includes his food, study materials, and lodging."

"Did you say two hundred and twenty-five dollars?" Kacie's voice rose higher than she expected. There was no way she could afford that amount of money, no matter how great the retreat would be for her son. "Look, I have to be honest, Minister Cecil. I have seven kids and I only work a part-time job. As much as I would love for Kenny to go, there's no way I can afford it."

"Hold on, Sister Kacie. Let me finish. I've already made the necessary arrangements for Kenny to receive one of the scholarships the program offers."

"What?" Kacie squealed into the phone.

"Kenny will not have to pay a dime, not even for food. All he'll need to bring is himself, some toiletries, bed linen and clothes."

"That's it? Are you sure?

"I'm very sure."

"Oh, thank you, Lord. Thank you, thank you, Lord. And thank you, Minister Cecil." Kacie started to cry with much joy.

"I take it that you're giving him permission to attend." Minister Cecil laughed lightly on the phone.

"Yes, of course, of course he can go."

"The retreat is next month from the fourth through sixth. Kenny will get more details about it, and so will you. I'm glad that he's going to be able to go. I hope we can get together to talk more about the retreat and some of the awesome things Kenny will have an opportunity to learn. Maybe we can meet one night after Bible Study. I promise, Miss Mayweather, you won't regret it." Minister Cecil cleared his throat. "I mean, allowing Kenny to go to the retreat, that is."

"I believe that." *Ooh wee. Mercy, mercy me,* Kacie reacted internally. "God has just been so good. I don't know what to say. I can't help it. I'm sorry I'm crying like a big baby."

"No need to apologize. God is in the blessing business, you know."

"Yes, He is. I'm so happy for my son. He's such a good child."

"Well, it's late. I'm going to let you go, Sister Kacie. I look forward to seeing you at church Sunday. Have a good night. And God bless you and your family."

"The same to you, Minister Cecil. Good night, and thanks again."

"My pleasure. Goodnight."

After Kacie heard the phone go silent, tears flooded. She lifted up her hands in total praise to God for opening up a door of blessing for her child.

She remained at the kitchen table, praising God, until her tears dried. Then she replayed Minister Cecil's Barry White voice over in her mind. He easily fit the profile of the man in her dream. She shook her head, pushing back thoughts of him out of her mind.

She tried reaching Envy again, but there was still no answer. "Where are you, Envy? And what are you up to?" she asked on Envy's voice mail.

Kacie retreated to her bedroom, climbed into her bed, and reached over for her Bible lying on the nightstand. She flipped through it until she came to the book of Habakkuk. It was the next chapter to read on the schedule for "Reading the Bible in One Year." Tomorrow she would try to settle things between Layla and Envy.

25

Betrayal does that—betrays the betrayer.—Erica Jong

"Hey, Kacie, you called me last night?" asked Envy.

"You know I did, but your phone kept going straight to voice mail."

"I had it turned off. Leonard was over there. So what has Layla told you?"

"I can't talk. I'm at work. Can you come by my house after you get off work? We can talk without interruptions."

"I can do that. I'll be leaving the office today between three and three-thirty. I can be at your place by four o'clock. How does that work for you?"

"That's perfect. The kids will be doing their homework and chores, so four is good. I'll see you then. I need to get back to work before my supervisor walks up on me."

"Okay, bye."

Envy spent most of the morning in meetings discussing new regulatory affairs and procedures sent from their headquarters. They catered lunch during the meeting, so she wasn't free until almost two o'clock.

She thought about calling on one of her other standbys, like Cedric, to spend some time with later on tonight. She hadn't let him cover over in a couple of months. She knew he would be thrilled to hear from her, he always was. But instead of dialing his number, she ended up with Leonard on the phone.

"Hi, beautiful," he said when he answered.

"Hi. How is your day going?" she asked.

"Busy, busy, and busy. After spending time with you last night, I feel energized, like I can conquer anything that comes my way. I've already met with my Direct Reports. Now I'm reviewing a retention report as we speak. I've got a pile of other stuff going on today."

"Humph, isn't that something? I didn't know I had it like that."

"Oh, yes you did. Think we can have a repeat performance tonight?"

"Umm, I don't know. I wouldn't want you to get spoiled. Plus, too much of anything is not good."

"I can never get too much of you. If only I could get you to feel the same way about me, then we could get married and spend the rest of our lives in total bliss with each other and a house filled with little Envy's and Leonard, Jr.'s running around." Leonard laughed.

She understood that Leonard was actually serious. He had a way of hinting around about what he wanted to happen between the two of them through joking, but it caused her to stiffen. She had too many hidden secrets in her life; so even if she wanted to settle down, she couldn't. Leonard wanted children, which was all but impossible for her. She couldn't see herself being a mother, anyway. She didn't trust herself, and after seeing the hard time Kacie had raising her kids, there was no way on earth she wanted to bring a child in the world again.

Regardless, all of the worries about marriage, children, and being in love had to be pushed to the side. She called on her own resolve to keep her from making what she honestly believed would be a mistake in her life.

"We'll see. I'll call you a little later. I told Kacie I would stop by her house for a few minutes this afternoon."

"Okay. I'll be looking forward to it."

"Bye," she said to Leonard.

Five minutes after four, Envy stood at Kacie's front door; her thumb pressed against the doorbell. She was greeted at the door by Kacie, Kassandra, Kyland, and Keith.

"Hi, Auntie Envy," each one of the precious kids said almost in unison.

"Hello, there," Envy said.

Kacie walked up. "Step back, y'all. Let Auntie Envy in.

The two of them hugged. "Hey, girl," said Envy.

"Come on in, girl. Let's go to my room so we can talk. That okay with you?"

"Sure."

"Do you want something to drink or a snack, anything? I haven't started dinner yet."

Envy threw up her hand. "Girl, don't worry about that. I'm fine. I don't want anything."

"Kids, go and finish your homework, and then I want you to clean your rooms. I need to talk to Auntie Envy in private for a little while. Okay?"

"Yes, ma'am," the kids said.

Envy was amazed. More like shocked, to put it mildly. The tone of Kacie's voice was almost angelic. The children were obedient and mannered. Envy couldn't believe it. Kacie truly had made a change for the better.

"How did you do it?" asked Envy.

"Do what?"

"Your whole personality, the way you talk to the children, the way the children respond to you—everything! I'm amazed."

"God did it. The day I walked up there and surrendered my all to God, I'm telling you, Envy, I felt myself being changed. I felt brand-new. I couldn't go back to the old Kacie. I have children that I'm responsible for. I can't allow my past mistakes to hinder me from raising them in the manner in which they deserve to be raised. I can't allow anger, fear, and hatred to rule my life."

They entered Kacie's bedroom, and Kacie pointed Layla to a red-and-navy bedroom chair close to her bed. Kacie sat on the bed and propped her legs up on it.

"I'm proud of you, Kacie. It's been a while since I've been over here around you and the kids. I love this new you."

"I can't go back to the way I was, sleeping around, having babies by this man and that man, looking at myself in the mirror every day and hating what I saw. I can't keep blaming God for my disability; rather, I'm learning how to praise Him for making me just the way I am. I am beautiful, I am kind, and I have a lot to give. I know that He did not make a mistake when He made me. He did not make a mistake when He allowed me to have seven children. I"—Kacie pointed to herself—"made so many wrong choices, but God exchanged my wrong choices for something good—my children."

Envy leaned over and hugged Kacie. "You are a good person, Kacie. You always have been."

"But this visit isn't about me. It's about you and Layla. Tell me what's going on between you two."

"Kacie, I don't know myself. Layla has changed. She's become this...this prima donna-like person. She's like an out-of-control diva. She even tried to blame me for the break up between her and Dennis."

"Are you?" asked Kacie.

"How could you ask me that? She was already talking about she was sick of Dennis, and you know it. If anybody is responsible, it's her. She's the one who chose to run around on the man. Yes, I messed up when I called his house. I should have left well enough alone. But I needed to talk to her about something."

"Come on, Envy. This is me you're talking to. First of all, Layla says that you called Dennis at one or two o'clock in the morning asking for her, when you already knew that she wasn't with him. That only made their already shaky relationship even rockier. And then she finds out that the guy she's been seeing is one of the men you were sleeping with. She says you're jealous. So what do you expect?"

"First, how could I be jealous of the likes of Layla with any man? Look at me. She can never be like me."

"Who says that she's trying to be you, Envy? And the girl is free to date whomever she chooses."

"Not if he belongs to me!" shouted Envy.

A look of disbelief came on Kacie's face. She pressed her lips together. "Why would you even say something like that? That man doesn't belong to you. He's not a pet or a piece of luggage. Come on now. If you were so tripped out about Layla and Tyreek hooking up, why didn't you let the girl know that you had been messing around with him when she first told us about him? Then all of this could have been avoided."

"I started to, but to be honest, I didn't think Tyreek would give her a moment's thought. But when she went to meet him that night, and then he started refusing to answer my text messages and phone calls, I was infuriated. I can't believe he actually fell for someone like her."

"Someone like her? Envy, listen to what you're saying. You're talking like Layla is some—some kind of misfit, or out of her league. It's words like yours that ruin people's lives. All of my life, people have made fun of me; pointing and staring. But you know this, because I've told you and Layla about it more than once. Now that Layla is hitting it off with Tyreek, you're all upset; so upset that you call her names? And you know the girl had no idea you were seeing that man. Come on now, Envy."

"No, she didn't know, but I told Tyreek, and he had the nerve to wave me off, like I was nobody. And how does she know about me and Tyreek anyway?"

"Hold up, that's irrelevant. First of all, you've never mentioned anything about this guy. It's not her fault or mine that you've chosen to keep your love life separate from our friendship. The only man we have ever known, and we really don't know him, is Leonard. You think we don't know you sleep around? Girl, puhleeze. You give the impression that you're the only one who can attract men. Granted, Layla flirts a bit now, and I hate that she did Dennis the way she did, but I am not the one to judge her, and neither should you. We certainly don't go around judging you."

"Still, she had no business fooling around with Tyreek," Envy snapped back. "But I'm so over it now, Kacie. I was over it after she called me up like she was going to do something to me. I admit that the situation had me going for a while, but no more. If they want to be together, so be it. There's nothing he can do for me, anyway."

"He is not your man. He is not your husband, and obviously he is not committed to you. If you would stop and think for a minute, the only reason you're probably so mad is because the man probably isn't at your beck and call anymore. You know you're wrong, Envy."

"Didn't you just hear anything I said? I said she can have him. And if you want to hear me say it, yes, I called Dennis. I wanted him to open his eyes and realize that Layla didn't love him."

"In other words, Layla is turning into a version of you?"

Envy stood up. "I knew you would take her side. You always do."

"Stop it, Envy. Now sit down," ordered Kacie.

Envy sat back down, hesitantly, while rolling her eyes.

"Now you listen to me. God has been good to you. He just brought you through one of the most traumatic events of your life. You could be locked away in a jail cell right now. Your name could be splashed all across the papers, but God worked it out for you. All these years you've been punishing yourself, thinking that sleeping with this man tonight and another one tomorrow gives you control. These men are not Stanton, nor are they your father. It's time to forgive yourself. You have to let go and let the love of God come in your heart."

"Don't you say anything about my daddy! And God is still the one who allowed all of this to happen in the first place. Things could have been so different if only God had been there the day I gave birth to my baby, to guide me—to tell me what to do and what not to do."

Kacie took hold of Envy's hand. "God was there and He's still by your side. There are many things in my life that I can't understand, but it doesn't mean that God has forsaken me. Quite the contrary, if it wasn't for Him, shoot there's no telling where I would be. I think of the men I've laid down with. I could have contracted AIDS. I could be dead and my children wouldn't have a mother. As for my cerebral palsy, there is nothing I can do about it. I am learning that God always knows what He is doing. The same goes for you, and for Layla too. Who are we to judge one another, Envy? And think about it, how can you blame Layla for something she didn't even know about? You have a man who is in love with you; yet you're spending time thinking about a man who you definitely don't love, but you're mad because he happens to have a thing for Layla?"

Envy started to cry. One of Kacie's kids knocked on the door.

"I'll be there, Kendra. Just give me a few more minutes, okay? Mommy's still talking to Auntie Envy."

"Okay, Mommy," said Kendra. "I want to show you something I colored."

"Awright, baby. I'll be there in a few minutes. Okay?"

"Okayyy."

Kacie went to the chair where Envy sat and leaned over to embrace her. She held her head against her chest and allowed her friend's tears to flow. "Give it to God, Envy. It's time to let go and allow Him to fix your life. It's the only way you can heal."

"But I've messed up so badly, Kacie. I've done so much wrong. I don't know how to begin to change."

"That's your problem. You can't change unless God changes you. That's when my life turned around, after I told God that I couldn't do it anymore. I needed Him. Girl, if He did it for me I know He'll do the same for you." Kacie laughed and gently nudged Envy who smiled."

"All you have to do is say His name. Say it, and mean it. Open your heart and let Him come inside and heal your brokenness."

Envy wept. "Please . . . God. Help me. I want to change. I don't want to feel ugly anymore. I want you to show me the true beauty that is inside me. Please."

Kacie continued to hold her. "God heard you. What you're going to have to do now is talk to Layla. Or we'll all get together and talk."

A dazed looking Envy looked up at Kacie with red, swelling eyes. "I don't know if I can. I just don't know, Kacie."

"You can do all things through Christ who strengthens you. Believe me, Envy—I know."

26

Fighting is essentially a masculine idea; a woman's weapon is her tongue. —Hermione Gingold

Saturday morning, shafts of sunlight parted the clouds. The three friends gathered around the breakfast nook at Kacie's. Today, the children were at church for a couple of hours spending time at the Children's Center. The church opened the new Children's Center a few weeks ago. Minister Cecil encouraged Kacie to drop off the kids, or come with them to the center on Saturdays to enjoy all the fun games and activities they had for children, if she didn't have to work.

"Listen, let me tell you two something," said Kacie. "I did not call y'all over here to bicker, fuss, and fight. I could have been with my kids at the Church Center, but I believed it was important that I do this first; it couldn't wait. Come on, y'all, we're friends," she said, and threw up her hands. "Now, the both of you want to sit here with your jaws on swoll and act like you're archenemies? I don't think so."

Layla spoke. Her words sounded like they had been sautéed in a bowl of vinegar. "She," Layla said, and pointed at Envy across the table, "started all of this mess. You know it, Envy. I would never treat you the way you've treated me, and all over some man? And one that I did not know was your personal bed warmer." Layla cut her eyes deeply at Envy.

"You don't know about me or my business. You don't know what was going on between me and Tyreek, so watch your words, sweetie," Envy snapped back, with both hands planted firmly on the table. "They might just come back to bite you."

"You're right, Envy. My point exactly. I didn't know about you and Tyreek. You're the one who made it a secret. When I first told you I met him, you had the freedom at that very moment to tell me that the two of you knew each other, and it wouldn't have been a big deal. I would've stepped aside with no problem, sweetheart. It's sad that Tyreek had to tell me what was going on and not my best friend. And you, you hate it so much that you go behind my back and do what you did to Dennis? But, you call yourself my best friend?"

"I didn't do anything to Dennis. Yeah, I admit I was wrong, but you were deceiving him. And it didn't just start with Tyreek. You were messing off on Dennis way before Tyreek came in the picture. So, hon...ey, that's on you. Actually, I feel sorry for you. You threw away a good man."

"If he's so good, then why don't you go pacify him and make it all better!" Layla yelled.

"Excuse me?" Envy leaned back and gave Layla an evil stare.

"You heard me. It was none of your business, nor was it your place to ask Dennis anything about me when you already knew I wasn't feeling him like he was feeling me. You were supposed to be my best friend, and best friends do not betray one another." Layla sounded hurt.

Kacie sat at the table and played referee. She listened as her two best friends in the entire world argued. But this time it was needed, if Envy and Layla were ever going to get past the hurt they had caused each other.

Kacie soon drifted from the ruckus between Layla and Envy. She hid the smile on her face as she thought about Minister Cecil. She thought about the man she had dreamed about some time ago. Could it have been Minister Cecil in her dream? No, no, no, that would be just too wild. She smiled while Layla and Envy went at each other.

"Kacie, what do you think?" asked Envy.

Kacie looked stunned. She had been in her own world. "What? I'm sorry, I didn't hear the question."

"I said, what do you think about Layla saying that having a relationship with Tyreek shouldn't matter to me, since I'm not in love with him?"

"I recall telling you a while ago that the time had come for us to reevaluate our lives. We all need to change." Kacie's frustration was obvious. "And what's even crazier is you're upset about a man that you care nothing about, but because he likes your best friend, who he didn't know was your best friend, and your best friend happens to like him, but she didn't know he was your lover, and you want to end the friendship with your best friend? Did you get all that?" Kacie sucked in her breath and chewed on her bottom lip.

Envy shook her head. Blood pounded in her temples.

"See, you can't deny it," Layla said to Envy.

Kacie showed no sign of relenting. "Envy, recall how good God has been to you. I don't like bringing up the past, but the truth is the truth, and sometimes it has to be spoken. You lived in your past by carrying it around into your future for a long time. You carried around guilt, self-hatred, and a number of other negative stuff in your life over something that happened when you were a young girl. How many times do I have to remind you how God turned everything around? Wake up. Shucks.

For the first time in all these years, you can finally live free. You don't have to be afraid to let love into your life. You don't have to walk around with a needless burden. And whether you want to admit it or not, you have someone who adores you."

"Who?" The edge was apparent in Envy's voice.

"You know who I'm talking about—Leonard. Maybe it's time you give the man a chance. He's been hanging around, chasing after you, running after you for a long time. I know you're feeling him too. Y'all go together like peanut butter and jelly," Kacie said, and started laughing.

Envy cracked a smile. "Okay. Never heard it put quite like that before. But I hear you."

"And you"—Kacie shifted her eyes toward Layla—"God has His reasons for what and who He allows to enter our lives. I think I can speak for us when I say I don't think any of us wanted to see Dennis get hurt. But that's something you have to settle in your own heart. Still, it doesn't mean that he's your mate. Only you and God know that."

Layla nodded.

"And back to you, Envy. I think you should apologize to Dennis for your act of deceit and to Tyreek, and Layla," she emphasized, "for trying to sew discord."

Envy looked down toward the table. "Who would have thought?" Envy said, and looked up to smile at Kacie, then at Layla, then back at Kacie.

"Thought what?" asked Kacie. Her eyebrows raised in question.

"That you would be the person to make sense of everything," Envy said. "But I must say, spoken like a true mother." They all laughed aloud for the first time since the three of them had gathered.

Envy stopped chuckling and turned serious. "Layla, Kacie is right. I have been wrong. I treated you unfairly. Will you forgive me for all of the nasty things I said, the trouble I caused?" Envy asked.

Layla cried and nodded. "Yes…and I'm sorry too."

Kacie got up from the table. "Come on, group hug."

27

Saying sorry doesn't mean there isn't guilt, and forgiving doesn't mean the pain is gone. —Unknown

Several weeks passed before Envy made up her mind to go and see Tyreek at Precious Cargo. Her plan was to make amends. At her first approach, Tyreek was apprehensive, but Layla had already told him about the make-up session she and Envy had at Kacie's.

Tyreek took a break so he could listen to what she had to say. Her voice sounded sincere and she held back tears that wanted to burst forth, but Envy was one who refused to be completely vulnerable.

"I was jealous. That's all it boils down to."

"I don't understand. You never wanted me. I had a thing for you, a serious thing for you at one time but I had to come to my senses because deep down I knew you didn't feel the same. I dealt with it because I wasn't serious about any other female myself." A broad smile filled Tyreek's face. Envy had to admit that Tyreek was a nice man. Maybe, just maybe, he and Layla would be good for one another.

"You're right. But not loving you made it easier for me to be with you intimately, if that makes sense. I didn't have to be concerned with falling in love. It was a way for me to hide the pain that I was suffering on the inside. I thought by sleeping with men, and using them instead of them using me, that I was proving something.

Turns out, all I proved was that I was promiscuous and setting myself to become a lonely, old, bitter woman one day. But I didn't come here to talk about me. I came to ask you to forgive me for hurting you, and for trying to ruin the relationship you obviously want to build with Layla. Both of you are good people. I wish you the best, Tyreek. Maybe we can be friends – without benefits."

Envy and Tyreek chuckled.

"Maybe. To hear you say you're sorry makes me feel that I can let go of the part I played in our relationship too. It's not like you forced me to do what I did; I wanted it too. But now, I know I want to move on to something more in my life."

I'm looking to start up another business. I've been managing this place long enough. I'm still going to maintain my partnership, but it's time to move on to something bigger and better."

Envy looked surprised. "I never knew you had a hand in Precious Cargo. Wow, good for you."

"I want to open another spot, more family style," said Tyreek. "I have a few leads on some places that some top realtors who come in here passed on to me. I'm going to follow up on them."

"You'll do it. Maybe I'll see you at church with your lady sometimes."

"Yeah, maybe," Tyreek said, and stood up to hug her.

She returned his embrace before she turned around, and walked out of Precious Cargo, without looking back.

~

Layla knocked on the door of Dennis's house. He opened the door and stood quietly, looking at her.

"May I come in?"

Dennis answered by stepping aside. He remained just on the other side of the door, and he didn't extend an invitation to go farther.

"To what do I owe this visit?"

"I need to talk to you."

"What do you want? If you're coming to gloat, or play the pitiful role, you can turn around and leave." He walked away from the door. Layla stepped inside but remained next to the entrance.

"Dennis, you were always good to me. I know you probably won't believe me when I tell you that I did love you. I still do."

"I know the old cliché, but you're not in love with me. Save it, Layla. Don't come over here trying to make yourself feel better."

Layla remained at the door. "It's not that way. I really was in love with you—for a time. And I still love you now. I'll always love you. People come and go in our lives for various reasons. "

"Don't give me that hogwash. I don't want to hear it."

"Please, don't turn me away. I need to say this."

Dennis stared. "Go on say what you have to say. The sooner you do, the sooner you can leave."

"Okay, I can't fault you for being angry."

"I'm not angry." His voice was cold. "I'm busy."

Layla took a deep breath. "Dennis, you came in my life when I was a victim, a victim at the hands of another person, but also a victim of myself. You helped me when I was still recovering physically and emotionally. You loved me when I was fat, and when I hated myself. You're the one God used to reveal to me that whether I was fat or not, I was not the ugly person who kept staring back at me in the mirror. You're the one who helped me begin to see that no matter what size I was, I was still beautiful."

Dennis sighed and turned his head away.

"Please don't turn away from me. All I'm here to ask is for your forgiveness. I'm sorry, so sorry that you had to be hurt in the process of me becoming new. Sure, I was caught up in doing all the things I thought normal-size women did. I could go into a department store and pick out dresses from the regular sizes instead of the plus sizes. For the first time, after losing all of the weight, I could wear boots and even walk in a pair of stilettos. Shucks, I could stand before the mirror and see a body that I used to pray that I could have. I had no idea it was going to happen during an attempted murder on my life. But it did, and I accepted it. Weight fell off me so fast that it made my head spin. And you, you were there to see the transformation."

"Yes, a transformation that changed you for the worse. You became conceited and self-centered." He shook his head regretfully. "To be honest, I liked the woman you were before you dropped all of the weight."

"I'm sure you did, and some of that woman is still inside me." Her cheeks burned in remembrance. "But when I lost weight, I turned away from God and stopped doing all the things I used to do for Him when I was big. I felt like I'd put in more than my share of serving Him during my fat days, and so it was time for me to do me." She pinched her lower lip with her teeth, and a look of dismay washed over her face. "I didn't have to sing in the choir anymore. I was part of it because it was the only thing I had to do. Don't you think I got tired of hearing 'fat people can sing'? Well, I can sing, and I'm not fat anymore. And I still love God, but I wanted to take a break from Him. So I flirted with men, something I never saw myself ever being able to do. I spent frivolously on clothes and shoes and purses." Layla cautiously took a step further inside.

Dennis walked to the door and closed it.

Layla's voice broke miserably. "I wanted to be free and beautiful like Envy and other pretty girls, and finally that day had arrived. But along the way, I hurt you; because in the end, I met someone whom I never expected to fall in love with."

"I'm glad for you, Layla. I won't deny that I'm hurt. My heart is heavy. I honestly believed that one day we would become husband and wife. I always knew you were a good woman. And I accept your apology." He sighed heavily, his voice filled with anguish. "I can't see you, or be friends with you, though. I need some time for me, time to heal. Because I do love you, I want the best for you. I want you to be happy, and most of all, I want you to have someone who loves you just as much as you love them." His expression was grim. "Even if I'm not that man," he said.

"I respect what you're saying, Dennis. I'll stay out of your way." She gulped hard, but the tears still found their way down her cheeks. "Just like you want the best for me, I want the best for you. I want you to have someone who loves you the way you deserve to be loved, and I'm going to be praying about that."

They stood at the door in silence. Layla saw Dennis's eyes become watery.

"I'd better go," she said.

"Yeah, I think that would be best."

Layla turned toward the door.

Dennis stepped in front of her and opened it. "Take care of yourself. Be happy."

"Thanks, Dennis. You don't know how much that means to me."

Layla left and drove to her parents. She went to talk to her mother about some of the things she had already shared with her about her breakup with Dennis and about her relationship with Tyreek. She sat in the den with her mother. Her father was still at work.

"Honey, I can't live your life for you," her mother said. "I can only pray for you and your brothers. Dennis is a good man, but I don't need to keep telling you that. I'm sure you've heard it over and over again. Now, this other man, you say he's a fine man; so again, I trust that you know what you're talking about. I'm glad to hear that you and Envy worked things out. Just like God forgives us, we must extend forgiveness toward one another. And y'all have been friends too long to let some mess come between you."

"You're right, Mother. You know something?"

"What?"

"I'm grateful to have godly parents. I'm just so grateful."

"Show God how grateful you are then."

"What do you mean, Mother? I'm back at church on a regular basis. I pray. And I know that I'm saved, so what else can I do?"

"Use your God-given gifts. Fulfill the purpose God has assigned to you. Now I have to get up and get your daddy's dinner ready. You're welcome to stay if you like."

"No, I have a couple more errands to run." Layla kissed her mother. "I'll let myself out."

"Okay. Remember what I say to you. Show God how grateful you are."

Layla walked away a little bit confused. What was her mother talking about? She locked the door behind her and drove off. The radio came on and she found herself singing along with the song, and suddenly she understood. It was time.

28

The hunger for love is much more difficult to remove than the hunger for bread. —Mother Teresa

Minister Cecil adored Kacie and her kids. The past months had brought an additional source of joy into his life in the form of the Mayweather family. He believed he was blessed because God allowed him to meet such a strong, inspirational, kind and gorgeous woman. He recognized her struggles, and was drawn in by her sense of naivety and how much she desired to grow spiritually. Her smile made him smile, something no woman had been able to do since his divorce. But Kacie was different.

The more they talked, the more he wanted to talk. Talking to one another after Bible Study had grown into talking on the phone about once or twice a week. Initially it was mostly about church events and her children. Kacie didn't care; she enjoyed talking to a male on the phone. It was refreshing. It felt good to have someone other than Kacie and Envy show genuine interest in her children and their well-being, as well as in hers.

"Have you ever been married?" he asked her one night during one of their phone chats. Phone chats that slowly turned more personal over time.

"No," she said in a tiny, shameful sounding whisper.

"I see," he said.

"Let me tell you up front." She spoke with light bitterness. "I've made a mess of my life, but I am not ashamed of my children."

"And you shouldn't be. I asked because I'm trying to get to know the remarkable woman responsible for such great kids. Anyway, we all have sinned and fallen short. But like I said, I'm just trying to get to know you, Sister Kacie."

"Sure," Kacie replied timidly. It still panged her to have to admit that she had seven children but never a husband. "There's nothing I've done that I haven't already gone to God and asked for His forgiveness."

"I like that. If only all of God's children could see how much He desires for us to pour ourselves out before Him, then we'd all be much better for having done so."

Kacie didn't want to exaggerate, but she felt like there was a physical attraction and spiritual connection between them. She enjoyed talking to Minister Cecil. It came out one evening while they were talking on the phone that he was a divorcé with no children.

Minister Cecil had volunteered to pick up her children early for the Children's Festival because Kacie had to work the morning shift. Even though it was for kids twelve and under, Kenny was excited, mostly because he would be working as one of the youth staff volunteers.

"I'll be at the church as soon as I get off work," she told the kids as they ran off and climbed in the church van. "Thank you, Minister Cecil, for doing this. I didn't want the kids to miss the festival. If it wasn't for you, they wouldn't have been able to go."

"Believe me, it's no problem. I'm more than glad to do it," he told Kacie as he stood at her door. He was a man of medium stature, in his late thirties, with refined, yet suave, good looks. His skin was dark as the night and spotless. His bald head added an extra oomph to his handsome profile, and his muscular arms looked perfect for rescuing a damsel in distress.

"I'll have to do something special for you," Kacie told him as she locked the door to her house.

"That's not necessary," he said. "But if you insist, I won't be one to turn you down." His voice flirtatious.

"Okay, what about letting me prepare dinner for you?" Kacie offered.

"You'd do that for me?" he asked, with teeth that glistened like sparkling pearls.

Kacie was so shaky and nervous, she thought she was about to faint. "Of course."

"Okay, I can't wait then," he said. His smile spoke a thousand words. "I'll see you this afternoon at the festival."

"I can't wait," she said and smiled.

And so was the start of a slow, tentative relationship between Sister Kacie and Minister Cecil. There was hardly a day that passed when they weren't on the phone giggling and having a great conversation.

~

One evening, Minister Cecil invited Kacie to dinner. Envy and Layla stayed with the kids.

"This is nice," Kacie told him as they sat in a booth at Macaroni Grill.

"I think so too," Minister Cecil replied. "I wonder how your friends are doing with the kids?" he asked as he put a forkful of pasta in his mouth.

Kacie threw her head back slightly and laughed. "You mean, how are the kids doing with them? Neither one of them is used to babysitting, so I'm sure I'm going to get an earful when I get home—from the kids, that is."

"Well, I bet Kenny is milking it for all it's worth," Minister Cecil said. "He's enjoying the company, I bet."

"Yeah, and Envy and Layla were ordering pizza, one of his favorite foods."

"Oh, good," said Minister Cecil. "Maybe we need to do this more often. You know, so the kids can get a break," he said, and then laughed, and so did Kacie. "But, seriously, do you mind if I speak from my heart for a minute?"

"Uh, no. Go ahead." Kacie hesitated. "I think," she added.

"Look, let me be real. Sister Kacie, it's no secret that I'm developing feelings for you."

Kacie detected a faint tremor in his voice, like some emotion had touched him. "Is that so? I, uh." She shifted her eyes away and looked down at her food. "I feel the same," she confessed.

"Ah, that's good to hear. I feel at ease and I want you to know that my feelings aren't just for you, Kacie. I'm concerned about your kids too. I certainly don't want to rush you into anything, but by the same token, I want you to be aware of my intentions."

Kacie gave a short, nervous laugh and then smiled. "Your intentions? What exactly are you saying?" she asked.

"I'm saying that I want to try to build something between us. That is, if you want to."

Kacie blushed. "I don't know what to say."

"Sister Kacie, I have been on three tours to Iraq and back. I've been married and divorced. I've been alone, not involved with anyone since my divorce four years ago. But it's all been good because I've been able to give my all to God and the ministry He's called me to. But God also knows that I desire someone in my life. Not just anyone, but someone with whom I can hope to build a future. I've been praying and asking Him for His guidance, Sister Kacie. And then you come along and it's like God just, just opened my heart. I don't know about you, but I take God at His word. And He's never steered me wrong."

Kacie remained transfixed. She couldn't believe the words she was hearing. Was there really someone, other than God, who could love her and see past all of her faults and shortcomings? Maybe he was really the man in her dreams. Could it be him?

"This is, uh, how should I put it? Weird is the only word I can think of right now."

"Ohhkay. I apologize. I didn't mean to come off like a...a...uh weirdo." He looked nervous.

"No," she put her hands up and shook her head and laughed. "I'm not saying you're weird. I'm saying the situation is weird, kind of."

"I'm not trying to pressure you into anything. I'm one of those fellows who wears his heart on his coat sleeve I guess. I believe in telling it like it is. And believe me, I respect you, Sister Kacie. I respect you a lot. I would never intentionally say or do anything to make you feel uncomfortable when you're around me."

"It's not that. But anyway, just let me say that since I met you, you've helped me along my journey toward the woman I believe God wants me to be. I have a better outlook on my life. I feel it's broader and more divinely positive. My knowledge of how special I am in God's eyes increases every day." She looked at him and chuckled.

"What's so funny?" he asked.

"I was just thinking."

"Thinking about what?"

"I have seven children — seven is the number of completion. Each one of my children is a blessing in the midst of my mess. God is truly doing a great work in my life."

"See, that's what I mean."

Kacie looked confused. "What are you talking about?"

"Listen to yourself. How can you blame me for wanting to get to know you better? And you give me too much credit, not that I don't like it." He giggled. "But it's God who's molding you, not me."

"I know it's God, but God uses people too. And I know He's using you in my life...in a good way of course."

Minister Cecil changed the subject. "Hey, I was excited when I heard you signed up to be one of the facilitators of the Single Parents Ministry." I know you're going to do an outstanding job." He reached over and gently laid his hand on top of hers.

Umph, I like this man. And not like I liked all the other ones. There's something different about him. "I tell you, signing up to be a facilitator took a giant leap of faith for me. But it was like something pulling me to volunteer to do it. I've only facilitated one time so far, but I enjoyed it. I really, really did. I have to facilitate again next month. I'm actually looking forward to it too."

"That's good, Sister Kacie. I'm proud of you." He lightly massaged her hand with his fingertips.

Kacie, Please. At least when we're by ourselves," she reminded him.

"I'm sorry. I keep forgetting. I'm so used to addressing the ladies as sisters."

"I understand. I know it's going to take some getting used to. It still feels weird calling you Cecil too." *But I'm getting used to it, mercy me,* were her thoughts.

Cecil was the kind of man that fed her spirit and helped her move from infancy in Christ toward His fullness. He seemed to look past her past. Didn't appear to be bothered about whether her children were by the same man or different men. He never asked, but during one of their phone conversations, Kacie told him that a different man fathered each of her children. He didn't sound disturbed by it, but she had no idea what kind of expression he wore on his face on the other side of the phone. She was just glad she told him. It wasn't that she felt she needed to tell him, she just did.

"Kacie, I'm not perfect. No one is." He interrupted her thoughts. "But I want to be part of your life and the lives of your children. I enjoy seeing you and them happy and smiling. It doesn't matter about your past. It doesn't matter that you have seven children. None of that matters. What matters is your sweet, sweet spirit. What matters is all the love I know you're waiting to give."

"Cecil, I don't know what to say. I wasn't expecting this," Kacie said.

"Why don't you start by not saying anything. Let it marinade for a few days." He flashed a dazzling white smile, which almost melted her heart like butter.

Kacie grinned. "Well, that's easy enough to do...I think." Her mind burned with the memory of the man in her dream. "I'd like that. I'd really like that."

"Nice," he said and squeezed her hand. A slight chill rushed through her body. Her spirit seemed to sync with his and she felt a tremendous peace consume her. He eased up slightly from his seat in the booth, leaned over, and kissed her. It was a light, tender, but lingering one.

She responded like she'd never been kissed. It was mesmerizing. Most of all, it felt right, oh so right.

When he pulled away, he took both of her hands in his.

Kacie's eyes were glued to his like she'd been hypnotized. She couldn't remember ever a man talking to her the way Cecil did. It felt good to have a man who wanted to take her out, who wanted to see her smile, who wanted to be around her, and who enjoyed her children. *Thank you, God for giving me exceeding, abundantly more than I can ever ask, hope, or think.*

29

None of us knows what the next change is going to be, what unexpected opportunity is just around the corner, waiting to change all the tenor of our lives. —Kathleen Norris

Kacie and Envy took their usual places in the sanctuary for Sunday morning worship service. They participated in the praise team songs and they held hands as they made their way down the aisle and to the altar for prayer.

A great change had occurred. Their very lives had been tested in ways that had been beyond their comprehension.

This morning, Minister Cecil read the scripture. Kacie blushed when he approached the podium in a striped cobalt blue and white polo shirt, with navy double-pleated dress pants. His dark navy loafers looked soft as lamb's skin. One of the things most people loved about Cummings Street was the fact that Pastor Betts encouraged people to come to church as you are. He also showed by example. It was seldom that he or his ministerial staff dressed in suits and ties.

Envy happened to look at Kacie. Kacie had a big smile on her face when Minister Cecil approached the podium. "I know that look," Envy said to Kacie.

Kacie broke into a wide open smile.

Envy giggled softly, then turned and focused her attention on Minister Cecil as he spoke.

"Please stand for the reading of the Word of God." Almost everyone in the sanctuary stood. "Turn your Bibles to Isaiah chapter forty-three and verse two. I'm reading from the New International Version, and it says, 'When you pass through the waters, I will be with you; and when you pass through the rivers, they will not sweep over you. When you walk through the fire, you will not be burned; the flames will not set you ablaze.'"

For a split second, her eyes appeared to connect with Minister Cecil's eyes. They looked at each other and smiled in earnest before she sat down. Her heart leaped because God had blessed her with a man like Cecil. He loved her children, and they loved him. This was an awesome year so far for Kacie. Just like the change of seasons, winter to spring to summer, so had Kacie's life taken on a remarkable, life-altering transformation.

Kacie and Minister Cecil became a recognizable couple at church. During the course of their budding relationship, he shared the intimate details concerning his divorce. Due to an injury he sustained during his first military deployment to Iraq, he was sterile.

He believed a miracle had occurred when his wife initially told him she was pregnant. But when the child was born, Cecil was met by another man at the hospital who claimed to be the child's father.

Cecil's' hopes were dashed after he went to the doctor to confirm whether the child his wife had given birth to could actually be his. Unfortunately, the news was not as he'd hoped, and it was then that his wife confessed that she'd been seeing someone else, the man at the hospital, and it was that man's child. She ended up leaving Cecil for her lover. Cecil explained to Kacie that he filed for divorce and prayed never to look back, and he hadn't.

He confessed to Kacie his desire from the time he was a young man to have a house full of children one day. However, he accepted being unable to have children as God's will and so devoted himself to working with the young people at church.

Kacie pleasantly thought about the dinner she had prepared for her children and Cecil. He would be there following church services, just like he had been doing quite a bit lately, unless he took her and the kids out to eat.

"Excuse me." Kacie looked up. Tyreek stood at the end of the pew, looking as fine as ever in a traditional black suit, starched white shirt, and a black tie.

Kacie's and Envy's mouths remained open while they moved down along the pew to make room for him.

"Layla didn't tell us you would be here today, but I'm glad you came," Kacie whispered.

"She doesn't know. I thought I'd surprise her. Oh, and you're going to have to scoot over a little more. We're going to need space for one more."

Envy didn't exactly feel awkward with Tyreek being at church but seeing him there was the last thing she expected, or so she thought.

"Who else is coming?" Envy leaned over and asked. Before Tyreek answered, another tall, well-dressed, handsome man walked up. This time it was Envy's turn to be surprised as Leonard excused himself and went farther down the pew to sit next to her.

Envy looked at him, then she allowed her eyes to rove around the sanctuary."

"Is that Leonard?" Kacie tugged on Envy's blouse.

"Yes," Envy answered through clenched teeth while her eyes followed Leonard as he sat down on the other side of her.

"Aren't you going to speak?" Leonard asked.

"Hi," she basically stammered. "Where's your lady?"

"Sitting next to me." He reached over and squeezed her hand.

Envy didn't resist. She felt all the years of reserve, of holding back, of being afraid to love, begin to thaw. No one had time to engage in conversation because Pastor Betts was in the pulpit.

Pastor Betts walked to the podium after Minister Cecil finished. "I know the choir has practiced what they're singing today. All I can say is that we're in for a treat. God is a good God. Oh yes, He is."

Layla's eyes locked with Tyreek's, and a huge, huge look of surprise came over her face before she started smiling. He nodded. Layla inhaled and then stood up and walked to the mic. The choir director got in position. The musicians began to play "You've Been So Faithful" by Minister Eddie James. For the first time in three years, Layla truly understood the meaning of the gift God had blessed her with. She began to sing the song, until the spirit of the Lord rained down on her. "'. . . Even though I've done wrong, You never left me alone,'" Layla sang, "'but You forgave me, and You kept on blessing me.'"

At the sound of her voice, Tyreek began to stare with a look of disbelief. It was powerful and anointed. His eyebrows rose with obvious pleasure and he looked like he was showing all thirty-two teeth. People all over the sanctuary stood up, clapping, singing along and praising God.

Envy and Kacie joined in. Next Tyreek and Leonard stood up and started clapping.

The spirit of God was moving. Change was definitely in the air.

After church ended, the vestibule was crowded with people in line to purchase tapes of the sermon, fellowshipping with one another, and leaving out the sanctuary.

"Layla ought to be coming out the choir room by the time Kacie comes back from getting the kids," Envy explained to Tyreek.

"Thanks," he said.

"And you Mr. Stein, you were another surprise today. Uh, did I miss something? Was there a special news flash or breaking news that told you to come to church today?"

"I'll do whatever it takes," he told her. "And I have to give it up to your pastor; the brother can teach and preach. What about me and you going out for a bite to eat?"

"Umm, I don't know," Envy replied.

"Why don't you know? I don't believe it's a tough decision. All you have to do is form the word, yes, let it come from your mouth and we'll be off." He looked directly in her eyes.

"Yes," Envy answered. "Come on, let's go. I'll follow you."

"I'll follow you to your house and you drop your car off. We'll go in mine – together."

"Umph, I heard that. I'll see you at my house in about fifteen minutes then."

"Sounds good to me." Leonard turned toward Tyreek. He had no idea that Tyreek had been one of Envy's past lovers. "Hey, man. It was nice meeting you."

"Same here, man," Tyreek said. They gave each other dap.

"See ya, Tyreek. Layla should be here any—"

Layla walked up. "I couldn't believe it when I saw you sitting out there with Kacie and Envy."

"And I couldn't believe you could blow like that either, woman," Tyreek said and embraced her.

"You ain't heard nothing yet," Envy told him. "Layla, I'm out of here."

"And who is this?" Layla asked looking at Leonard.

"Oh, I forgot you've never met Leonard. Leonard this is Layla. Now you've met the three musketeers."

"Nice to meet you. Hey, he's right," Leonard said pointing to Tyreek. "You can sing, girl."

"Thank you. And it's nice to finally meet you. We've heard a lot about you. All good of course."

"Oh, is that right? That's good to know, especially since you say it was all good." Leonard moved in closer to Envy and wrapped his hand around her waist.

Tyreek appeared to flinch but if Layla or Envy noticed, neither of them said anything.

"Layla, me and Leonard are going to get something to eat. I'll talk to you later."

"Okay. Y'all have a good time. Oh, has Kacie come out here yet?"

"No, she must be still getting the kids."

"Or getting the kids and her man," Layla teased.

"You're probably right. Anyway, I'm outta here. I'll talk to you later on. Bye."

"Bye. And, Leonard, I hope this won't be the last time you come to Cummings Street."

"It won't. Nice to meet you."

"You too. Bye, y'all."

"Look, I'm going to vamp. I just wanted to surprise you, that's all," Tyreek told Layla.

"Well, mission accomplished. Thank you for coming."

"I had a good time. Felt like the good old days."

"What are you getting ready to do now?"

"I'm meeting some friends and we're going to watch the game. I'll call you later, okay?"

"Sure," Layla said, but sounded somewhat disappointed.

"What?" Tyreek asked.

"Nothing. I just thought we could spend some time together this afternoon."

"Baby, I already had this planned. But we'll get together, maybe later on tonight." He kissed her on the cheek. "You going to wait on your friend?"

"Naw, I guess I'm going to go by my parents' house and spend a little time with them."

"Good," Tyreek said and they started to move toward the exit and out of the vestibule. "I'll walk you to your car."

"Okay."

~

Kacie gathered the kids and headed toward the vestibule. It had taken longer than usual for her to meet up with Layla and Envy, but Cecil had stopped her just as she was coming from the nursery.

"Hey, I'll see you in about an hour," he told her while playing around with the smaller kids.

"Sounds good. That'll give us time to get home and changed. Pastor spoke a powerful message today, didn't he?"

"Yes, he did and it was right on time too."

"Did you happen to see two men sitting by me and Envy?"

"Yeah. You know 'em?"

"Not really. I officially met them today. One of 'em was Envy's friend and the other one was Layla's. Layla and Envy didn't know they were coming. Envy's friend has been here before."

"Oh, that's good. Maybe we'll gain two more members. It's always good to have men come and give God His due service."

"Well, honey, I'm going to go and see if they're still waiting on me in the vestibule, then I'm headed home. I'll see you in a few."

"Okay. Bye, kids," he said.

Minister Cecil turned and walked back toward the sanctuary. He was stopped by one of his friends who was also on the ministerial staff.

"Man, you really are into Sister Kacie, aren't you?"

"Yea, man. I'm crazy about that woman."

"I just don't see it. How can you deal with a woman who already has a ready-made basketball team?" he said sarcastically.

"What's wrong with her?"

"Man, you know how many women in this church that's after you? You're a single man and you want to get caught up with a female with seven kids. And I don't know if you know this or not, but I heard every one of them kids have different daddies. I don't have to tell you what that means." He looked at his friend like he'd just committed a serious crime.

"Terrence, I don't like what you're insinuating," he responded as they entered the sanctuary. "Kacie is a great woman. And some of these women running around here, all they want is to snag themselves a man."

"And you trying to say she's not one of 'em? Come on now, Cecil. Don't fall for the okie doke, man. Sister Kacie, fine as she is, looking for someone to help with all of them little rugbrats." Terrence laughed.

"Stop it, man. I won't stand here and listen to you talk about her like that. That's disrespectful, man. And you don't know anything about her because if you did, you would see that she isn't like all these other females running up in my face. We all have a past, man. You and I know that for sure. We've been friends for a long time and we weren't always men of God. We still don't always act like men of God. You know it and I know it."

"I'm just saying, man. I was just trying to look out for you. I don't want you going all crazy over here because of those kids. I know you love children, and I know your condition, man, but hey, I hope you go to God on this one, for real. That's all I'm talking about. Be sure about what you're doing and what you're getting yourself into with a chick like that."

"I have gone to God, on this one, as you put it. And what God spoke to me about a chick like that is between me and Him. So back off."

Terrance raised both hands. "Cool, man. You happy – I'm happy."

They gave each other dap.

"Come on, man; let's finish up in here. I don't know about you, but I'm starving. Cherise and I are going out to eat. You want to come along?"

"No, I have a dinner date already." Cecil patted his friend on the back and smiled.

"I heard that. Look, man. I didn't mean any harm. Sister Kacie does seem cool. I'm sorry I stepped to you like that. You're a smart man, and I know you know what you're doing. I just don't want to see you get hurt; that's all."

"No problem, man. But believe me, I'm good. Real good."

Maybe Terrance couldn't understand the love he had developed toward Kacie. Maybe it would be difficult for people to see him with a woman that many labeled as loose. But Minister Cecil was glad that God looked beyond the faults of His children and saw their hearts.

Minister Cecil talked to Pastor Betts about his growing feelings toward Kacie during one of their private times together. Pastor Betts reminded him about the story of Hosea and Gomer.

After listening to Pastor Betts' wise, Godly counsel, Minister Cecil was further convinced that Kacie was the woman for him. Maybe she was a Gomer in her own way. But the wonderful consolation he found in Kacie was that no matter who she was or what she'd done, God had prepared her just for him.

30

"His hands are saying that he wants to hold her. His feet are saying that he wants to chase after her... He's probably forgotten that I'm here, beside him." Ai Yazawa

Layla lay underneath the sanctity of Tyreek's arm, which was wrapped securely around her shoulders. Their lovemaking had left Layla sure, more than ever, that she was falling deeply in love with him. She snuggled closer to him, her backside nestled against his front, so close that there was no space between them. Looking up toward him, their eyes locked.

He leaned forward and kissed her on her lips. "What are you thinking about?"

"Oh, just about how happy I am right now." She shifted her body over to directly face him. "Everything is finally going right in my life. I mean, don't get me wrong, things have definitely been better than ever, but it's like the icing on the cake now. I've met someone who makes me feel whole, complete." Tears glistened in both corners of her eyes. "I can't help it, I'm in love with you, Tyreek."

Tyreek's relaxed body stiffened. He lifted himself up and rested on his elbow. Looking down at Layla he sighed then said, "I don't think what you feel for me is love. At least I hope it isn't."

Layla moved her naked body until she was sitting upright in the bed. Tyreek sat up too. She looked at him with disdain. "Why do you hope it's not like that? I can't help it if I love you. Don't you feel the same?"

"I like you. I like you a lot. But love, it's way too soon for me to say those words. And it should be the same for you."

Layla stared. A look of disbelief plastered on her face. "I cannot believe this." She pushed the sheets off of her and preceded to grab her clothes from the nearby bedroom chaise.

"What are you doing?" he asked. "I know you aren't calling yourself getting an attitude because I don't want you to be in love with me."

"Oh, it's more than an attitude." She continued talking while she hurriedly dressed like she was late for a flight. "I cannot believe I let myself fall for your crap. I see why you hit it off with Envy so well."

"And what is that supposed to mean? You women kill me. You always say you want a man who will tell you the truth, then when you run across one, you blow up when he doesn't say what you want to hear. I said I like you, Layla. I like you a lot. But I am not in love with you. I'm not trying to hurt you, or upset you, but I won't lie to you either. Who knows, maybe one day my feelings will change, but right now, I'm not trying to fall in love, sweetheart."

By the time Tyreek finished talking, he was standing next to Layla in what he came into the world wearing.

"You should have told me that in the beginning then." Layla yelled. "I don't lay down with just anybody. You waltz up into church like you're a changed man, filling my head with your game, pretending like you're just so wrapped up in me. Well, never again. You can count on that. Lose my number."

Layla stepped in her pumps and headed toward Tyreek's living room where she grabbed her purse off the end table. She stomped toward the door, digging frantically inside her purse with each step, until she pulled out her car keys.

"So this is how you want things to end between us?" Tyreek's hands stretched toward her. "Just because I don't want things moving too fast? Why can't we take things slow? We don't have to get all caught up. Let's enjoy one another. That's all I'm saying. I just got a little nervous hearing you talk that love stuff."

She swallowed hard and squared her shoulders. "I can't help the way I feel, Tyreek. Maybe you've become so used to being used by Envy, that you've actually become a male version of her. Well, I can't, and I won't be some sleep buddy for you. You've got the wrong one, baby." She put on her last stitch of clothes and proceeded to walk out of his bedroom and toward the back door.

Tyreek followed behind her – still stark naked. With outstretched hands he said when she reached the door, "So this how you're going to act? You're just going to walk away from the best man you've ever had in your life? Yeah, I know all about how fat you used to be, and how you lost all that weight. You never had someone to make love to you the way I do. Admit it, Layla."

Layla remained absolutely motionless for a moment before she grabbed the door handle. "I wish I could say what I want to say to you. But my momma always told me that God don't like ugly. And if I stay here one minute longer, you're going to see just how ugly I can get.

Layla fought back tears as she climbed in her car, nervously fumbled until she got the key in the ignition, shifted to reverse and hit the pedal to the medal. "I will not cry. I will not cry." She could not believe that she had allowed herself to fall for Tyreek so quickly. Maybe she didn't know what true love was after all. Tyreek had certainly pulled the wool over her eyes. As she continued to clock miles that separated her from Tyreek, her thinking slowly changed. She admitted that there was some validity to what he said. He never professed to love her, only that he liked her. She was the one who lost control. Had she confused sex with love? How could she blame him for being honest about his feelings? She had given up the love of Dennis for the kind of man she thought she wanted. She was wrong and now she had no one to turn to. No one that is, accept for – God. "Lord, I've done it again. I've messed up. Forgive me again for putting a man before you. I'm hurt, but this time I realize that you've got me in the palms of your hands – and I will survive."

By the time she pulled into her driveway twenty minutes later, she succumbed to the hurt that was steadily mounting. Her heart pounded and her head rested heavily on the steering wheel. She released the tears that she had fought hard to hold back.

Her cell phone ringing startled her. She answered it without recognizing the number.

"Hello."

"My mind fell on you the other day. I don't know why; I just know it did. I'm not calling to bug you, I just want to know how you're doing," Dennis said.

Layla's red, swollen eyes grew even larger. She quickly wiped her runny nose with an old tissue she found in her purse.

"Dennis?" She tried to sound as normal as possible.

"Yeah, look, I just want to know how you're doing."

"I'm…I'm fine." She barely got the words out. She couldn't believe it was Dennis, But why now? Why did he have to call her now after what she'd just gone through with Tyreek? "How are you?"

"I'm okay. Well, now that I know you're doing okay, I won't hold you. It's good to hear your voice, Layla. Sorry if I disturbed you."

"Wait, Dennis. You didn't disturb me. I was just pulling up in my driveway. I'm about to go inside. I didn't recognize your number."

"I switched cell phone carriers. I started to keep the same number, but I changed my mind and just told them to give me a new one."

"Oh, I see." She was at a loss for words. Hearing Dennis's voice was soothing to her. She walked up to her apartment, unlocked the door, closed it behind her and went straight to her favorite chair and sat down. What could she say to Dennis? She was still reeling from the night's events with Tyreek. Did Dennis feel as bad as she did right now when she broke things off with him? Was this payback of some kind?

Silence invaded the connection between them.

"Listen, take care of yourself, Layla. Be happy."

Layla felt an onslaught of fresh tears about to surface. She fought hard to hold them back because she didn't want Dennis to hear the hurt in her voice.

"Dennis—"

"Yeah?"

She wanted to tell him she was sorry for hurting him the way that she did. She wanted to rush over to his house and bury herself inside the sanctity of his arms, but she couldn't. It wouldn't be fair to him. Anyway, knowing Dennis, or rather knowing the women out there he encountered on a daily basis, she was almost sure that someone had snatched him up. Any woman with a lick of sense could see that Dennis was a great catch. Any woman but her that is. She'd messed up a good thing and there was no way she could expect him to want her back in his life.

"Maybe we can have lunch sometime," she blurted out.

She could hear Dennis sigh. "Uh, wouldn't that be a little awkward? I mean you're in a relationship, aren't you?"

"You know me," she said trying to feign happiness. "This is the new and improved Layla. I'm not committed to anyone. But I totally understand if you don't want to. I know you've moved on."

"I'll call you later this week about lunch."

"Oh, uh."

"You sound surprised," he said.

"I guess I am. After the way I've treated you."

"Layla, I love you." His voice was still full of tenderness. "I always have. And to be honest, I miss you."

Layla let the tear drops fall. What a fool she'd been. Yet, here this man was still telling her that he loved her and missed her.

"Dennis, I don't know what to say. I never meant to hurt—"

"Let's not go there. I'll call you in a few days, okay?"

"I'm looking forward to it."

"Goodnight, Layla."

"Goodnight, Dennis."

Layla hit the End button on her cell. She curled up in her chair and cried until her phone rang again. It was Tyreek. She couldn't talk to him now. She didn't want to hear anything he had to say. He'd said more than enough already. She turned off her cell phone, got up and went to her bedroom and prepared to take a shower.

Dennis, Dennis, Dennis. How can you still love me?

The jet streams of water washed her outward body, while her inner spirit was being renewed by something stronger than she was. Maybe she didn't quite know it or understand it just yet. But in the grand scheme of things, Layla would have to come to learn that beauty goes far deeper than outward appearances.

When she got out of the shower, she dried off and put on her pj's. She got ready to get in bed, hoping sleep would come quickly so she wouldn't have to relive the day's events.

Turning her cover back, Layla climbed underneath the sheet and comforter. As she reached for the remote, she saw her opened Bible on the nightstand. Her parents taught her to always keep a Bible in the house, and always keep it open so the word of God would be visible and plain. Every few days, without really thinking, Layla flipped the pages of the Bible. Without giving it much thought she picked it up and it was the book of Jeremiah. She saw a verse she must have highlighted during one of Pastor Betts' sermons, or maybe it was a special passage she'd read at an earlier time. Jeremiah twenty-nine verses eleven and twelve were highlighted. Layla read the two verses with intensity.

"For I know the plans I have for you," declares the Lord, "plans to prosper you and not to harm you, plans to give you hope and a future. Then you will call on me and come and pray to me, and I will listen to you. You will seek me and find me when you seek me with all your heart."

God was speaking to her. It was so plain. Why else out of all the places she could have had opened in her Bible was it on Jeremiah and these two verses highlighted? The hurt she had been feeling began to slowly disappear. Layla got down on her knees and began seeking the man her parents had taught her about since she and her siblings were toddlers. Somehow after she finished praying, Layla knew that no matter what tomorrow held, she was going to be just fine.

31

"Fight one more round. When your arms are so tired that you can hardly lift your hands to come on guard, fight one more round, remembering that the one who always fights one more round is never whipped." James Corbett

The three friends gathered at a little spot called GG's for Girls' Night Out. It was a totally different scene from the places they used to go for their get together. They ordered their food and while they waited the quaint restaurant known for superb service and food was filled to the brim with their chatter.

Layla told them about her lunch date with Dennis. "We had a good time. I don't know where or if it's going to lead to anything, but it's like we're starting all over again."

"What about you and Tyreek," remarked Kacie. "Have you heard from him lately?"

"He's been calling and I keep telling him the same thing. I'm not going to subject myself to his kind. For him to even think that I should be lucky to have him?" Layla crinkled her lips and waved her hand. "I don't think so. There's nothing more I have to say to him."

"Good for you," replied Kacie.

"I agree," added Envy. "Your worth is not based on what he thinks about you. Take some time and learn who you are, Layla. Since I released my past mistakes, I feel better, so much better. I'm enjoying spending time really getting closer to God. I'm not sitting here trying to sound like I'm all perfect and everything. I still have lots of growing to do."

"And what about Leonard?" asked Layla.

"Yeah," said Kacie. "What's up with you two?"

"I guess I have to admit to you two that, well, how do I say this. Umm, I'm enjoying spending time with Leonard, getting to know him and he's getting to know me. Who knows where our relationship is going, but for now, I can tell you that I really do care about him."

"Ooooo, I'll be praying some more for y'all then." Kacie chuckled.

"Yes, First Lady," teased Envy. "But seriously," Envy said and looked at Layla. "Layla, there's something I've been meaning to say for a long time now."

"What?" Layla remarked.

"About everything that happened between me, you and Tyreek."

"Girl, please. That's all in the past."

"I still have to say this. None of it was worth jeopardizing our friendship over. God has blessed me with freedom from my past, yet I was still being spiteful and vindictive."

"Envy, there's no need to bring that up again. Tyreek is a goner anyway, and you and Kacie are my girls. Nothing will ever change that."

"I know, but it's like God has been impressing upon my heart to tell you this, so please let me say it. It's time that I do better and act better."

"You are doing better. We all are, in my opinion," Kacie interjected.

"Yes, we are. And I think it all started when you stepped out that day in church and rededicated your life to God. It's like soon after that, I understood the

importance of getting my soul rig
straight, my heart right, and my prese

I'm tired of holding back my hear
love I want desperately to give. I
bitter and angry person."

Layla giggled and jokingly rema
right."

Kacie laughed too. "Go on, Envy. We were just messing with you. Finish saying what's on your heart."

"Well, to think that I had the capacity to treat you the way I did, Layla. My best friend too? Someone whose been by my side through all of what I've been going through? I mean what was the big deal if you and Tyreek did make some good happen in your lives? Who was I to try to ruin it? But I tried, and thank God I failed miserably. I've really learned a lot about myself over these past months. Sometimes we can hang on to the past so tight that we can't move into the future that God has designed for us. I just want to tell both of you how much I love you and how sorry for all the foolish things I've done to you. Won't you all forgive me?" Envy asked looking at Kacie and then allowing her eyes to rest on Layla.

"How can we not forgive you," replied Layla. "I think I can speak for both me and Kacie when I say that all of us have done things toward each other that hasn't always been in the other ones best interest. But it's part of growing and getting to know one another. It's part of friendship. We share the ups and the downs – together. And there are going to probably be other times when we have our knock out drag out disagreements, but as long as we don't let it keep us apart, we'll be fine."

"I agree," said Kacie. "Every day we're allowed to be here on this earth is another opportunity to live to the fullest. There's not time to hold petty grudges against

other. You two are my rocks, well, other than
il." Kacie beamed and started laughing.

"Yea, tell us about it," said Envy. "We know that
Minister Cecil has taken our top spot. But it's cool. I
ain't mad at you."

"I know I'm not," said Layla.

"So, now can we eat? My catfish is getting cold and I
think a tear just fell in it," said Envy.

They all laughed and began to eat.

It was amazing. The lives of three friends were being
transformed. They once had self-made definitions of true
beauty, but slowly they were beginning to see
themselves the way God sees them. Kacie, Envy, and
Layla felt it, but more importantly, they believed it was
good—ALL good.

The End

Words from the Author

Kacie, Layla, and Envy experienced situations in their lives that shook them to the core. Some of the mistakes they made were of their own making, some were because of the circumstances of life, and others were brought on because of other people.

They equated beauty with the way they looked, the way they walked, the possessions they owned. They mistook love for something that was meant to hurt, kill, steal, and destroy; when the Word of God says that the devil is the one who is out to kill, steal, and destroy. God is a God of love. No matter what He allows to enter into your life, He remains in total control.

When God told Satan that he could try Job, Satan was given certain instructions and rules to abide by. One of them was that he could not kill Job.

Many times in our lives we believe that when problems, troubles, and tragedy enter our lives, we are down for the count. We don't ever see how we can get up again—but God can take any bad situation and transform it into something that will turn around and glorify Him.

Kacie had seven children by seven different men. She had a physical handicap too; yet God used her to help renew and restore her friends. He showed her both sides of what being a mother meant.

Layla lived most of her life severely obese. But in the midst of someone out to murder her, to bring harm to her, God used something horrific and changed it into some healing in Layla's life.

Envy carried the burden of her past on her shoulders for eighteen years, until God began to deal with her personally. She tried to escape the pain by seeking refuge from it in the arms of men, but God showed her that He was the Man she was looking for. Once she set her eyes on Him, then God could bring a man into her life that could show her what true love was.

Each of them, in her own way, experienced the divine, true beauty that God had placed in each of them.

A Special Invitation from the Author

If you have not made a decision to accept Jesus Christ as your personal Lord and Savior, God Himself extends this invitation to you.

If you have not trusted Him and believed Him to be the giver of eternal life, you can do so right now. We do not know the second, the minute, the hour, the moment, or the day that God will come to claim us. Will you be ready?

The Word of God says,

If you confess with your mouth, "Jesus is Lord," and believe in your heart that God raised him from the dead, you will be saved. For it is with your heart that you believe and are justified, and it is with your mouth that you confess and are saved (Romans 10:9–10 NIV).

About the Author

Shelia E. Lipsey is the award-winning, best-selling author of the Christian fiction titles: *Into Each Life, Sinsatiable, Beautiful Ugly, My Son's Wife, My Son's Ex-Wife: The Aftermath, My Son's Next Wife, Always, Now and Forever Love Hurts,* and *True Beauty.* Lipsey also contributed a story in the Christian based anthology, *Bended Knees* (Hollygrove Publishing). Among some of Lipsey's list of literary accomplishments and affiliations, Black Expressions Top 100, Top 25 and Top 20 Bestsellers lists numerous times, Black Christian News Network #1 bestseller (Beautiful Ugly), Top 50 Bestsellers List (Independent and National) multiple times, Conversations Book Club 2008 Author of the Year (thebestbookclub.info), Dallas Morning News Bestselling Author, Urban Knowledge Bestselling Author. Honoree for 2011 Kindle Awards for giving back to the community; recipient of the Book Clubs Unite 2011 Literary Arts Award for her contribution to the literary arts, 2010 Pink Diamond Award presented by the national chapter of SistahFriend Book Club, recipient of EDC Creations Top Shelf Book Award, Top 2010 Best Books Award, and numerous other accolades. She is founding president of Memphis African American Writers Group (MAAW), president of UC His Glory Book Club (uchisglorybookclub.net), contributing writer for Black Pearls Magazine, contributing blogger on Black Christian News Network (BCNN1), Shelia's Blog at www.shelialipsey.com/blog), as well as several other online literary groups.

READERS' DISCUSSION GUIDE

1. How do you feel about the change in Layla's personality and outlook on life?

2. Why do Envy and Kacie feel the way they do about the change in Layla?

3. Does Dennis come off as too good to be true? Why or why not?

4. Would a man (or woman) accept someone with seven children in today's society, especially if that person has never been married?

5. Discuss your opinions about the men in each of the friends' lives: Tyreek, Dennis, Leonard, Thomas, Minister Cecil.

6. What do Layla, Kacie, and Envy have in common?

7. What are your feelings about Envy's secret and the decision she made to tell her friends about it?

8. Does God honor the prayers of those who knowingly continue to commit sinful acts and then run to Him to ask for His forgiveness? Why or Why not?

9. Do you believe teenagers in today's society really feel like Kenny and Jackie about sex? Discuss.

10. Why are there some subjects that many pastors steer away from preaching about in the pulpit? Alternatively, do you believe that subjects about sexual acts should not be talked about in church?

11. What are your thoughts about sibling rivalry? In True Beauty, who is to blame for the sibling rivalry—Nikkei or Envy?

12. What is your favorite part of this story?

13. Are there any characters that you do not like or that you like more than others in this novel? Why?

14. Do you believe Layla, Envy, and Kacie are true Christians? Why or why not?

15. What is your definition of true beauty?

16. Do men look at women through physical eyes, like Kacie seems to think? If so, is Kacie right to feel the way she does about her disability? Why or why not?

To arrange signings, book events, speaking engagements, seminars with the author, or to send your comments to the author,
Contact
books@shelialipsey.com
www.shelialipsey.com
http://www.twitter.com/shelialipsey

Book Order Form

Quantity	Description	Cost	Total
	True Beauty	$14.95 (ea.)	

BOOK SHIPPING INFORMATION (PRINT PLEASE)

Name_____

Address_____

City_____

State/ Zip_____

Email _____

Phone (+ area code)_____

Money orders or cashier's checks only	Total
Subtotal	
S&H (add to total)	2.25
Taxes (TN Residents Only) Add 9.25% tax	
Total amount enclosed	

Make money orders and cashiers' checks payable to
Bonita and Hodge Publishing
Mail to:
P. O. Box 280202
Memphis, TN 38128

Thank You for Your Support

What's Blood Got To Do With It?
By Shelia E. Lipsey
<u>National Release Date February 29, 2012</u>

Bonus Chapter

November 1, 1987.

Upon exiting the womb, the newborn uttered a barely audible cry. Was it born of prophetic significance? Everyone nearby heard it. Immediately, it was whisked away. A flurry of nurses preened, sucked, injected and wiped this one so small, so fragile, so precious.

Tears slowly cascaded down the mother's pink cheeks as she whispered, "Adanya."

"Come again?" said a nurse nearby.

"Adanya."

"What is she saying?" the teenage girl's mother asked.

"Oh, Adanya is that going to be your baby's name."

"Umm," replied the mother with a nod.

"What a lovely name," the compassionate nurse told the adolescent girl lying drowsily before her.

The difficult delivery left the mother's braided hair a glowing, damp mess. An autistic mother and an unknowing father were not likely candidates to raise this child.

What lay ahead for Adanya? Who would the caregivers be? What kinds of tragedies would befall such a one? Certainly only God knew the answers. The hard delivery, coupled with a sedative put the mother into a deep, deep sleep.

Chapter One

"Pity is stronger than love." Unknown
February 4, 2010

Tar black heels attached to shapely brown legs click-clacked across the cement floor. Self-assuredness marked each step. She was the personification of confidence. A black and white thigh-length dress typified her aura. A high-powered executive? She was not. A self-made millionaire? She was not. A well-kept mistress? She was not. A successful businessman's wife? Not that either. A high-priced call girl? Nope. Born with a silver spoon? Sort of.

Adanya Katherine Anniston lived in a world of her own. One that was surrounded by lushness, where the sight of money and power was an everyday occurrence, and one that included love of God and family. She graduated from a prestigious all girls' preparatory school in Memphis at the age of sixteen and immediately entered Spellman College. Adanya appeared to have everything a twenty-two year old Spellman College Communications and Cultural Master's graduate could imagine. She was raised by loving parents who were not severed by divorce like millions of other families. The Anniston's were successful in their own rites.

Adanya adored her naturally curly, coarse, brown hair, along with her pronounced Puerto Rican and African ancestral facial features. She was gorgeous in her own classification of how physical beauty was often defined.

Her Puerto Rican mother, born in the Bronx of New York; and her father, a black man from the heart of Memphis, the Bible Belt some called it, defined her in ways she would learn throughout life.

Her maternal grandparents, Eva and Maurice Kaplan, Sr. much like a story book tale, met and fell in love while attending Lemoyne Owen College. For years, the Kaplan's played a pivotal role in education as college professors, fought for civil rights as young people of color; and stood boldly to proclaim their faith and belief in what was right. The Kaplan's were the proud parents of identical twin girls, Annalisse whose name carried on the Puerto Rican heritage of their family and Anaya, the African side.

Adanya had an inquisitive nature since she was a toddler. She seemed to have a questioning curiosity, for no apparent reason, about her family circle. She had a keen sense, even at a tender age that far outweighed the intellect and wisdom of many of her cousins and relatives, startling her parents constantly with her innate ability to perceive every day happenings within her family and outside in the vast world. Her parents often remarked that Adanya acted older than her young years. In many instances, it was true.

Adanya strolled in the small classroom full of college students. Many were like Adanya, from the affluent, society driven, rich crowd. She gracefully approached her desk, placed her iPhone on top of it and set her gray leather briefcase next to it.

"Good afternoon. I trust each of you had an adventurous and pleasant weekend." Adanya smiled slightly. Without further salutations, Adanya began lecturing the lecture hall full of students. Most of them, especially the men sat attentively as she lectured. Adanya had considered teaching public high school after she graduated but quickly decided against it after she consulted with her dearest confidante, her father.

Adanya and her father, Kenneth John Anniston were definitely a close pair. Kenneth absolutely adored his only child and daughter. He loved her infectious smile, the wave pattern of her hair, the innocence she portrayed, her gracefulness and the love she had for him, which was immeasurable. Anything he could do for her, Kenneth was willing to do.

Adanya, after all, was a precious gift from God. Her name alone appeared to instill within Kenneth a source of pride because of its Nigerian meaning - 'her father's daughter.'

The family background and how her name was derived was not a talked about subject, nor was it part of Kenneth's past that he chose to discuss. But true to his heritage, and much like Annalisse's parents, his spiritual beliefs had brought him through the rungs of the past.

Not only were the Anniston's wealthy monetarily, but they were wealthy in the blessings of their relationship. A strong couple, Annalisse and Kenneth remained faithful to each other even in lieu of their successful lifestyle. Many times money and power ruined marriages but not the

Anniston's. They were known throughout their community and the city for their philanthropic work.

Adanya was the type of child that soaked up everything her father told her. She was daddy's girl, one whom when she was little, loved to climb on his lap whether he was at work in his huge office overlooking the mid-south or at home resting comfortably in the family library in his favorite pillow-soft indigo recliner. Adanya was an adult, a young woman, but she still relied heavily on her father's love, guidance and direction.

She slowly strolled back and forth from one end of the classroom to the other as she lectured. "Gunther Kress in Communications and Culture states 'Communication, the idea is a matter of great interest. Kress goes on to tell us that ours is the information age, where everything depends on communication. Great jobs are linked to the skill level of communication. Promotion in a job depends on it."

Adanya's form of college lecturing seemed to have a magnetic effect on her students. If one searched around the state-of-the art class room at the faces of the students, all eyes were pointed in her direction with an uncanny type of magnetism. Adanya, after all, wasn't much older than many of them. Sometimes it was hard for her to make that distinction and to maintain professionalism after being approached by some very handsome, smart, going somewhere young men, in not only her class but throughout the college campus. Being a professor at such a young age was tough, but she wouldn't trade her job or position for anything in the world.

Her first lecture of the day ended right before noon, just in time to meet her best girlfriend, Nanette, at the coffee shop less than a block away from campus.

Nanette was director of counseling for a private all boys' school a few blocks away from where Adanya taught. She texted Nanette and told her she was on her way. Nanette texted back that she was walking into the coffee shop and she'd get them a seat before it got crowded.

"Hey, girl," said Nanette when Adanya approached the table. "I already ordered your turkey burger combo and Arnold Palmer."

Adanya sat down in the chair across the table from Nanette. "Thanks. I 'appreciate it."

"No problem. So, how has your day been so far?"

"Umm, pretty calm. Nothing much going on. I have a couple of more lectures and then I'll be finished for the day. What about you?" asked Adanya.

Nanette shrugged her shoulders. "Same old same old. I'm not complaining about a thing." The waitress brought both of their lunch orders. Before eating, Nanette stretched out her hand and automatically Adanya grabbed hold of it. They bowed their heads and Nanette blessed their food.

"Amen," they said in unison after the short prayer.

"Hey, would you like to go to a Grizzlies game with me and Poppy tonight?" asked Adanya. Poppy's best friend is out of town at one of their company conventions, so he has an extra season ticket seat."

"I don't think so. I have quite a few college essays to read. You mean your daddy isn't out of town at one of those tech conventions he frequents. I thought he rarely missed them."

"Believe it or not, he's decided to spend more time in the office rather than flying around the country like he usually does, unless it's absolutely necessary, of course. He finally has a pretty good group of loyal employees that he hired from some of the cities he usually travels to. It's decreased his work load tremendously."

"I know you're glad. You act like you and your poppy are joined at the hip." Nanette giggled.

"Yeah, I'm more than glad. I don't want Poppy to be heartbroken because I'm not enthralled with the IT business to the extent that he is. I mean, I have nothing against it, because it's provided us with the comfortable lifestyle that we have," Adanya said between taking a bite and chewing her juicy grilled turkey burger. "I'll probably become more involved a few years down the line, but not right now. Too hectic for me." Adanya smiled, and took a handful of fries and stuffed them in her round mouth.

"It's still good to know you have your father's IT business to fall back on if you ever decide to choose another career." Nanette sipped from her iced decaf coffee, followed by a bite from her sandwich. "Hey, forget about work, maybe it's time we get a love life, girl." Nanette grinned. "Or should I say, maybe it's time you get one." Nanette pointed a finger at Adanya for emphasis.

Adanya giggled and wiped her mouth with her napkin. "Where did that come from? I don't need a man in my life right now. I do not have time, even if I wanted one. It'll only complicate matters. When it's time, he'll find me."

"Love is never complicated, dawdling," Nanette said in an exaggerated southern drawl and with one hand flowing in the air.

Adanya waved her off. "You are too crazy for me. Anyway, Poppy says I have plenty of time for a relationship. He wants me to concentrate totally on me for now," Adanya emphasized by placing her hand flat against her busty chest.

"Your poppy, your poppy. To listen to you talk, the only person in your life is your poppy. I never hear you say anything about Mrs. Anniston. We've been best friends for two years, and I can count on one hand the times you've talked about her. And she's such a nice woman too. And talking about pretty, you've got her looks."

"Thanks. But really, Nanette, there is nothing wrong. I love my mommy. You know that, but you also know that she can go off on a tangent sometimes. She has select friends she deals with, and you know it. So I do not interfere with that. Plus, I can't help it if I'm a daddy's girl. I have his blood running through these voluptuous veins," said Adanya without a hint of conceitedness. She ran her hand up and down the length of her arm and smiled.

"You are so silly. You have both of your parents' blood running through your veins, as you put it," answered Nanette and shook her head.

The two friends continued eating lunch. They commented in whispers about several cute guys that walked into the deli. Some of them were total hotties, whom they tried to guess if they worked at the Executive Plaza a couple of blocks away, or at the college campus or some other nearby business. A couple of them Adanya had seen before eating lunch at the popular deli spot. Several more, Adanya recognized as students from campus.

A few minutes into their girly game, Adanya's eyes engaged with a pair of eyes that reminded her of the ocean and skin that likes the sands of Siesta Key.

She watched as he walked toward their table.

Nanette followed Adanya's eyes. "What are you looking at?"

Adanya didn't have time to response because green eyes were gazing into hers. "Hello, how are you lovely ladies doing this afternoon?"

Adanya shifted her gaze and locked eyes with Nanette.

Nanette, speechless, looked at the hunk standing before them and shrugged her shoulders.

"Are you talking to us?" Adanya glanced over her shoulder.

"Of course," he answered. "Definitely you," he said in a flirtatious tone.

Nanette cleared her throat and took her napkin and poised it over her mouth to shield the smile Adanya saw form on her face.

"I'm fine. Thank you."

"Me too," quipped Nanette and took a sip from her straw.

"My name is Bleak...Bleak Kissinger," he said and extended his hand toward Adanya.

Adanya hesitated, glanced over at Nanette like she was pleading for help. Nanette gave none so Adanya shook his hand.

"Hello," answered Adanya without giving up her name." Uh, how can we help you?"

"Well, you can help me by telling me your name," he said in a flirty manner.

"I don't think so," responded Adanya. She suddenly felt a light but swift kick on her shins from Nanette.

"Ouch," she said.

"Something wrong?" he asked.

"No, not at all. But if you'll excuse us, we only have a few more minutes to finish our lunch."

"Oh, of course. I'm sorry. I didn't mean to be rude. But I've seen you somewhere before. I can't quite remember where."

"Ohh, that's ashamed," answered Adanya in a rather sarcastic tone. Nanette continued to sip on her soda, not mumbling a word.

Adanya made a mental note to let Nanette have a mouth full as soon as she could get rid of Bleak.

"Well, Bleak, I'm not sure where you've seen me, but I really don't have the time for conversation right now."

"Sure. Understood. Maybe I'll run into you again."

"Yeah, maybe," responded Adanya and then turned her back toward him.

Bleak walked away and headed out of the crowded restaurant.

"Girl, he was fine," said Nanette. "I can't believe you wouldn't tell him your name."

"Are you crazy? That was nothing more than a cheap pick up line. He's probably one of the college students on campus. Just being a flirt, that's all." Adanya took the last bite from her sandwich and washed it down with her remaining soda. "Let's get out of here."

They paid their checks and proceeded outside. Stopping on the side of the entrance to the deli, they chatted some more. "Since you're going to the game, I guess I won't be talking to you tonight," Nanette told Adanya and huddled herself inside her thick top coat to ward off the cold temperature.

"Probably not. I'll be enjoying some daddy-daughter time." A glow spread across Adanya's face.

"We'll talk tomorrow then. Do you want to meet back here for lunch around the same time?" asked Nanette.

"Sure. That'll be great." The two friends hugged each other tightly.

"Maybe you're run into Bleak again. Wouldn't that be cool?" remarked Nanette.

"No, that wouldn't be cool. Not at all. Maybe for you."

"Come on, Adanya, you have to admit that he was a cutie. Those curly locks of blonde hair and those piercing baby blues, girl he had it going on."

"I won't deny that, but I'm not about to entertain the thought of getting involved with anyone from campus. Honestly, I'm not interested in being involved with a man period, and most definitely not a white boy. I have too many other things on my mind. Having a boyfriend or dating would just complicate matters."

"First, you don't know whether he's from the university, Adanya. Stop shooting down men before you even give them a chance. And I know you are not trying to pull the race card. You're the one that's always talking against prejudice. You are so green. It's time to have some fun, get a boyfriend, go out on some dates and enjoy your life."

"Just because you love the dating scene, don't try to put that label on me. Anyway, I don't have time to stand here and indulge in useless banter. We both have to get back to work. I'll see you tomorrow," said Adanya.

"Whatever." Nanette waved one hand in the air. "But one day you're going to be swept away and when it happens, I'm going to be bouncing off the ceilings with I told you so's." Nanette laughed and started to walk away. "But you're right; we need to get back to work. Have a good time at the game tonight."

"I will. Bye." The girls walked away in opposite directions.

CPSIA i
Printed i
BVOW0
2837

893509